Praise for Steven Womack and his Harry James Denton mysteries

DEAD FOLKS' BLUES

"A deft, atmosphere-rich novel: smart, funny, and filled with a sense of wry heartbreak. Steven Womack's Nashville stands out—it is a beautifully drawn backdrop."

—JAMES ELLROY
New York Times bestselling author of
L.A. Confidential

"*Dead Folks' Blues* is a virtuoso performance."
—*The Virginian-Pilot and Ledger-Star*

TORCH TOWN BOOGIE

"A sure winner . . . Many critics . . . have lauded Womack's sense of setting. In *Torch Town Boogie*, his rendering of Nashville is almost palpable."

—*The Tennessean*

*Please turn the page
for more reviews. . . .*

WAY PAST DEAD

"As an exotic setting for a regional mystery series, Nashville's got it all. . . . For the local color alone, Steven Womack's *Way Past Dead* is a real hoot."
—*The New York Times Book Review*

"*Way Past Dead* has action and mystery enough to keep the reader eagerly turning pages all night."
—*Southern Book Trade*

"The third Denton mystery is a little jewel. Denton is a Rockford-like private eye who'd like to avoid danger but has just enough integrity to follow his cases through to the end."
—*Booklist*

CHAIN OF FOOLS

"*Chain of Fools* is the fourth, most tightly written, and best novel yet in the Denton series."
—*Nashville Life*

"If you're looking for hard-boiled, you need look no further than Steven Womack's latest, *Chain of Fools*. . . . A memorable mean-streets tale."
—*Alfred Hitchcock Mystery Magazine*

"Womack's books feature strong, believable characters, fast-paced, multifaceted plots, a well-defined Nashville setting, and humorous insights galore. *Chain of Fools* is the latest and best in the Harry James Denton saga, a great series by an extraordinarily talented writer."
—*The Armchair Detective*

MURDER MANUAL

"Another fast-paced whodunit . . . How will Harry escape the tightening web of intrigue he's caught in? Read the book. . . . You'll enjoy it. Edgar winner Steve Womack spins a captivating story."
—*The Knoxville News-Sentinel*

"[An] empathetic and believable hero. . . . The best of Womack's five Denton books."
—*Mystery News*

By Steven Womack:

The Harry James Denton Books
DEAD FOLKS' BLUES*
TORCH TOWN BOOGIE*
WAY PAST DEAD*
CHAIN OF FOOLS*
MURDER MANUAL*
DIRTY MONEY*

The Jack Lynch Trilogy
MURPHY'S FAULT
SMASH CUT
THE SOFTWARE BOMB

Published by Ballantine Books

DIRTY MONEY

Steven Womack

FAWCETT • NEW YORK

A Fawcett Book
Published by The Ballantine Publishing Group
Copyright © 2000 by Steven Womack

www.randomhouse.com/BB/

Library of Congress Catalog Card Number: 99-091096

ISBN 0-345-41448-9

Manufactured in the United States of America

First Edition: January 2000

10 9 8 7 6 5 4 3 2 1

To the memory of Theodore "Woody" Eargle.
As someone once said, "Free at last . . . free at last."

Acknowledgments

I'm deeply indebted to a number of folks who helped me with research, story, editing, inspiration, and support. *Dirty Money* would never have been written if Mike Price hadn't encouraged me to go to Reno and try it on for size. He was a wealth of information and ideas and, as always, incredible wisdom and insights.

While in Reno, Detective Sergeant Todd Shipley of the Reno, Nevada, Police Department gave me invaluable resource material, firsthand tours, and the benefit of his years of experience. I'm very grateful to him.

Sara Cruz and Joy Snowden of the Eureka County Economic Development Council supplied me with everything I needed to re-create Eureka, Nevada, in the pages of this book. I owe them a lot.

My friends and colleagues in the Nashville Writers Alliance were a tremendous help, as they have been throughout the years. Their support and patience has been a great gift.

I'm very fortunate to have several friends who are also eagle-eyed copy editors. Jim Veatch and Justine Honeyman have now copyedited at least five books for me, and if they get any better at it, I'm going to have to start paying them. Laurie Parker's keen editorial eye and sensitivities also were a great help.

Willy Stern, ace investigative reporter for the Nashville *Scene*, supplied me with a lot of background information on the crime of money-laundering, and I thank him.

And, as always, I'm grateful to Joe Blades and Nancy Yost for their support and encouragement.

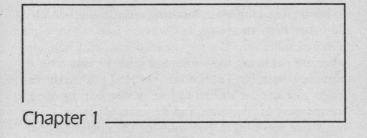

Chapter 1

The Mustang finally died somewhere west of Ely, Nevada, on U.S. 50 just past the Little Antelope Summit.

God, don't ask me how I got here. I left Nashville four days ago—or was it five? Hell, I can't remember! I was en route to Reno, trying to get there in time for the birth of my first child, and I should have been there by now. When my girlfriend, Marsha, called me last week, she was eight months plus, just waiting to, as she put it, explode with baby. She—we already know it's a girl—could come any day.

The trip was just over twenty-two hundred miles, door to door. I'd hoped to make it in three days, maybe four. Unfortunately, I didn't factor in the noise and aggravation that comes from driving a car that's only about a dozen years younger than I am. A '68 Mustang that's already seen better days is a ride that's not much better than a Fifties-era pickup truck. You get about eight driving hours a day before hallucinations start to set in.

Still, I was doing okay all the way to Kansas City. That's when the heater core blew, so in addition to all the other discomforts, I now got to freeze my ass off as soon as the sun went down. That ended my nighttime driving, but by then I was so exhausted, I needed a few hours in a Motel 6 anyway.

Then around Lincoln, Nebraska, the Mustang seemed

to be running a little hot. Nothing serious, but I decided I'd better keep an eye on it. I was on I-80, about eight hundred miles into the trip headed toward Cheyenne, when the car began to sputter and miss. I wrote it off to altitude at first, but I noticed that when I pushed the car much past sixty, it started to lose power fast. I stopped for gas west of Cheyenne and the carb vapor-locked on me. I had to sit there and wait for the engine to completely cool down before it would start again. Lost about two hours to that.

By now, I'm getting tired and really cranky. I wanted to do about seven or eight hundred miles a day, and I'm getting maybe half that. I called my buddy Lonnie in Nashville. Lonnie's the repo man/bounty hunter/jack-of-all-trades who sold me the car and rebuilt the engine a few months back. I was broke at the time, needed a cheap car, and this one was fine for knocking around Music City. Guess I should have traded it in before I left.

I called Lonnie and got his answering machine, so I tried his cell phone, then his beeper, and finally the special number he has that only a few other people even know. Nothing. Lonnie's probably off somewhere with his girlfriend, Sheba. Either that or he's sneaking through somebody's backyard getting ready to slim jim a car open because some jamoke's missed one too many payments and he's just too busy to answer the phone.

So I limp on through day three or four—like I said, I'm starting to lose track of time—and manage to make it all the way through Salt Lake City, only by now the Mustang's got a top speed of about forty-five miles an hour and I'm starting to get some pretty seriously nasty looks from the other freeway drivers. Going up a steep incline near the Utah-Nevada border, some trucker tries to pass me, only he's carrying a load of steel and he can't get any speed going up the mountain either. So here's this guy in an old White Freightliner going side by side with me for about ten miles, with the traffic behind us lined up flashing lights, laying on horns, flipping us both off.

Finally we get to the summit, the highway levels off, and the Freightliner gets past me. Traffic's whizzing by about ninety now. Some guy in a Porsche rolls down his passenger window and chucks a plastic cup full of soda out the window at me as he goes by. The next guy draws down on me. I mean, literally, he waves a pistol out the window and we make eye contact and I guess I sent him the right message, because he never fired it at me. Just wanted to make sure I got a good look at it.

I took that as divine intervention, and the word I got from on high was to get the hell off the interstate. So I pull off I-80 at a rest stop just across the Nevada state line, near Wendover Air Force Base. Some kid at the gas station takes a look at the Mustang for me, but he's an oil-change guy and a battery installer, not a serious mechanic. We let the car cool down and I check the radiator. There's a thin, foamy layer of slippery stuff on the surface of the coolant. That's not good. And on the dipstick there's a thin sheen of water and oil mixed together.

"That's real bad, I think," the kid says. I agree with him. Probably a head gasket that's on its way to blowing.

Still, there's nobody there who can fix it and the car is still running, at least for now. I figure if I can limp across Nevada into Reno, I can get it repaired there no matter how long it takes. Only no more freeway for me. I check the map and see that if I take 93 down to Ely, then take State 50 west, I'll go straight into Reno and miss some of the worst of the mountains. Plus it's a two-lane state road; I can drive forty-five without getting my head blown off.

Done deal, I think, so after the car cools down and I eat a quick lunch, I head south. It's only about one hundred thirty miles, maybe a bit over two hours in a normal car, but it takes me nearly four. It's high desert country here, stark and beautiful, with the clearest blue sky I've ever seen. This time of year back home in Nashville, we get a lot of gray. Gray clouds, gray skies, gray psyches. I've never seen anything this color: a piercing, intense blue that's almost unreal painted above the scrub brush and the bare brown earth. I'm already in love with this country despite my trouble getting across it, so I figure what the hell, it takes as long as it takes. I'll call Marsha when I stop tonight and be in Reno late tomorrow.

Maybe she can hold that baby in another day or two, I think, smiling at the thought.

So I'm about an hour west of Ely when I hear this clunking sound from just in front of the firewall, followed by a grinding noise and this feeling like there's no power at all left in the car. In the rearview mirror, I see smoke, blue smoke. That means oil; that's bad. I push in on the clutch and the moment I do, the engine's dead as a rock and I'm coasting to a stop.

I climb out of the car and do what every idiot does in a situation like this: I raise the hood and stare down at the engine. Like I can do something to it. I don't even have a toolbox in the trunk, not to mention that I wouldn't know what to do with it if I had one.

It's four o'clock in the afternoon, the sun still high in the sky but not as high as it was an hour or two ago. I can see behind me on State 50 all the way to the eastern horizon, two lanes of asphalt without a living two-legged thing on it except me. Ahead of me, to the west, the two lanes stretch out for miles, finally dropping out of sight in a line of mountains that look sharp, craggy, impassable.

I do a quick inventory, my mind trying to focus on my

increasingly narrow set of options. I check the odometer, which I just happened to glance at when I filled the gas tank just outside of Ely. I've put somewhere between forty and fifty miles on the car since then.

Way too far to walk back . . .

I pull out the map, check out where I've been and what's in front of me. A while ago I went through what a sign said was the Robinson Summit, elevation 7,588 feet. The engine blew on the western downhill side of the Little Antelope Summit. To my immediate left—in fact, practically across the road—is the Humboldt National Forest. According to the map, Mount Hamilton should be off to the south and, at an elevation of nearly 11,000 feet, pretty visible.

I set the map down on the roof of the car and turn. Yeah, there it is, huge and sharp and covered in white at the top.

Great, I think, *snow.*

The mental inventory continues. I've got no food in the car, no water, just one-half of a twenty-ounce Coke in a plastic bottle, no doubt flatter than hell. I've got no cell phone, no radio, no way to contact anybody. And when the temperature starts to drop in another hour or two, I've got a couple of sweaters and a leather jacket in my suitcase, but no blanket and nothing else to cover up with.

And let's see, there's a car with a heater that won't run anyway. I could siphon some gas out of the tank to start a fire, but I don't have a hose. There aren't any matches either, and come to think of it, I even took the cigarette lighter out of the car because I don't smoke.

I turn back to the map, studying it as closely as I can while there's still enough light. Then, for the first time, I notice in small print these little letters that run below the thin red line that is Route 50 on the map. I trace the letters as they dance across the page with my right index finger. Then it all comes together for me.

The little letters spell out the words THE LONELI-EST ROAD.

I look to my left and then to my right. No sign of life anywhere. Not even a sound. If I strain real hard, I can hear the wind gently blowing past my ears; at least I think I can. Maybe I'm hallucinating.

"Holy shit," I whisper. If this road is so deserted that they even call it the loneliest road on the map, then I really am in some trouble. Right now, it's just a question of how much.

I fold up the map and toss it onto the driver's seat, then pull my jacket out and put it on, zipping it all the way up to my neck. I'd always heard people say this, but only now was I beginning to get a sense of what they were talking about: the desert gets cold as hell at night. Just in the last half-hour, I could feel it. It was midfifties, maybe low sixties a couple of hours ago. Now I'd bet the rent the temperature was in the forties and just beginning to fall.

On top of that, the air's so thin up here it's giving me a headache. And it's so dry I can feel it sucking the moisture out of me as I stand here on the side of the road. My lips are cracking and my eyes feel dry, like there're no tears left.

One thing you can say for a thirty-one-year-old Ford: it's made out of stouter stuff than today's plastic cars. I hop up on the bumper, then across the hood, then onto the roof of the car, my weight causing only the slightest indentation in the metal. I put my hands to my forehead and strain to see as far off to the east as I can, where the purple and blue of dusk is already rising up from the ground like ink. A few stars are visible as sharp, distinct points of life maybe an inch off the horizon.

Nothing.

I scan the horizon a full three-hundred-sixty degrees, thinking maybe there's a house or a ranch or a trailer or even a well or something off the side of the road. Give me a hiker or a cowboy or Gabby Hayes mining for gold with his burro back in the hills—anybody with a canteen and a cell phone.

I'm from back east. I'm a city boy; my idea of roughing it is when room service closes at eleven. Even in Nashville, your car breaks down and the worst you've got is a pain-in-the-ass walk to the nearest pay phone and a tow-truck bill. But here, in land as barren and empty as a John Ford set, I get the feeling that this is the kind of country that can kill you if you're not ready for it.

But here's the weird part; for some reason or other, I'm not scared. I should be. There should be panic, yelling for help, wailing, and screaming. Only there's not, and I don't know why. Maybe it's the awesomeness of it all: that after being reduced to such insignificance, my whole life is only a spark against such a sky, there's nothing to fear because all is lost anyway.

I stand there, leaning against the Mustang, scanning the road in either direction, until the sun sets below the western horizon and the purple and blue fade into black. By now it's just plain cold outside, but it's not that wet, humid cold we get back east, the kind that eats through your skin and muscle and all the way to the bone and then even deeper, into the marrow, until it's impossible to ever warm up. This is different; there's something about it that's invigorating.

All the same, I pull off the jacket, unzip the suitcase again, and pull out both sweaters, then put them on. The jacket goes on top of that. Now I've got five layers on from the belt up, which ought to be enough to get me through the night. I crawl back in the car and roll up the windows and hunker down for the night. I drink half the flat Coke, which leaves a sweet, syrupy, disgusting taste in my mouth, but at least it's not dust.

I look out the car window and can't see the road barely three feet below me. Above me, there's no moon, but the sky is bright with the sparkle of countless stars. Silence is everywhere, broken only by the rustle of my clothes as I move.

For a moment I worry about the car battery running down, then figure that's a useless concern since the engine's dead anyway. I pull the knob on the steering column and the hazard lights start flashing. I can see the rhythmic bursts of white parking lights, while in the rearview mirror corresponding spurts of red glow off the back end. There's something comforting about it, except that the clicking of the relay sounds like a hammer hitting metal, and I wonder how long I can stand it.

I reach behind me, into a small grocery sack full of paperback books, and pull one out, then flick on the tiny dome light inside the car. I'm getting kind of hungry and really cold. I can't feel my feet much anymore. I check my watch: It's 7:30. I've been sitting here for over three hours. It must be nearly freezing out.

I settle into the driver's seat and readjust the rearview mirror so that I can look out the front and back of the Mustang at the same time without moving. Right now, I'd take a ride in either direction. If somebody would take me back east to Ely, I'd be thrilled.

The first book my hand comes to is Henry Miller's *Tropic of Cancer*. I don't know what made me throw the book into the car as I left. I'd tried to read it once as an undergraduate and it was too dense, too thick, for me to get much out of it. I'd taken a shot at it because of its racy reputation, but the truth was, Miller is so philosophical about sex that most of it wasn't much of a turn-on. The writing had seemed surreal, convoluted, and I'd finally put the book down and forgotten about it. It stayed with me, though, in a box of books that I moved from place to place, through my years as an investigative reporter and from the beginning to the end of my marriage. Then my career crashed and burned and I got my license as a private detective. And always, this ever-present box of books that I dragged around with me as I descended one rung at a time down the socio-economic ladder.

And now here I was, on the loneliest road in America, broken down and lost, and the only question remaining was which would get me first: the lack of water or the cold.

I cracked the window to get a little air and began reading.

It is now the fall of my second year in Paris. I was sent here for a reason I have not yet been able to fathom. I have no money, no resources, no hopes. I am the happiest man alive.

I looked out the windshield, at the vague black shapes that came up out of the ground and melded into the night sky and above them at the endless tiny pinpoints of light. I climbed out of the car, onto the asphalt that still glowed and radiated with a faint heat, and stood in the middle of the highway, my feet straddling the dotted white line that marked the lanes. At that moment, when I was totally alone and cognizant somewhere in the intellect part of my brain that I was facing a situation that would eventually get serious if it didn't change, I felt freer and happier and lighter than I'd ever felt in my life. I laughed out loud, surprised to hear my own voice cutting through the darkness. I yelled again and then spun around deliriously in the middle of the road, a lost soul on a desert highway.

The loneliest road. The loneliest road in America, and here I was, right smack-dab in the middle of it, dancing in time to the rhythmic flashing of hazard lights.

Dancing for as long as they lasted, and then somewhere near dawn, when the flashing slowed and the lights dimmed, maybe I would dim as well. Maybe my lights would go out, the rhythmic flashing of my heartbeat fading slowly just as the day faded into night. And if they did, would anyone ever find me, or what was left of me? Would any of it matter, beneath this sky, this universe, which reduced everything in it to insignificance?

And then I thought of my unborn child, my daughter, and was suddenly very saddened. If I were to die out here in the middle of this high-country desert, I'd never see her, never know who the child was, what she would or could become.

I didn't feel like dancing in the middle of the highway anymore. From far off to my left, I heard a howling, like a coyote or a lost dog. I couldn't tell which. From behind me, another howl erupted in answer to the first. Then from the distant brush in front of me, I heard a squalling sound, a horrible, high-pitched caterwauling, like a horny tomcat trying to get to his girlfriend's house, only the tomcat's the size of an NFL linebacker and ain't nobody's going to stop him.

Shivering, I climbed back into the car. Suddenly, the night desert erupted in a symphony of noise. During the day the desert is almost completely silent except for the gentle hissing of wind; that is, of course, until the wind picks up into a howl of its own. But that's about all you can hear.

But at night—at night the desert comes alive. I rolled down the window, despite the cold, and listened until the wind picked up and my face felt like it was resting against a pillow full of broken glass.

I rolled the window up, then read until I drifted off to sleep.

I came up out of a restless, troubled half-sleep just as the blinking of the hazard lights was slowing down to nothingness. I came to, my lips cracked and dry, my throat parched. My sinuses had swollen shut from the cold and the dry air, so I'd been breathing through my mouth for who knew how long. I ran my tongue across my cracked lips, raked it across the roof of my mouth, trying to collect any little bit of moisture that could be found.

I checked my watch: 4:30. The sun would be up soon. I knew that a car battery would recharge itself a tiny bit as long as it wasn't completely drained. No one had passed all night; I knew that because even when asleep my senses were attuned to any car noise. I reached down and pressed the button to turn off the hazard lights. Immediately, the faint white blinking at the front of the car stopped. I shifted, sat up on the bench seat to check in the rearview mirror. But the lights were still there. I reached down and pressed the button again. But it was already in the off position. I looked up again, half asleep, dazed even, trying to make sense of the white lights in the rearview mirror.

But the rear hazard lights were supposed to be red.

My heart seemed to jump in my chest as I strained to focus on the mirror, then turned and stared out the dusty back window. In the distance, two tiny pinpricks of light were growing larger by the moment.

My mouth opened, but nothing came out. I shook my head, trying to get my brain to work. I was dehydrated, blood sugar shot to hell, still half asleep. I stared again.

Yes . . . Lights.

I cracked the car door open and that's when I heard

it—the faint whining of a car's engine, growing louder by the moment as the lights grew brighter. As I reached in to turn the hazard lights back on, I thought again of Henry Miller, starving in Paris, penniless, no hope and no prospects, and the happiest man alive.

Finally, I understood.

Chapter 2

The driver's-side door squealed as I pushed it all the way open into the freezing Nevada desert night, frigid metal on metal grating painfully. I stepped out onto the pavement, still half asleep, not sure if I'd dreamed or imagined the twin beams of light moving toward me from the horizon.

Suddenly, a blast of wind sent me into the same kind of chill I used to get as a child when fever would set in and there was nothing anyone could do to stop it. I shook from within, from deep in my core, teeth rattling uncontrollably, shoulders bent, my whole body vibrating like a plucked bowstring. It hurt all over, but the thought of rescue was enough to lessen the pain.

The engine noise grew louder and I could see the outline of the approaching car. Only it wasn't a car; it was a truck, a large pickup, and it was less than a mile off.

I stepped into the middle of the highway, jumping up and down to try to stave off the chill, to generate any kind of heat I could, and waved my arms wildly above my head.

"Please," I yelled, my teeth chattering, "please stop! C'mon, baby, hit those brakes! Come to Papa!"

I bent over away from the wind, wrapping my arms around my torso, hugging myself, trying to get the pilot light lit again. The truck was getting closer. I forced myself to open my arms again and wave, even though that meant another tsunami of chills and shakes.

The truck grew closer and then, like a miracle, its right blinker started flashing and it began to slow. I waved, grinned, strained to get a better look at the truck just as the blue-orange light of dawn began to shimmer in the east, like a halo around the truck. The pitch and volume of the engine changed as the driver slowed, and then a few moments later the crunch of gravel and sand flying broke the night as the truck braked to a stop just behind the Mustang.

I ran to the driver's side as he lowered the window. He was in his late twenties, early thirties, but with a face that was already beginning to line from too much time in the sun. His greasy blond hair was long and tangled and he looked like the kind of guy who'd always made a living with his hands. The truck was an old Ford F150, faded blue with bubbled rust all over the hood and fenders, but to me it looked like a stretch limo pulling up in front of the Plaza.

"Thanks, man," I sputtered. "I really appreciate this."

He looked me over, then the Mustang. "How long you been out here?" he asked.

"All night. Since late yesterday afternoon."

The guy next to the driver turned, examined me in silence. He was a few years older than the driver, with long shiny black hair pulled back and tied in a ponytail. He looked Native American to me, but I didn't know for sure.

"Nice '68," the driver said. "What happened?"

"Engine blew, I think."

"Ain't that a bitch? Tennessee plates," he observed. "Where you from?"

"Nashville," I answered. "I was trying to get to Reno."

"Music City," he said in the standard response to

hearing where I was from. "I love country music. That Garth, he's something else."

"Me, too." I nodded. "Yeah, I'm crazy about Garth." Hell, I'd be crazy about Egyptian hieroglyphics and underwater basket-weaving if that's what it took to get this guy to take my freezing ass off this road.

"When's the last time you had any water?" he asked.

I thought for a moment. "Jeez, I don't know. Sometime yesterday, maybe lunchtime."

The driver turned to his buddy, grinned. "Tourists," he said contemptuously. The Native American–looking guy just grunted.

The driver turned back to me. "We can take you as far as Eureka. You can get a tow truck there."

"Super," I said, grinning from ear to ear. "Thanks, guys, I really appreciate it. Let me get my bag."

Just in case I couldn't find a tow truck, I decided to grab my small carry-on and bring it with me. I had a couple of other suitcases and boxes of stuff I'd brought along, but they were all locked in the trunk and would be okay for now.

The passenger opened the door and stepped out as I ran over to the Mustang, grabbed my bag out of the backseat, and locked the car up. As I moved quickly back to the pickup, I noticed the guy was huge, maybe six-four, chiseled, and wore a denim jacket and a work shirt. Only the work shirt was pulled out of his pants, with the tails hanging down below the bottom of the jacket. He also had this way of standing that's hard to describe, but it was a stance that put walls up around him. Body language that said, more than anything else, *Don't fuck with me.*

Suddenly, I had this wave of apprehension. The only other place I'd ever seen a man stand like that—with shirttails obsessively out to cover up anything that might be tucked into a waistband—was when I interviewed guys in prison.

Then when he held out a clear glass bottle to me, all the apprehension vanished and in a moment I'd tossed my bag into the back of the truck, climbed into the cab between the driver and his bud, and was unscrewing the cap on an empty Jack Daniel's bottle full of clear, beautiful, gorgeous cold water.

As the driver slammed the truck into gear and pulled out onto the highway, I lifted the bottle to my lips and had the best long swallow of water I'd ever had. It felt like heaven. I savored each sensation: its coolness over my parched lips, the feel of it going down my throat, the rush of sensation when it hit my gut. Almost instantly, I felt more alert, more awake, more alive.

"Better be careful with that," the driver said. "You don't want it coming back on you."

I lowered the square glass bottle, pressed my weight back into the seat. "I'll be careful," I said, trying not to shiver. "But, man, that's good."

"You know," he said, "you gonna be driving out here in the desert, you oughta carry water with you. The locals always carry water and blankets in the car. Me, I got ten more gallons in the back."

The driver motioned with his thumb out the back window. The interior noise in the truck's cab made conversation difficult. I just nodded, exhausted and grateful and determined to remember the lesson.

The driver leaned over, turned the heater up, and I felt warm air wafting from behind the dashboard, over my feet, gently blowing up my pants legs. I looked around the inside of the cab. The truck was easily fifteen, maybe twenty years old, worn and battered. Small hand tools littered the floor and the tan vinyl dashboard was scarred with rips, grease smudges, cigarette burns. I looked over at the speedometer; the driver had edged the truck up to about seventy-five, the asphalt speeding by below us just barely ahead of the dawn. The landscape in front of us seemed to open up with the rising light, unfolding in a panorama of exquisite beauty. I tried to relax, fatigue catching up with me now that I wasn't freezing to death. We drove on for maybe five more minutes and I started to drift off. My head nodded; I felt my chin lowering to my chest.

The driver shifted his weight and, out of the corner of my eye, I saw him look past me and toward his buddy. The tall guy nodded back at him and the driver lifted his foot off the accelerator. The truck slowed.

I looked up, out the windshield, as the driver braked the truck and steered it off the pavement and onto the shoulder. The sun seemed to be coming up behind us even faster now. I could sense the warmth on my neck through the back window of the truck.

I had a bad feeling about this.

The driver pulled the parking brake and killed the engine. I looked down and to my right. The Indian was holding on to the door handle so tight, the skin of his hand was stretched across the knuckles.

"What's your name, buddy?" the driver asked.

I turned, my face suddenly numb, my voice blank and matter-of-fact. "Harry," I said. "Harry Denton."

He smiled broadly, revealing a jumble of stained, rotten teeth below the mop of greasy hair. "How much money you got on you, Harry Denton?"

"Not much," I answered. "Couple hundred, maybe."

He leaned forward on the steering wheel, looked at his buddy. "You hear that, Wolf?" he asked. "Harry's only got a couple hundred on him."

Wolf, I thought. Name fits.

The Wolf nodded. He had yet to say a word the whole trip.

"So what you're telling us, Harry, is that we saved your fucking life back there and all you've got on you is a couple hundred bucks. No water, no food, and a couple hundred bucks. You weren't exactly ready for this part of the country, were you, Harry?"

"Guess not," I said, my mind starting to work in about ten directions at once. I was tired, weakened. The driver was right; I wasn't prepared for this country, and I sure as hell couldn't take these two. I couldn't fight them, couldn't outrun them. This might be a case where I'd just have to talk my way out.

If that's possible . . .

"I can get some more," I said. "I've got an ATM card. We get to Eureka, go to a teller machine. I'd be happy to pay you guys for helping me out. Pay you well, in fact."

Greasy Blond laughed. "An ATM in Eureka. Yeah, right." Then he stopped laughing, the grin disappearing. "You travel all the way across country with just two hundred bucks on you, Harry?"

"Well," I interjected quickly, "you know, I got credit cards. You don't need a lot of cash these days."

Greasy Blond looked over at the Wolf again. "You're wrong, Harry, everybody needs a lot of cash these days. The Wolf would agree with me. Right, Wolf?"

The Wolf raised an eyebrow, gave a subtle nod of his head.

The driver, whose name I still hadn't gotten, suddenly lifted up the door handle and kicked the door open. He hopped out of the truck, turned to me.

"Get the fuck out, Harry," he said.

I turned to the Wolf. His stare was stone cold, his eyes dead. I started to go into that altered state, that "this isn't happening" mindset that Mother Nature puts you in when some really bad shit's about to go down and she knows you can't come anywhere near handling it in your normal frame of mind.

"Guys," I said, "what—"

"Shut up, Harry!" Greasy Blond ordered. "Just get out of the truck. Now."

I slid slowly across the seat, my mind racing. I thought of the Smith & Wesson Bodyguard Airweight I'd once borrowed from Lonnie and wished I still had it. I'd always hated guns before, but I sure could use one right now. Maybe that's the way guns are. They're like lawyers; you hate them until you need a good one and then you thank God for them.

The driver had left the keys in the ignition. If I could slam the driver's door, lock it, somehow manage to get the Wolf out . . .

But he wasn't going anywhere. Jackie Chan and Arnold and that Steven Seagal guy can pull that kind of shit in the movies, but here on Planet Earth it doesn't quite work that way.

I held on to the steering wheel for balance and eased down out of the truck, my feet once again on U.S. 50.

"Listen, pal, I'm happy to pay you to take me to Eureka. You don't have to do this."

"Hand it over," he said.

"Wha—"

His hand shot out, catching me on the left side of the face in a glancing blow, his knuckles scraping across my unshaven jaw with just enough force to slam me against the bed of the truck.

"Hand it over, motherfucker!" he yelled.

I reached into my back pocket, removed my wallet, held it out to him. He took it, opened it up, and peeked inside, then grinned.

"Couple hundred bucks is a couple hundred bucks,"

he announced to the cab of the truck. The Wolf stepped out of the truck and grabbed my bag from the truck bed. He unzipped the bag and rifled through it quickly. A moment later he looked up at Greasy Blond and shook his head. Nothing worth keeping . . .

Greasy Blond folded the wallet and stuck it into his front pocket. I took a long look at him, at his bloodshot blue eyes, his tangled, dirty blond hair. And something in me went cold, then hot with a fury that I fought to contain. So far I hadn't seen a gun on either of them, although it was a sure bet that a couple of scuzballs like these two probably wouldn't hit a public bathroom without flicking the safety off first.

Still, I was just about ready to take my chances. As my mind churned through one scenario after another, one plan after another, one fantasy or fear after another, I realized that the most logical thing to expect was that they were going to march me into the desert and put one into the back of my head. A body fifty yards off the loneliest road in America, beneath a pile of scrub brush or rocks, might never be found.

So what did I have to lose?

My jaw was numb and I realized my left eye was swelling and starting to water.

You bastards, I thought, *you miserable, cowardly sacks of shit.*

Then, off in the distance ahead of me, I heard the faint noise of another car engine, the second one in fourteen hours. Must be rush hour on U.S. 50 . . .

That seemed to get their attention. The driver looked over at the Wolf, nodded his head. The Wolf grabbed my bag by the shoulder strap and flung it off the road as far as he could. Clothes went flying everywhere.

"Harry," the driver said, turning to climb back into the truck. "Have a nice day."

The Wolf got in next to him and the pickup truck roared to life. The tires spun gravel and sandy dirt all over me as they pulled away, and in a few moments they were gone, the truck diminishing in size until I couldn't see it anymore.

Damn, I thought. *I'm still alive.*

I reached down, felt the front of my jacket, patted my arms. The rising sun behind me was warm on my back, my head, the nape of my neck, and I felt wonderfully, marvelously alive. Still mad as hell, still violated, wounded but alive. The car coming toward me was getting closer by the second. I wanted to wave the guy down, whoever he was, and thank him for being, for just being, and especially for being right here, right now.

I raised my hands, waved back and forth, rolling up and down on the balls of my feet. The car was closer, streaking by, and then was gone.

Gone.

I turned, faced the morning sun as the car rode into it. Maybe the guy didn't see me, I thought. Maybe he was blinded by the sun as he drove eastward at dawn. Maybe I was only a silhouette that appeared too late for him to stop.

And maybe he didn't give a damn.

No matter; any day aboveground's a good one. I stepped off the road, across a narrow shoulder of crushed gravel, larger rocks, and sand and into a thicket of brown, dry grass about knee high. I found my bag, then took maybe five minutes to gather up my socks, underwear, and T-shirts that used to be clean. I loosened the shoulder strap, slung the bag over my right shoulder, and climbed back up onto the highway. The sun was a couple of inches off the horizon now, its warmth a comfort on my sore face.

I did a quick appraisal of my situation. The upside was that at least I'd gotten a little water in me before the Wolf and his boyfriend decided to rob me. So I wasn't going to die of thirst, at least not for a while. I'd read that humans can go a long time without food, that the body's metabolism adjusts itself to accommodate the calories, or the lack of them. I had the feeling I was going to get a chance to test that theory.

On the downside, I was stranded in the middle of the loneliest road in America, with no wallet, no identification, no credit cards, no cash. But the two punks who had taken all that away from me had neglected to take the one thing I needed the most: the keys to the Mustang. I didn't blame them. Who wants the keys to a car with a blown engine?

I started walking east, slowly at first to conserve energy and loosen up the tired muscles of my body. As I walked, I settled into a smooth, flowing rhythm. It felt good to be moving. And as I did so, I jingled the keys in my pocket, the car keys that the Wolf and Greasy Blond hadn't bothered to fool with.

Wonder what they'd have done if I'd thought to mention the two grand in traveler's checks I had locked in the trunk, hidden under the spare tire?

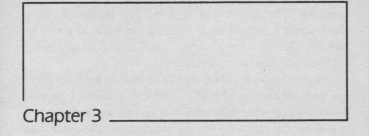

Chapter 3

Time gets weird in the desert.

I mean, first it seems to drag by. I wasn't wearing my watch, so there was no way to count it, no way to measure it. You just know it's passing incredibly slowly. I felt like I'd walked for hours and hours, but the sun had only climbed about an inch higher on the horizon.

Then, after a while, it starts slipping by so quickly, you can't remember where it went. One moment the sun was barely up and I was forcing myself to walk faster to keep from freezing; the next the sun's in my face, beating me to death, holding me back. I unzipped the jacket, took off the sweaters, and packed them back in my shoulder bag. Later the jacket came off and I tied the sleeves around my waist. I started getting dry again, my lips cracking, my skin chapping. It had to be near noon, but noon of which day, which month, which year?

After a while, your mind goes blank and you're not aware of time passing anymore. You just walk.

I had stopped to rest on the side of the road, had taken a seat on a boulder about the size of a beanbag chair that was so smooth and rounded, it could have been polished and set there just for me. My guts were starting to gnaw at me now. It had been over twenty-four hours since I last ate. About an hour earlier a tractor-trailer rig had

23

gone by. The driver had ignored my frantic waving, then nearly knocked me over with the blast of air as he passed. By that time it hadn't much mattered anymore. I'd been too tired to fuss about it.

Something skittered off into the brush behind me and I jumped off the rock as if it had come alive. I backed away, trying to see whatever it was that had moved, but it was far too quick for me. I picked up the shoulder bag, hefted it slowly to my shoulder, and turned back east.

That's when I saw it.

It was just a glimmer at first, like a glance at a mirror in the next room just as the sun was coming through the window at just the right angle to shoot a spark of light in your direction, which nearly blinds you. I leaned down, squinted, tried to find another angle.

It was gold, gold metal, the color of the Mustang.

I smiled even though it hurt and made my lips crack even further. I began walking, too tired to run, hoping to hold out until I made the car. I kept thinking about the rest of that flat Coke that was sitting on the seat. Even flat and stale, it meant liquid and it meant sugar.

As I walked on, getting closer with each step, the image of the car grew larger. And the larger it got, the more sharply focused it became. And as it came into focus, I saw that there was something else next to it.

Another car . . .

Now I don't mean to sound paranoid, but you've got to understand, the last day or so the karma hadn't exactly run in my direction. Maybe it was a good Samaritan. Maybe it was a cop or a highway patrolman.

Or maybe it was Greasy Blond and the Wolf, circling back to check out the car and see if there was anything left worth stealing.

I stopped, set the bag on the side of the road, and bent forward, straining my middle-aged eyes as hard as I could to see what was going on. I estimated the car was about a mile or so in front of me, barely more than a speck, but who knew how accurate a guess that was? I picked up the bag again and started walking at an even pace, the car and whatever was next to it growing larger with each step.

A few minutes later I could make out distinctly the sharp lines of another vehicle, pulled off the road at a cockeyed angle to the Mustang. The hood was up on the Mustang, and there was a body leaning over the front grille.

Disconnecting the battery, I guessed. There wasn't much inside the engine compartment to pull out. It was a new battery, though, barely two months old, and the thought of some redneck bastard running off with it was enough to piss me off even in my strung-out condition. I reached down, picked up a few choice rocks and stuffed them in my pocket, then quickened my pace. With a little luck, the guy would keep his head down in my engine compartment until I got close enough to bounce a rock off his head.

About two hundred yards or so away, I sped up again until I'd worked up to a slow trot. The bag bounced off my leg as I jogged along, panting, trying not to stumble on the loose gravel at the side of the road. I stepped onto the asphalt and continued, only I knew my knees weren't going to take too much more pounding before they gave out.

I watched as the guy straightened up from the engine compartment with the battery cradled in his hands. Then he turned and spotted me. I stepped up my pace until I was as close to running as I was ever going to manage. I couldn't get a good look at him or the truck he was driving. But I could tell he was alone.

He seemed to stand still for a few moments, staring at

me, and then he moved quickly. He bent over the side-rails of the truck bed, set the battery down, and came up with something in each hand. I couldn't see what was in his right, but his left held an object that was small and red. He set that down on the ground near the Mustang, then raised his right hand and brought what was in it down hard on the windshield. Even from a distance I heard the crystalline, sharp sounds of glass shattering. The hood was still up on the Mustang, so I couldn't see the spiderweb that was no doubt painted in the glass across the front of my car, but I felt it almost as if I'd been standing there.

Time seemed to stand still and each pounding step of my shoes on the asphalt took forever. I could see the guy better now. He was wearing jeans and a bright red western-style shirt. He sent the hammer into the driver's-door window, and I saw pieces of glass glimmering like metal as they showered out and rained down on the highway. The guy turned, tossed the hammer into the bed of the truck, then leaned over and picked the red, boxy container up off the road.

Then he held it over the engine compartment and tilted it.

Damn it! I yelled inside my head. *No, damn it! You got what you came for! Don't do this!*

The guy's arms danced as he continued pouring liquid all over the front of the car, then into the car's interior through the busted window. I dropped the bag, pumped my arms as fast as I could, ran like a sixteen-year-old toward the guy. If I could just get close enough to get my hands on him . . .

He turned, and for a moment I thought I spotted panic race across his face, as if he'd miscalculated and I was getting closer than he thought I'd get.

He tossed the red container into the bed of his truck, then ran around the back of it and climbed into the cab.

I could see his face now. He was a kid, a teenager, a sick, twisted little shit of a kid.

The black pickup pulled forward, toward me, then U-turned in the middle of the highway. The kid pulled up next to the Mustang and I saw his brake lights flash.

I was almost close enough to read the license plate. It was green with white letters, but I couldn't make the letters out.

He turned, looked out the back window at me, and grinned. Then he raised a middle finger in salute.

And with the other hand he tossed out a lit match, just as the brake lights went out and the truck jerked forward.

I screamed. *"You son of a bitch!"*

But he never heard me. There was a *whomp* and a ball of orange seemed to flash up out of nowhere as the truck peeled rubber and squealed away from me. I thought for a second—no, *hoped* for a second—that the kid really had miscalculated and his truck was standing just a bit too close to the car when it went off.

No such luck. I stopped, exhausted, spent, my chest heaving, straining for air, and watched through the ball of flame that had once been my '68 Mustang as the kid pulled safely away and was gone.

I stared, dumbfounded, almost numb, as the color of the flame went from orange to red to blue, then with some purple and green thrown in, followed by thick black smoke as the interior of the car went up.

Loud popping sounds, tires exploding, glass shattering.

All I could do was watch, just stand there and watch.

"This day is really starting to suck," I croaked dryly, then turned around and started trekking back to pick up my shoulder bag before somebody ripped that off.

* * *

I was lying in the brush a few yards off the road, with the bag serving as a pillow, watching the Mustang smolder, when I heard another car off in the distance. For some reason or other, the Mustang's gas tank never blew. I don't understand the physics of these things, but I'd seen the kid pour gas all over the engine compartment and then splash some in the interior. Maybe he hadn't had that much gasoline to begin with. In any case, the front three-quarters of the car was charred and blackened, while the rear of the car was only scorched, the gold paint peeling off in long, thin strips.

I was waiting for the damn thing to cool off so that I could see if by some miracle the traveler's checks had survived. They were in a small metal lockbox, mashed down under the spare tire.

With a little bit of luck . . .

I laughed at the thought, figuring a little bit of luck was more than I could hope for lately. I almost started giggling—half out of my head, I guess—when I thought I heard the distant sound of another engine.

"Jesus," I muttered. "Not again."

I eased myself up into a half-crouch, staring carefully up over the top of the car. Heat waves still undulated and shimmered off the cooling metal. Through the waves I saw another car, miles down the road, moving toward me fast.

This time I wasn't taking any chances. I still had the rocks in my pocket. I fingered them, my eyes narrowing into a squint as the car approached. I turned, crawled quickly into the brush, and hunkered down as low as I could get. My head was starting to do funny things to me, like thinking that they've finally come back for me. This time they won't make any mistakes. This time they'll get me for sure.

And at the same time some other part of my brain, some other level of whatever innate intelligence I still had, told me this was nonsense. There was no one out to get me. No one was after me. I'd just had a run of bad luck, a couple of chance encounters on a lonely, deserted stretch of highway with a few ethically challenged males who had been forced to grow up without adequate guidance.

But this time, the other side said, *Don't take any chances!*

I pushed aside a clump of dried brown grass and peeked out through the brush. A car the deep blue of new Levi's before they've been washed, trimmed in gold, pulled to a stop behind the Mustang. I heard gravel crunching and then the sound of the engine settling into a high idle. A door opened and a man wearing mirrored sunglasses and a brown uniform stepped cautiously out of the car and scanned the area.

I carefully arranged a clump of brush in front of me just as his eyes rotated around to my hiding place.

My mouth burned, my eyes felt as dry as the rocks I held tightly in the palm of my hand. There was this little hot sphere of pain right at the top of my neck that throbbed rhythmically in time to my heartbeat.

My God! I thought. *They've sent the brownshirts after me. The bastards!*

The storm trooper sauntered around his car and over to the Mustang. He was on the opposite side of the car, staring down inside it. Looking for a body, I guess. His polished boots shone bright silver shards of light straight at my eyes from under the car.

Must lie still . . . must lie very still.

I rubbed my eyes with my dusty fingers, which for some reason or other I thought would feel good but in fact felt like I was scraping sandpaper across them. As dry as they were, my eyes started to tear up.

Hold on! Don't lose it. They'll have you for sure then.

Then the other part of my mind kicked back in, if only for a few moments. Why would they be after me? What have I done to them? Why are the bastards after me?

Then I realized, with that one last little bit of sane mind I had left, they're not.

They're not after me! I didn't do anything wrong!

The thought made me choke with emotion, relief, and joy, mixed with a turmoil deep inside the likes of which I could not remember ever experiencing before. I coughed, cleared my throat, struggled to regain my composure.

I looked up. The brownshirt was looking out over the top of the car in my direction, searching for the source of the sound he'd just heard.

I stood up slowly, my hands raised. He saw me, put his right hand on his holster but never drew his gun. I took a couple of steps toward him as he came around the front of the Mustang.

"Mister," he said, "are you all right?"

"Yeah," I whispered, so softly I was sure he couldn't hear me, but it was the best I could do. "Yeah, I'm fine. Now."

I nodded to him and took another step forward. And then everything went all sparkly and black. Shards of gold and purple and green closed in on me from all sides, and that's the last I remember.

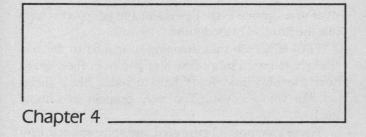

Chapter 4

I woke up bathed in white, surrounded in white. White lights, white sheets, white ceiling above me.

Or was it sky?

Was I dead?

A moment of panic erupted before I realized that no, I couldn't be dead. I felt too shitty to be dead, and there was a tube running out of my arm that led to a plastic bag full of clear liquid, which was hanging from a chrome pole. I don't think they have IVs in the afterlife.

I tried to raise my head but was still too weak and sore. I moaned, heard the noise coming out of my throat as a detached entity, as if it came from somewhere else.

I licked my lips. They were still cracked, but I wasn't as thirsty, as parched, as I had been before.

"So you're awake," a voice said. A woman's voice, low and sweet. I rolled over a couple of inches.

She stood at an angle to me, fooling with something on a metal table. She was maybe in her early thirties, thin, attractive, long red hair almost down to her waist, braided in some kind of intricate pattern.

"I hate to sound like a cliché," I said weakly, "but where am I?"

She turned, smiled at me. Her skin was pale, her teeth glaringly white, straight. Obviously, she didn't spend a lot of time outside in the desert sun and her parents were able to afford an orthodontist.

"I'm Kelly," she said, stepping over next to the bed. "Kelly Graham. I'm a nurse and you're in the Nevada Rural Health Clinic. And I hate to sound like a cliché, too, but who are you? You were brought in without any ID."

"Name's Denton," I answered, my voice still scratchy. "Harry Denton. I was robbed. They took my wallet."

"That's what we figured, Mr. Denton," she said. "I'll send the clerk in here in a few minutes to get your paperwork started."

I thought for a moment. "How long have I been here?"

"Not long," she said, pulling a blood pressure cuff off a rack on the wall behind me. She continued talking as she wrapped the cuff around my left bicep and began pumping.

"Couple of hours. You were brought in here semiconscious, dehydrated, pretty empty all over. You feel up to a cup of ice chips, maybe a light lunch?"

"Yeah," I answered. "I'm starving."

She scribbled some numbers down on a form attached to a clipboard, then removed the cuff.

"There's a gentleman outside that would like to talk to you," she said. "Seems you've got a nasty little bump on the side of your head and I think he'd like to find out how it got there."

I settled back into the pillow as she scooped some ice chips from a plastic pitcher into a small cup and handed it to me.

"Yeah, be glad to talk to him," I said, shaking a few of the ice chips into my mouth. The sensation was so wonderful, so delightful, that for a moment I felt nothing but sheer, unadulterated joy.

"Also," she added, pulling aside the white curtain that surrounded my bed, "it seems you were found next to a freshly torched car. I believe the gentleman outside would like to ask you about that, too."

I closed my eyes, savoring the ice chips and moaning softly.

"I'll phone over to the café and ask them to send something over. I'll make sure they get you something light. Soup and sandwich, maybe?"

I nodded. "That'd be great."

She turned to leave. "Oh, Kelly?" I said.

Kelly turned back to me, a sweet smile on her face. God, I was glad to be alive.

"Yes?"

"Thanks."

"And that's about all I can remember," I said, pulling myself into a sitting position on the side of the bed. "I saw you pull up to the car and then I think I must have passed out."

"You did," Sergeant Dell Kanon of the Nevada Highway Patrol said to me. "I managed to get you into the back of my cruiser and you pretty much slept the whole way here."

"Where is here?" I asked, pulling my shirt on.

"Eureka, Nevada," he answered. "About thirty miles west of where I found you. Have you got a record of your credit-card numbers and anything else you'll need to report?"

"I've only got a couple. I'll just have to call the toll-free number and get them to cancel the cards with my name and address. I'm sure they've dealt with this kind of situation before."

"The Eureka County Sheriff's Department is just down

the road a bit. I'll give you a ride there. The sheriff'll want to fill out a complete report. You can phone in on the credit cards from there, too."

"Any chance of finding those two?" I asked. "Actually, three, counting the kid with the matches . . ."

"The license plate of the kid who torched your car sounds like a Colorado one. I've got your description and I'll get it out over the network. The other two guys? Who knows? A tall, dark Indian who goes by the name of Wolf and a greasy blond-haired Anglo. Ought to be pretty easy to spot. But if they're on the run, they're probably long gone."

I stood, still a little shaky, and finished buttoning my shirt. "Where will they tow the Mustang, or what's left of it?"

"It'll be at the sheriff's department, down by the E-Z Stop."

"The what?" I asked.

Kanon smiled. "You'll see. It's down at the other end of town. Sort of a local landmark."

"I've got some things in the trunk of that car. If they're not burned up, I'd like to get them."

"No problem. Just one other question, Mr. Denton?" he asked.

I turned in his direction, raised an eyebrow.

"You a cop?"

I smiled. "No, why do you ask?"

He closed his notebook, clicked his pen, slid it back into the slot on his front-pocket flap. "The way you described these guys. You went right down the line, noting each characteristic in the same order. Everything very precise, right in line. Just like a law-enforcement professional would."

"Thanks for the compliment, I guess. But I used to be a reporter."

"Used to be?"

I tucked in my shirt, tried to straighten myself up as much as I could. "Yeah, I'm a licensed P.I. in Nashville. Got my own shingle."

Sergeant Kanon reached down and picked up my shoulder bag for me. He was a good guy. I liked him, and he'd come along at a time when I hadn't been sure there were many good guys left. He'd been a little suspicious of me at first; after all, a shell-shocked guy next to a burned-out car in the middle of the desert tends to make law-enforcement officers a bit skeptical. I think I managed to convince him that I was just an ordinary guy who'd had a run of bad luck.

"I know you'll find this hard to believe," he said as I signed the last of the forms that would allow me to leave the clinic. "But you really were lucky."

"Lucky?" I asked. "Help me out here with that one."

"To begin with, those two could have marched you off into the bush, killed you, and there's a chance no one would ever have found you."

A chill ran up the back of my neck. "That thought already occurred to me."

"Second, the gas tank on the Mustang could have gone up while you were standing next to it."

"Guess you're right," I agreed.

"And then there's the fact that a trucker pulled into the café back in Ruth, just off 50, and said he saw an abandoned car about twenty miles back. Which is why I showed up. I wasn't scheduled to work 50 today. I was supposed to be patrolling south on Route 6."

I handed the clipboard full of signed forms to the silent lady behind the desk, then followed the sergeant out into the late-afternoon Nevada sun.

"Yeah," I said, taking a deep lung full of the crisp, clear, dry Nevada air. "Guess you're right."

"Welcome to Eureka," Kanon said as I eased into the NHP patrol car. "Truth is, this's a really nice little town. One of the wealthiest per capita places in the state."

"Really," I said. "Good place to get robbed."

"Those two guys who robbed you weren't from here," he said with just a hint of scolding in his voice. "I'd be willing to bet the rent money on that."

The engine started with a grinding that settled quickly into a powerful, deep-throated rumble. The car was a big Ford, a Crown Victoria Special, no doubt with cop engine, cop suspension, cop brakes, cop tires. Kanon put the car into reverse and backed out of a parking spot in front of the building.

"That looks new," I said, motioning toward the clinic.

"It is. Just got started last year. Like I said, there's a lot of money in Eureka."

"Where's it come from?" I didn't really care; it just felt good to hear a voice talking. I'd had a lot of silence in the past few days and it was starting to wear on me.

The heavy car swung out onto Main Street, which was what they called Route 50 through the middle of town, and turned north. "A hundred thirty years or so ago, there were ten thousand people in this town," Kanon explained. "Eureka was a stop on the Pony Express route. Prospectors, gamblers, saloon girls, gunfighters. Just like in the movies. Then it all gave out and the town nearly died. A few people hung on. This is hard country, but once you get settled here, you can't give it up."

I watched out the window as we drove through town. The building storefronts were straight out of the Old West, brick and masonry construction with wooden balconies overlooking the street, balustrades intricately carved and painted white. It looked like a movie set, except that it was real, and despite my experiences of the last twenty-four hours, I liked it.

"Then a few years ago," he continued, " 'round about '94, I think, they hit another gold strike up in the hills. Homestate Cortez and Newmont moved back in. Probably got about a hundred locals working the mines now. Good pay, good tax base. We got the best-paid teachers in the state here."

I turned, smiled at Kanon. He was maybe early fifties, weather-beaten, could stand to lose about thirty pounds, with short graying hair in a buzz cut.

"So what, do you, like, moonlight for the Chamber of Commerce?" I asked.

"No, nothing like that."

"You must live here then," I said. "Nobody talks about a place the way you do this place unless he lives here or is paid to do it."

"Got a little ranch north of town, just off 278, on the east side of the Sulphur Spring Range."

"Little ranch?"

"Yeah," he said, slowing as we approached a tanker truck moving slowly up the street. "Only about twenty-five hundred acres."

"Twenty-five hundred acres!" I said. "My lot back in Nashville measures seventy-eight feet by a hundred."

He shook his head. "Man, no way I could live like that. My neighbors right on top of me . . . No way."

"Makes for easy lawn maintenance," I said.

We drove on in silence for a few minutes, coming to the west side of town, where the sheriff's department and local jail were within spitting distance of the E-Z Stop and across the street from the small fire house.

"So that's the place you mentioned," I said.

"Yeah, that's where the van can pick you up, when it comes by in a few days."

"Few days," I snapped, sitting upright from the relaxed

slouching position I'd eased into. "What do you mean, 'few days'?"

"Nevada Express operates service from Ely to Reno, but it only comes through a couple of times a week," he explained.

"What am I supposed to do until then?" I asked. "Can I rent a car?"

Kanon eased the patrol car into a slot in front of the police department and shifted into park. "Not without a driver's license and a credit card, you can't," he said as he exited.

I climbed out of the car, hefting my bag onto my shoulder.

"Besides," he added, "the nearest car rental place is Ely, little over seventy-five miles that way."

Kanon pointed east, away from the late-afternoon sun.

"Yeah, I know where it is," I grumbled. "What am I going to do until the bus comes?"

"There's a place here in town," he said. "Sort of a boardinghouse—the Colonnade Hotel. It's clean and affordable, if you don't mind walking down the hall to go to the bathroom. While you're talking to the sheriff, I'll call the woman who owns it. I'll drop you off there later."

"It's pretty nice," he added, "and you look like you could use a hot bath and a soft bed."

"You forget, Sergeant," I said. "No credit cards, no money, no driver's license."

He stopped at the door to the sheriff's office and held it open for me.

"Got anybody who can wire you some cash?" he asked.

The Eureka County Sheriff's Department deputy took a complete report, let me call the credit-card companies, and even let me make a toll call to my insurance company. Not that I had any insurance on the Mustang beyond the bare minimum legal limit, but at least I could cancel the policy and get part of my premium back. After that I tried calling Marsha collect in Reno, but there was still no answer. I was beginning to wonder what was going on and if I'd be able to find her once I got there.

Assuming, of course, I ever got there.

Then Kanon, the deputy, and I walked a couple of blocks over to where they'd towed the car. I discovered that the other suitcase and the two boxes in the trunk were scorched but largely okay. My clothes were going to need several trips through the wash to get the smell out, but other than that they would survive.

And better still, the lockbox under the spare tire had protected the traveler's checks.

Okay, Sergeant Kanon was right. I am lucky.

On top of that, the deputy had a buddy who ran a scrapyard on the outskirts of town who drove his tow truck in and gave me fifty bucks for the Mustang as scrap metal, more as a favor to his pal than anything else. So I pocketed the traveler's checks and had enough cash to buy dinner and a bus ticket to Reno.

The deputy handed me a copy of the police report in case I wanted to write off the loss of the Mustang on my taxes, then wished me well, telling me not to expect too much in terms of finding any of these guys and to have a pleasant stay in Nevada. I thanked him, grabbed my stuff, and followed Kanon out the door into the deepening Nevada shadows.

As I climbed back into the NHP cruiser with Kanon, I realized I'd forgotten to check the interior of the Mustang to see if by some chance my copy of *Tropic of*

Cancer had survived. I started to ask him if we could go back to the lot, but by now the tow-truck driver had probably hauled the Mustang off to the car knacker's.

Damn.

Chapter 5

Sergeant Kanon and I said goodbye after he drove me to the hotel, which was a block off Main Street at the corner of Monroe and Clark. The building was a two-story brick, painted white, with those tall, narrow windows that are characteristic of nineteenth-century western buildings. The name—COLONNADE HOTEL—was painted directly on the bricks, red on white, and another painted sign read ENTRANCE with an arrow pointing left toward the narrow front door. With each moment I spent in Eureka, I felt more and more like I'd simply been dropped a century or two back in time. Kanon explained my circumstances to the woman who ran the hotel. Good thing, too, because I hadn't shaved or showered in a couple of days, smelled of smoke and gasoline, and my clothes were worn and dirty. My bags were scuffed and slightly scorched, and all I had in the way of assets was a handful of traveler's checks and no way to prove they were mine.

"Well, if you say so, Dell," she whispered, eyeing me from the other end of the front desk, where she'd gone to confab with the sergeant. "I guess it's okay."

I signed a hundred dollars' worth of the checks over to establish some credit and thanked her profusely. I wanted her on my side, if that was possible. I had no idea how long I'd be stranded here. In any case, she gave me a room; that was all that mattered, and Sergeant Kanon was kind enough to help me with my stuff. At the door, I told him once again how grateful I was and wished him well. He handed me his card and told me to call him if I ever needed anything.

Then he was gone and I was alone in a small yet warm and clean room, with indoor plumbing and a hot bath waiting for me just down the hall. I unpacked my clothes and did an inventory of my belongings. Fortunately, nothing was seriously damaged. A few things didn't even smell. I picked out a pair of jeans and a blue-checked sport shirt to put on later. Then I tried calling Marsha one more time, collect.

Still no answer. I wondered if I should start calling hospitals, but I had no way of even knowing what hospitals were in Reno.

I opened the window and stared out to a range of hills on the horizon. The setting sun had painted the sky deep shades of blue, headed toward purple, then black, sprayed with orange and silver. It was beautiful, awesome, and for a few moments I managed to find some kind of quiet inside myself.

Then I went down the hall to the bathroom, turned the bathwater on, and stripped out of my clothes. I took a good, long look in the mirror and didn't particularly like what I saw. My eyes were bloodshot and tired, with deep black circles below the sockets that looked like pouches. Lines ran out from the corners of my eyes; not quite crow's-feet, I thought, but lines that even a year ago hadn't been there. I didn't have the bone structure or the youth to get that sexy *Miami Vice* look from not shaving. I just looked like hell. And down the side of my face the ugly bruise from where Greasy Blond had taken a swipe at me lay on my skin like a careless smudge.

Damn, I'm getting old. Too old for this . . .

Steam began to fill the bathroom and, in one of Mother Nature's more gracious gestures, cloud up the mirror. As the reflection of my face gradually lost its sharpness in the mirror's fog, the ravages of the last few days seemed to melt away a bit, even if it was only an illusion.

I grabbed my shaving cream and razor, then slid into the hot water slowly. The water temperature was right where I wanted it, as hot as I could stand it, on that thin line between exquisitely hot pleasure and scalding. The tension in my shoulders dissolved into the water, which went all the way up to my chin, barely an inch away from overflowing. Everything in me went limp, my mind went blank, in this incredibly sweet release from the last few days. Or maybe it was weeks . . .

Marsha's offer—request, really—that I come to Reno for the baby's birth had been a surprise to me, along with the fact that the baby was a girl. Marsha'd left Nashville in a hurry and might have gone without telling me if I hadn't happened to find out almost serendipitously of her plans. Things had been tense, strained, between us for a long time before that.

It had been a bad time and I didn't want to think about it. But I had survived it and my life had settled down. I was in a resting phase, I guess, with a long period of downtime. I'd closed up shop as a private investigator and spent a few months renovating a house I'd inherited from a friend. Along with that house came enough cash from the inheritance, so that for the first time in years I had a little breathing room. I could afford to take some time off, recoup my energy, figure out what to do next.

And then she'd called. Her voice had been plaintive, maybe even scared, and certainly lonely. Marsha had gone to live with her aunt Marty in Reno. Aunt Marty, I knew, was loaded, with apartments in New York City and L.A., along with the house in Reno. When Marsha'd called, she told me she was staying there alone except for a live-in Hispanic maid who wasn't much company.

Marsha had asked me to come out to Reno for our daughter's birth, but I didn't have any illusions about my future as a husband and father. No white picket fences for us, I knew. No parent-teacher conferences and Girl Scout meetings and pictures before the prom, with the two of us waiting nervously for our little-girl-who-grew-up-too-fast to return home safely. Marsha had made it very clear that this was not in the cards for us. And I'm not sure why I agreed to come out here, except for the fact that I'd had some part in the creation of this new human being and was curious to see how it would all work out.

My mind drifted along with my body in the hot water. I sat up, lathered my face, and shaved slowly, carefully. There's something about the ritual of shaving, especially when you have the time to do it slowly, that is a strange kind of comfort.

By now it was dark outside and I was beginning to get hungry. The light meal at the clinic had been wonderful at the time, but I was ravenous again. I wanted steak and potatoes and wine and cheesecake afterward. I've never been a big eater; for me, I only ate because if you don't, you'll eventually fall over. But my two days in the desert had given me a whole new appreciation for food. When you don't have food and water, pretty soon it becomes all you can think about. You obsess about it. Politics and money and literature and art don't matter anymore; it's, *Where can I get a meal?*

I could also use a few other things, like a big bottle of aspirin and some eyedrops. I walked downstairs, out into the cool night air, and began strolling the block over to Main Street. The street was quiet. No cars passed me the whole block. Music played faintly somewhere behind me, like a saloon piano's tinkling. I imagined myself a gunfighter, new in town, parading down these mean streets looking for trouble.

Only they weren't so mean, these narrow streets of a nineteenth-century mining town. Eureka, Nevada, seemed like a good place to live, a good place to hide. Maybe, I wondered, I should just stay here. Call Lonnie and have him put the house on the market and send me the cash.

I reached the intersection of Clark and Main and turned left around the Lucky Stiff Bar. Across the street, the Masonic Lodge loomed in red brick turning black in the shadows. It felt good to walk, to know that a hot meal was just ahead and a warm bed just behind me.

But as I walked on, I wondered how long I'd be here. How much trouble would it be to find a way to Reno, not to mention getting another driver's license and solving all the other problems Greasy Blond and the Wolf had left me with.

I tried not to think about those two, about the fear and humiliation that comes from being assaulted, robbed. You'd think in this day and age it wouldn't be that big a deal. Hell, we're Americans; we imprison more people than any other civilized nation on earth. We're descended from criminals; our ancestors were on the run from every decent culture on the planet. We ought to be used to it by now.

On my right a block or so ahead was the E-Z Stop, the combination convenience market, café, pool hall, slot-machine parlor, and God-knew-what-else Kanon and I had passed earlier this afternoon. I stepped in through the door to the sound of a jukebox playing and the resonant clicking of balls bouncing off each other on a pool table. Someone in another room laughed loudly at something someone else had just said and suddenly I felt terribly alone.

I was hungry but didn't feel like eating here. There were too many people having too much fun and I couldn't be a part of it. I walked through the grocery area and grabbed a few things from the shelves, then stepped over to the checkout counter to pay. As I was fishing some money out of my jeans pocket, I heard someone behind me daintily clear a throat and then a low, feminine voice.

"Mr. Denton?"

I turned. A pale young woman, couple of inches shorter than me, with long red hair pulled behind her, stood there in a pair of jeans, blue work shirt, and jeans jacket.

"Hello, Nurse Graham," I said.

"Please, it's Kelly." She stuck out her hand to me. "How's the head?"

I took her hand, smiled broadly, and shook it. "Much better," I said. "Much better. Hey, thanks for taking such good care of me today. I was feeling pretty lousy."

"How was the lunch?" She smiled at me, that pretty smile I remembered from earlier.

"Fine, only it didn't last that long. I was kind of thinking about getting some dinner, but I don't know the secret handshake."

"The what?"

"You know," I said, handing the clerk a twenty as he finished sacking the things I'd bought. "Where the locals eat, the secret places that aren't in the tourist guide."

The clerk handed me my change and a brown paper bag. I stepped aside but continued to talk to Kelly as the clerk toted up her things.

"Depends on what you want," she said. "For a small

town, we've got quite a lot of choices here. We got your Chinese, a good Italian deli, and then there's the steak-and-potato places."

"Ordinarily, I'd jump at the chance to eat Chinese. I'm a sucker for good Szechuan."

"Oh, me, too," she said. "I can't get enough of it. But there's not much good Szechuan here."

"There's a place back home you'd love," I said, suddenly homesick. "Mrs. Lee's. Best cheap Szechuan food this side of the Yangtze River."

She smiled. "I'm glad you're feeling better. How long are you going to be in town?"

"Oh," I said, turning back to the clerk. "That's what I meant to ask. Somebody told me there's a bus or a van service through Eureka and you catch it here."

"Yeah," the clerk said. "Only he came through yesterday headed west. He goes to Reno, comes back late tomorrow headed east, then takes Sunday off, and heads back to Reno on Monday."

"I don't even know what day it is today," I admitted.

"Friday," Kelly said. "How bad a hit did you take?"

I turned to her. "I've been on the road, driving four days, maybe five. Not much sleep. It all starts to run together after a while."

"You're really determined to get there, aren't you?"

"Yeah, just didn't know how much trouble it was going to be."

"Maybe you should have flown," she said.

"Well," I said offhandedly, "then I wouldn't have gotten to see . . . Eureka."

"Yes, and you can see an awful lot of Eureka in three days, which is how long you've got to wait for the van service."

She opened a leather shoulder bag and pulled out her

wallet, then paid the clerk for her things. Kelly picked up her shopping bag, but I was blocking her way.

"Excuse me," I said clumsily, "I'm sorry. I'm in your way." I stepped to the side and then followed her out the door. Once outside, she stopped.

"Good night, Mr. Denton," she said. "Good luck."

"Please, it's Harry," I said. "And thanks again for this afternoon. I really appreciate it."

"It's my job," she said. "No need to thank me." Then she turned to walk away.

"Kelly," I said. She turned back. "I, uh, well, I don't . . . Well, I'm sort of at a loss for someone to talk to over dinner and I hate to eat alone, and you were so kind to me today. Can I buy you dinner?"

Her eyes seemed to get a little bigger and she shook a long hank of hair off her left shoulder.

"No strings attached," I said, maybe a little too quickly. "Just somebody to talk to over dinner. That is, if you don't have any other plans."

She stepped back over to me and stood there for a moment, her bag of groceries like a toddler cocked on her hip.

"You never did tell me what you felt like eating."

I grinned, probably stupidly, but I couldn't help it and I didn't care.

"Anything," I offered. "You name it, as long as they'll take traveler's checks without an ID."

"How about a steak?" she asked. "You could use a little meat on those bones of yours, you know. Have you always been so skinny?"

"Steak it is," I said. "Lead the way."

We dropped our bags off in the backseat of Kelly's Saturn, then strolled the two blocks or so down Main

Street to the Jackson House, which billed itself as HOTEL, SALOON, AND CAFÉ on the square sign mounted on the second-floor balcony overlooking the street.

This being a Friday night, we were going to have to wait a while for a table, which suited me fine. We ordered drinks at the bar, then took them outside to the front gallery and sat down in the cool night air. I sipped on a tall scotch and soda while Kelly nursed a glass of wine. She pulled her long red hair in front of her, then pinned it up into a bun unself-consciously. It seemed a long time since I had simply sat and studied the movements of a woman. There was a grace and smooth fluidity to her movements. I'd forgotten what it was like to talk lightly and aimlessly with a woman with whom I had no baggage, no weight, no history. It was almost like a casual date, although I tried not to let myself think in those terms.

"So," Kelly asked, "why are you headed to Reno?"

Oh, hell, I thought. *So much for the nice, pleasant evening.*

"If you don't mind my asking," she said, sensing my hesitation. "I mean, if it's none of my business . . . I don't mean to pry."

I smiled, sipped my drink. "It's not that," I said. "It's just that it's a little awkward."

I studied her face. She had high cheekbones, her skin dotted with light freckles, and her eyes were a bright hazel that seemed to be even brighter in the dim light.

"My situation is a little unusual," I said after a moment. "You see, I'm supposed to be in Reno for the birth of my first child."

She looked down for just a moment, then back up at me as if I'd said nothing of consequence. "Oh, I see."

"I'm not so sure that you do. You see, it's a woman I

used to be involved with who got pregnant. I mean, she did it on purpose, but she didn't tell me she was going to. When I found out, I was actually kind of excited. I mean, I thought we'd get married. Only she didn't want to. In fact, she kind of, well, dumped me and moved out here."

"Wait," Kelly said. "She got pregnant. You wanted to get married. She said no and dumped you?"

"That's about it." It felt strange to tell a complete stranger in a couple of sentences the abstract of the last year of my life and discover that I was beginning to feel completely detached from it.

She looked away, almost confused. "Okay, that's not your standard boy-meets-girl, boy-knocks-up-girl, boy-runs-away story."

I grinned. "Hadn't thought of it that way."

"What's this chick's problem, anyway?"

I shrugged. "Oh, it's complicated. It was a bad time for both of us."

"Look, if I'm prying, just tell me. But why are you even going out there if she doesn't want you?"

"She asked me," I said. "I think she's trying to do the right thing."

"Maybe," she said. "And maybe you still love her." She lifted the wineglass to her lips, took an easy swallow. The hollow of her neck bobbed as the wine went down and I couldn't help but wonder what it would feel like to—

Stop that!

"So," I said, interrupting my own train of thought. "Are you from Eureka? This your hometown?"

"Yeah, I was born here. Lived here until I went to college at UNLV."

"Go Rebels," I said.

"A man after my own heart," she quipped. And then,

embarrassed, she looked away. "Anyway, I got my degree in nursing about the time my dad got sick, so I moved back here to take care of him and just never left."

"So you must like it." Out of the corner of my eye, I saw the hostess motioning to us. "I think our table's ready."

We stood up and walked back into the hotel, continuing the small talk that passes for dinner conversation between two people who don't know each other very well. Kelly related almost offhandedly her mother's death in an auto accident when she was five and her father's death last year. She had been married once while in college, for only a couple of years, and had been divorced for so long, she barely remembered what marriage was like. She lived alone in a house she'd inherited from her parents and alternated weeks working at the clinic in Eureka and for the LifeFlight service out of Ely. She liked being a helicopter-borne emergency nurse.

"Satisfies my adrenaline addiction, I guess," she said over coffee after dinner. "Sort of like when you're on a case, right?"

I smiled. "There's usually not much adrenaline raised when I'm on a case. Most of the time I'm parked down the street waiting for some guy who's supposed to be wheelchair-bound to walk his dog so that I can take pictures of him and get paid by the insurance company."

"If you don't mind my asking," she said, "what are you going to do after your daughter's born? Will you stay in Reno?"

I shook my head. "Not likely, I'm afraid. I've got a house and friends back in Nashville. And Marsha doesn't want me around. She's made that pretty clear."

Kelly leaned back in her chair and for a moment was silent, looking contemplative. "I don't get it, Harry," she said after a bit. "You seem like a decent guy, and decent guys are hard to come by these days. Doesn't make much sense to toss one aside."

"Thanks. I appreciate that. But Marsha and I were together a long time and I think things just started to go off after a while. We were more different than we thought we were, I guess. I know she didn't like the line of work I was in."

"Yeah? What did she do?"

"She's an M.D.," I answered. "A forensic pathologist. She was the assistant medical examiner in Nashville for years."

"God! She cuts up dead bodies for a living and gave you a hard time about your line of work?"

"Yeah," I said. "Go figure."

When the waitress brought the check, I realized we'd been sitting over dinner for nearly two hours. It was getting late; I was sated with food and good wine, but I was having so much fun, I hated to let go of the evening.

"Let me help you with that," Kelly said, pointing toward the bill.

"Wouldn't hear of it," I said, pulling four twenty-dollar traveler's checks out of my wallet. "I asked you to dinner and it was a real pleasure. Thank you."

"Thank you," she said sweetly.

I handed the checks to the waitress and told her to keep the change, then Kelly and I walked out into the night air.

"Here," I said, "I'll walk you back to your car."

"You don't have to do that," she said.

"No, it's late. It's better not to walk alone. Besides, you've still got my groceries."

We began strolling. The temperature had dropped down to about forty, but the air was so crisp and dry, it felt good. Off in the distance, a coyote howled and behind us a chorus of barking dogs answered.

We got to the Saturn and I stood there as she unlocked the car.

"Hop in, I'll drive you back to the Colonnade."

"You don't mind?" I asked, grateful to have the chance to hang around her a little while longer.

"Course not." She started the car as I got in and latched the seat belt around me. In about ninety seconds, we pulled up in front of the hotel.

"I've enjoyed this," I said. "Thank you."

Kelly stared out over the steering wheel for a moment, her lips pursed, her forehead wrinkled just a bit. I wondered what was going on.

"Harry, I've got the next three days off. I don't have to be anywhere until four o'clock Monday. Why don't I just drive you to Reno tomorrow?"

"I couldn't ask you to do that. It's too far. It's got to be—"

"It's two hundred and forty miles," she said. "About three hours' drive."

"But that's five hundred miles there and back," I said. "And I don't have a place for you to stay, really. I don't even know if I have a place to stay, and I couldn't ask you to go there and back in one day."

"Look, I like Reno. I'll get a hotel room, play a little blackjack, get a massage. I could use the break."

"But it's so far." My protests were getting weaker by the syllable.

"Harry, this is the west. We drive a hundred miles to pick up milk, bread, and diapers for the baby."

I smiled at her. "Okay, if you're sure."

"I'm sure. I'll pick you up at nine tomorrow. We'll get some coffee, a quick bite, and make Reno in time for a late lunch."

I nodded my head. "Great," I said, feeling numb at my good fortune. "Fantastic."

"Hey, pal," she said, placing her hand on my shoulder, "we gotta get you there for that baby."

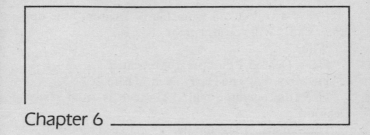

Chapter 6

I walked out of the Colonnade Hotel at ten minutes to nine the next morning just as Kelly pulled up in her green Saturn. She wore a T-shirt and a pair of jeans with a light brown suede coat over them. She looked bright, cheery, well scrubbed, young, and pretty—all the things I hadn't seen much of in a long time.

I stowed my two boxes and two bags in the backseat, and within minutes we were on our way out of town.

"Okay," I said, "somebody told me once that all the locals carry water and survival gear when they travel."

"Ten gallons in the trunk," she said, turning north onto Main Street. "Plus some MREs, a first-aid kit, and two blankets. Plus extra batteries for the cell phone."

I stared at her a moment before speaking. "Guess I heard right."

We saw maybe ten cars on the road before we got to the edge of town. Eureka's rush hour, I guess. We pulled into a slot in front of the E-Z Stop and bought a couple of large coffees and a box of doughnuts. While Kelly made a trip to the ladies', I tried one more collect call to Reno.

The phone rang five times before a woman's voice, heavily accented in Spanish, answered.

"Hello?"

"I have a collect call from Harry Denton," the operator said. "Will you accept the charges?"

"Who?"

"Harry Denton," the operator repeated.

"I'm sorry, they's no Harry Denton here."

"No," the operator said. "The call is from Harry Denton."

"For Marsha," I said loudly.

"Oh," the voice answered. "Dr. Marsha not here. She up on the mountain."

"Can you accept the charges?" the operator asked again, this time with a note of frustration in her voice.

"Oh, *sí*," she said. "*Sí*, I can accept."

"Go ahead," the operator said, no doubt relieved to be rid of this one.

"Thank you," I said quickly. "I'm trying to reach Dr. Helms, Dr. Marsha Helms. Is she there?"

"No, she up on the mountain," the woman said.

Up on the mountain . . . What the hell does she mean, up on the mountain?

"Well, who is this?"

"Estella," she said. "I work for Señora Marty."

"Well, where is she?"

"What?"

I struggled to recall my high-school Spanish. "*Dónde está la Señora Marty?*"

Big mistake. Estella went off in Spanish at about ninety miles an hour and I think I picked up maybe two words.

"Wait," I stammered. "I don't really speak Spanish—"

She kept right on going. Nothing was stopping this lady. "Excuse me, uh, *por favor, señora, no hablo español . . .*"

"Oh, then how come you be talking it at me?"

I felt my face turning red. "I'm sorry. I'm just trying to

find Dr. Marsha Helms. Can you tell me where I can find her?"

"*Sí, sí*, she up on the mountain."

Kelly came up behind me, mouthed "What's up?" I turned, shrugged in frustration.

"What do you mean, she's up on the mountain?"

"She up on the mountain," Estella insisted.

I had to try another tack. "Do you have her number up there?"

"*Qué?*"

"The telephone number!" I said, trying not to shout. Kelly broke into a broad grin; I made a face at her. "Have you got the telephone number?"

"Oh, *sí*, I got the number."

I stood there for a few seconds, shaking my head. "Would you mind giving it to me?"

"Oh, *sí*," she said, and then rattled off a string of numbers in Spanish. I repeated them back to her. For some reason or other, they were easier to remember in Spanish than they would have been in English.

"Thank you, Estella," I said. "Goodbye."

I hung up the phone. "Nothing's ever easy," I grumbled.

"Did you find her?"

"I don't know," I admitted. I picked up the cup of coffee, blew gently across the top, then took a sip. It was hot, strong, and badly needed after that phone call.

"She kept saying she's 'up on the mountain,' she's 'up on the mountain.' Whatever the hell that means . . .".

Kelly held her hands out, palms up. "Who knows? Somehow I don't see a pregnant woman mountain-climbing the week she's supposed to give birth."

I picked up the phone, dialed the operator. "I better at least try the number she gave me."

I told the operator my name and the number and she placed the call. On the third ring, Marsha picked up.

"Yes, yes!" Marsha said excitedly to the operator's question. "I'll take it!"

"Hi," I said.

"Harry, is it you? Is it really you?"

"Yeah, I've been trying to get you."

"I've been so worried," she said. "I haven't heard from you. Didn't know where you were."

"I kept trying this number, see, and—"

"That was my mistake. Aunt Marty's got an apartment in Reno that she keeps for when the weather gets nasty up here. I accidentally gave you that number. I'm so sorry. There's seldom anybody there."

"I finally got this Hispanic woman—"

"Yes, that's Estella. She's very sweet, but her English, *she ain't so good . . .*"

Marsha sounded chipper, in good spirits. Too good.

"How are you?" I asked. "Have you had that baby yet?"

"No, no baby yet. And I'm okay, I guess. If you don't mind looking like the Goodyear blimp and feeling nearly that big. The doctor put me in bed a week ago, told me to stay put until the baby's born."

"Is your aunt staying with you?"

"No, Aunt Marty's in L.A. But she's due in late tonight. Where are you?"

"Eureka," I said.

"Eureka, California? What are you doing there? Did you miss Nevada and drive on through?"

"No, I'm in Eureka, Nevada. The Mustang died and I got stranded. But I'm on my way in now."

"I didn't even know there was a Eureka, Nevada. Are you okay?"

"Yeah, I am now," I said. "Been a long couple of days. But I'll be in Reno later today."

"How? Is there a bus?"

I turned, looked at Kelly. "No, I made a buddy who's giving me a ride."

"Great. When you get to town, call this number, okay? I'll get Estella or Jake to come pick you up."

"Jake?"

"Yeah, Shaky Jake," Marsha said. "He sort of works for Aunt Marty, part-time. You'll like him. He's a character."

"Okay, I'll call. Should be sometime after lunch."

"I'll be waiting. And Harry?"

"Yeah?"

"I've missed you."

I sat there, holding the phone to my ear like I couldn't quite figure out what it was.

"Harry? Are you there?" Her voice held a note of apprehension, maybe even fear, like she was afraid I was going to hang up on her and disappear.

"Yeah, I'm here," I answered. "I'll call you when I get in."

They don't call this the loneliest road in America for nothing. Kelly plugged the radar detector into the cigarette lighter, licked the suction cup, and slapped it onto the dash, then floored it once we got out of town. We were doing eighty-five, ninety the whole way. You go north out of town on U.S. 50 and then it doglegs west and for the next seventy miles you go up and down, over mountain ranges and summits, through passes, but except for a few easy shifts of angle, the road is as straight as a needle. We saw maybe four cars during those first seventy miles, over the Hot Creek Range and through

Antelope Valley, and we didn't even slow down until we got through the Hickison Summit and jogged northwest through the Toiyabe Range. The land was clean and dry and crisp and cold and the day was beautiful, with the sky above so blue, you couldn't stare at it too long. We went over a ridge just before the Austin Summit and Kelly pointed out over the hood.

"Oh, look," she said, surprised.

"What?"

"A cloud . . ."

I followed her finger with my eyes, straining to focus on the horizon. And then I saw it, a thin, bumpy, little cotton ball in the sky.

"Cumulus, I think," she said. "We really don't see much of that here. Lots of high-altitude, wispy clouds. You know, cirrus, stratus, like that."

I watched her as she kept one eye on the road while watching the cloud in the distance. She sounded like a middle-school student reciting a science lesson.

Our conversation drifted in a relaxed and easy manner as the asphalt rolled by under us. Kelly Graham was easy to talk to and to listen to as well. I told her of my first and only marriage and how it had ended, and she spoke of how hard it had been to end her marriage. She had found marriage suffocating; her husband had been a fellow student at UNLV. Basically a cowboy, he had wanted her to drop out of school and take care of him and get pregnant as quickly as possible. They'd fought over her staying in school and only lived together about six months after the marriage. Her father had warned her about the danger, but she'd been in love.

"And then very quickly out of love," she said, only a trace of wistfulness in her voice. Time had clearly made it easier for her to talk about the losses she'd suffered. She and her ex-husband had actually stayed friends for a few years, exchanging phone calls and Christmas cards, and then he'd remarried, moved to Wyoming, and they'd lost touch.

"It's hard to make these things work," I said.

"Ah, but when it does," she said. "When it does."

We slowed down through the tiny town of Austin, which was even smaller than Eureka. Kelly kept a running commentary on this part of the state as we drove through the town, then sped back up on the west side.

"Highway 50 roughly follows the same route first used by the Pony Express riders in pioneer days," she said.

"God, imagine riding twenty, thirty miles at breakneck speed on a horse, pulling into a corral, slapping your mailbag on a fresh horse, and taking off again in ten minutes."

"Yeah, pretty amazing," she said.

"My ass is going to be sore from riding in this car," I said.

Kelly laughed out loud. In fact, we were both laughing a lot as we drove, our conversation flowing in a way that I hadn't experienced in a long time.

"So, Harry," she said during a rare quiet moment. "What are you going to do with the rest of your life after Reno?"

I shifted down in the seat and settled my head on the headrest. "I don't know," I admitted. "I've been drifting lately."

Kelly leaned over, adjusted the thermostat on the car heater. The sun was well up now and the car was warm and toasty. Without too much prompting, I could probably take a nap.

"Do you want to stay with this woman?" she asked. "I mean, I know that's a real personal question, and you don't have to get into it if you don't want to. I'm just curious."

"I wish there was some way I could answer that."

"So you really don't know?"

I rolled my head on the headrest and faced her. "Kelly, when I first met her I was so sure that this was it, that she was the one I was going to spend the rest of my life with. I mean, I was pushing forty, and when you're that old, you really think you're past all that feeling-in-love stuff, that mushy, hormone-driven roller-coaster ride. But I had it with her. I was so . . . so crazy about her. The last time I felt anything like it was when I had a crush on some babe in high school."

"I wonder if I'll ever feel like that again," Kelly confessed. "It's been a long time. Years."

"Oh, yeah, it's possible. I can prove it. I've been there. And in a lot of ways it's even better, because you're a grownup, at least technically . . ."

She turned, a smirk on her face. "Technically . . ."

"Well, as grown up as we'll ever be, right? And it's great. You feel alive in ways that you never felt before. Food tastes better, the air smells better, you wake up in the morning and you're just raring to take on the world."

"Hormones, Harry," she said. "It's all just hormones."

"Whatever," I agreed. "The experience is the same. You talk to someone on a more intimate level than you ever thought possible. You feel the other person's heart beating in time to yours. You know what's going on inside them and they know what's inside you, if only briefly, if only for a few special, wonderful moments. It's the only time in a human life when you don't feel alone."

"But it never lasts, right? That's the problem. Nobody can make it last. Like my dad, for instance. He was crazy about my mom, and when some drunk-assed cowboy in a GMC pickup drifted across the center line and killed her, I thought my dad was going to die, too. I understand now as a grownup that the only reason he didn't was because of me. He had to keep going because he had a little girl he didn't want to become a complete orphan."

I stared at her a moment as she looked intently out over the steering wheel.

"But who knows, Harry? Who knows if it would have lasted? For the rest of his life, he missed her and mourned her and got by on her memory. But if she hadn't been killed, for all I know, they would have driven each other crazy and got divorced."

Her lower lip seemed to quiver for a moment, and I couldn't tell if it was from emotion or road vibration. On impulse, I raised my left arm, brushing it across the seat fabric, placed my hand gently on her shoulder, then squeezed it.

"I don't know," I said, "but from what you've told me about them, I have a feeling they'd have worked it out."

Not quite two hours later we hit I-80 in Fernley. We'd been in some serious traffic for about an hour, ever since we got close to Fallon. Now the traffic was more like what I was used to, more like Nashville on a good day. Tractor-trailer rigs roared by doing eighty, six inches off each other's bumpers, and the cars zipped in and out like fighter jets in a war movie.

The freeway heads southeast into Reno through a kind of valley, with high mountain ranges on the left and somewhat smaller ones on the right funneling us toward the city. Some of the mountaintops were already capped in white, although down where we were the ground was dry and brown, mixed with bursts of light green where plants grew. The town, Kelly explained, was growing like crazy, with Sparks and Reno essentially becoming one city. Suburban sprawl was in evidence as clusters of half-built houses dotted the hillsides. As the skyline of the city came into view, I turned to Kelly.

"It's smaller than I thought it would be."

"Hey, Harry, this is the biggest little city in the world, don't you know?"

"Guess I forgot."

"It's too bad what's happening here," she commented.

"What do you mean? Something bad's happening?"

"Depends on how you look at it." Kelly slammed on the brakes to avoid a wooden crate that had fallen off the back of a pickup eight or ten lengths ahead of us.

"There're only two states left in the continental U.S. that don't have any kind of gambling at all," she said. "Yours and Utah. Every other state has some kind of legalized gambling."

"You serious? I didn't know that," I admitted.

"Yeah, and a year or so ago they had one of those propositions in California—I forget the number—but it made it legal for the tribes in Northern California to open casinos."

"I didn't know they couldn't already."

"No, it's new," Kelly said, scanning the view in front of us. "If I'm not careful, I'll miss our exit."

"By the way, where are we going?" I asked.

"I come to Reno often," she said. "I always stay at the same place. The Peppermill. I'll check in and you can call your lady friend from my room. How's that?"

"Works for me."

"So, anyway, Northern California's just the other side of the highway from Reno. Tons of Californians used to come here to gamble. Now they don't have to. They can stay at home."

"So what's happening here?"

"Hard times a-comin', my friend," she said. "Hard times a-comin'."

Chapter 7

I'll give people out west this much: When they say they're going somewhere, they go. None of this stopping every hundred miles or so to stretch your legs, go to the bathroom, grab a soda. You get in the car and you don't stop until you get to where you're going or you have to stop for gas, whichever comes first.

"If you'd wanted to stop," Kelly said, admonishing me as we pulled into the parking lot of the Peppermill, "all you had to do was say so."

"*Rest stop!*" I said in a mock Spanish accent. "*We don't gotta show you no steenkin' rest stop!*"

"Behave yourself," she said.

We'd turned off South Virginia Street into the huge parking lot of an even larger hotel. The Peppermill was enormous, I thought, although I guess by Las Vegas standards it was probably only ordinary in size. The parking lot was full and the cars were lined up half a block for valet parking. Running around the outside of the building was a red metal band with large white letters advertising the delights awaiting inside: SINGLE-DECK 21, 1,500 SLOTS, KENO, SPORTS BOOK, STEAKHOUSE, FOOD COURT, POKER, ROULETTE . . .

On and on it went, with me climbing out of the car and staring up at it like a real hayseed. Truth is, I've never been to a gambling town, either in Nevada or anywhere else. I'd been able to maintain an aura of cool throughout my time in Nevada when faced with things like slot machines in grocery stores and drugstores—hell, doctor's offices and church sanctuaries for all I knew. I'd stopped for gas at one place just across the state line and been confronted with a bank of slots and video poker machines next to a rack full of liquor and wine selections and next to that a complete display of adult videos with a handwritten sign: PORNIES—$7.00.

What the hell, one-stop shopping . . . Still, I had just enough of my southern conservative upbringing left over to feel slightly shocked and embarrassed by what my grandparents would have called a blatant display of sinful wickedness. I was able to hide that genetic legacy with some success, but I could admit it to myself.

Kelly pulled her bag out of the trunk and handed it to me as the parking valet walked up. I slung the bag over my shoulder and walked into the lobby of the Peppermill. It was the middle of the day, yet my eyes were almost blinded by the lights. It was like a thousand flashbulbs going off in your face at one time. Mirrors everywhere, flashing lights of every color imaginable, and each color more vibrant and vivid and loud than anything I'd ever seen before. Although I never indulged while in college, the only thing I could relate this to were the descriptions my classmates had told me about the experience of taking LSD.

And the noise. Bells clanging, metal coins slamming on aluminum trays, the incessant din of chatter, with the occasional jackpot—whistles and horns and people yelling and screaming thrown in for good measure. We were on the edge of the casino, walking toward the registration desk. I turned and strained to see as far into the casino as

I could and couldn't see the end of it. It was a phantas-magoria on speed.

The hallway to the registration desk was lined on both sides with hundreds of slots. To my left, an enormous lady wearing a faded muumuu, her long, stringy gray hair badly in need of washing, a half-smoked cigarette dangling from her lips, sat in a wheelchair and fed coin after coin into a machine, oblivious to the rest of the world. Next to her, standing on a stool, a dwarf wearing a red stocking cap reached up on tiptoes to grab the handle of another machine, bending over as he yanked it down.

Farther up, a young couple—well groomed, preppie, healthy—held on to each other tightly as the blonde woman pumped in quarter after quarter. Next to them a fat, bald man smoking a cigar that smelled like a burning rag stared into a video poker screen, studying the hand he'd been dealt. The two kids next to him paid no atten-tion to him or his acrid, rank cigar.

By now I had just enough of a road buzz to start to lose it in all this insanity. I'd been told that casinos were by design and by definition unreal, with no windows, no clocks, no way of recording the passing of time. The drinks and the cigarettes are free and the dealers are gor-geous and the food is cheap and all you have to do is gamble and toke well and it's all perfectly respectable.

Reality? Who needs it?

I followed close behind Kelly as we went past the packed bar, a half-dozen large television screens blaring, each with a different game on, holding the crowd's atten-tion. A thin old lady with a head full of curlers, thick eye-glasses, and a walking stick hobbled out of the coffee shop. I stared at her. I think it'd been decades since I'd seen anyone wear curlers in public.

"Do people even wear curlers anymore?" I said out loud.

"What?" Kelly turned, just as we worked our way into a crowd getting off a tour bus.

"Never mind," I said as I was bumped and jostled and tossed around in the throng.

We waited in line for twenty minutes to check in, which went by in a daze as I stood there watching the passing circus. Circus or a Fellini movie—I wasn't sure which. Finally, Kelly handed the Filipino man behind the counter her credit card and we were able to escape the madness.

"You okay?" Kelly asked, as we rode the elevator up to the fourth floor.

"Yeah," I said, a bit dazed. "Guess I'm a little tired."

She looked at me. "The last few days have been a little weird for you, haven't they?"

I nodded. "I think so. I'm no longer sure."

The elevator door opened and we walked out into a hall that was carpeted in thick, fuzzy bright blue, with engaging horizontal stripes of numerous colors painted along the walls. Kelly led the way, scanning the room numbers, until we got to a door near the end of the hall. A large window looked out over the parking lot, a segment of which had been cordoned off and was filled with matching RVs.

"Must be a convention," I muttered, as Kelly swiped her electronic key through the reader and opened the door.

The room was cool, comfortable, with a large king in the middle of the room in front of a mirrored wall. A plush blue sofa was pushed against another wall with a lampshade hanging down over one side. I sat down on the sofa, rested my head against the wall.

"You don't look so good," Kelly said, sitting on the edge of the bed in front of me.

"Gee, that's too bad," I said, smiling weakly at her. "Because you look great."

This almost bashful smile crossed her face and she looked down at the floor. "I think your blood sugar's crashing. Why don't we go downstairs and get some lunch?"

"You're not sick of my company?" I asked.

She reached over, took my hands in hers, and held them. They were soft, smaller than mine, and very thin. We sat there silently for a moment, looking at each other, wondering, I think, what the hell was going on.

"No, Harry. I enjoy your company very much, but I don't think I want you passing out on me again."

We sat there for a few moments longer, then got up and took the elevator down to the casino. Kelly took my hand in the crowd and led me through it. Clearly, she knew her way around here. We walked through an area that seemed like it held thousands of slots of so many types that I lost track of them after a while, then past a stage where a Rod Stewart imitator was doing a rendition of "Do Ya Think I'm Sexy?" that was better than the original.

Then we strolled through row after row of blackjack tables, crap tables, roulette wheels, something called Caribbean Poker—games and variations on games I'd never heard of. And everywhere noise and the frenetic bustle, shouts of delight and anguish, craziness.

We grabbed trays at the food court and loaded them up with Chinese food, then sat down.

"Kelly, you tipped the rice guy," I said. "Is that standard operating procedure?"

"I spent summers in college, before I got my nursing degree, first as a change girl, then as a drink girl, and finally, my last summer, I dealt blackjack. Sometimes I still miss it, Harry, but it can't compare to life-flighting an injured kid out of a car wreck."

"Yeah, but I—"

"No, listen, this has a point."

I shrugged, stabbed a forkful of cashew chicken.

"Most of the jobs in this town are minimum wage. I know that's hard to believe coming from back east, but it's true. You live and die by the toke here. Everybody tips everybody. Guy parks my car, I tip him. Lady brings me a coffee, I tip her. Dealer deals me a blackjack, I bet a buck for him on the next hand."

I swallowed a mouthful of not-bad Chinese. Can't hold a candle to my buddy Mrs. Lee back in East Nashville, but not bad.

"Just passing around the same money from one hand to another," I said.

She smiled at me. "What do you think the economy is, Harry? One hand passes money to another, who passes it on to another, and on and on."

"Until the money gets too dirty and has to be retired."

"You got it, pal."

We talked on like that, in the same easy, relaxed fashion that we had for the last two days. And as we sat there for a couple of hours over lunch, just talking, I realized that I needed to call Marsha. Wherever she was, I had promised to go to her, to wait by her side for the birth of our baby, and to take care of her and help her in any way I could. But I also remembered the last year when things really hadn't been so great for us. I'd gone through a bad time and managed to survive it with, frankly, not much help from her. I mean, we loved each other and all, at least I think we did.

But as I sat there talking, laughing, and joking with

Kelly, I began to realize that I was having more fun sitting right there with her than I had had in a long time, an awful long time.

And I didn't want it to stop.

It was three o'clock by the time we got back to Kelly's room. We'd taken a tour of the casino, with me getting my first instruction in the finer points of blackjack and losing my first twenty bucks at a gaming table in the process. I also hit my first blackjack, though, and got a three-to-two payout that made me want to jump up and down like an eight-year-old.

"I feel like taking a shower," Kelly said, opening her bag and pulling out a few things. "I'll jump in the bathroom and you can have some privacy on the phone. How's that?"

"Great, Kel. Thanks." I settled onto the couch and dialed Marsha's number. She sounded sleepy when she answered.

"Did I catch you at a bad time?"

"No, I just drifted off. I'm into afternoon naps these days. Not much else to do, given that I'm mostly confined to bed."

"I guess this has been pretty rough on you, hasn't it?"

"It'll work out. So where are you?" Marsha asked.

"At the Peppermill," I said. "The person who gave me a ride's staying here."

"So who gave you the ride?"

"A nurse I met in Eureka."

"Oh," she said, an almost imperceptible shift in her voice. "You've taken to picking up nurses now."

"Actually, she took care of me when I was in the hospital."

"You were in the hospital?" she demanded, her voice suddenly more serious.

"Clinic, really. You see, I . . ."

And I gave her the twenty-five-words-or-less summary of the last couple of days of my life.

"My God," Marsha said, sighing. "I'm just so glad you're okay. But good God, Harry, how do you manage to get yourself into these scrapes?"

"Just lucky, I suppose. Hey, Estella kept saying something about you being up on the mountain. She kept saying that over and over. Up on the mountain."

"Yeah, Aunt Marty's got a place up here on Mount Rose. It's real nice. You'll like it. Kind of off in the woods."

"I didn't know there were many woods around here. Thought it was mostly desert."

"There's enough snow and rain up here to support tree growth," Marsha explained. "Lots of pines. Ponderosa, mostly. It's very beautiful."

"I'll bet. Is there room for me up there?"

"Of course, goofy, where did you think you were staying?"

"I wasn't sure."

"Harry, I asked you to come out here because I want you here with me. I want you to see your daughter and I want her to see you. And I miss you and it's lonely. I don't know anyone up here but Aunt Marty and a couple other people, none of whom are ever around much."

I shifted on the couch, kicked off my shoes, and stretched out. I heard the water start through the wall next to my head and tried not to imagine Kelly in the shower. Without much success . . .

"So what happens after the baby?" I asked. "What happens to us?"

She hesitated a few moments. "I don't know," she finally

admitted. "We've got a lot to talk about. A lot of things have happened, between us and outside of us."

"I know that. Are you coming back home, back to Nashville?"

"I don't see how I could ever go back there, Harry. My name's Mudd back there."

"C'mon," I said, "it's not that bad. Nashville's a big city now. And not everybody knows about the problems at the M.E.'s office."

"Enough people who matter know so that I could probably never get a job there again."

"You could teach, consult, write," I said, wondering why I was trying to convince her of something I wasn't entirely convinced of myself.

"Besides, I'm not from Nashville. I was only there a dozen years or so. Now that I'm gone, it doesn't feel like home anymore."

"So where is home? Is it here? Reno?"

"No, not really. I mean—" She stopped, clearly uncomfortable, and hesitated. "Harry, I don't know what I'm going to do and I'm too tired to think about it now. Can we talk about it when you get here?"

"Sure," I said. The strain in her voice was real enough for me to realize that I had to back off.

"And when's that going to be?"

"Soon," I answered. "How far is it to your aunt's place on—what was it?—Mount Rose?"

"Yes, that's it. Estella's not here right now, but I can call Jake and get him to pick you up."

"Don't do that," I said. "I'll try to find a ride up there. Worse comes to worst, I'll grab a cab. How do I get there?"

"You sure you want to do that, Harry?"

"Yeah. It's better this way. I don't want to be a bother

to anyone." I also didn't feel like answering a stranger's questions.

"Okay, it's real easy to get here." I grabbed a pen and the hotel stationery pad and began writing. "The Peppermill's on South Virginia. You just head south on that road and you'll see signs for 395. Just get on 395 until it ends and you'll see Mount Rose in front of you. Take the Mount Rose highway—that's also 441—exactly eight-and-a-half miles until you come to . . ."

I scribbled the directions down as she finished dictating. I'm a bit navigationally challenged at times but thought I could find the place without too much trouble.

"All right," I said. "I'll get up there one way or the other."

"Okay, love. Just be careful. And Harry—"

"Yes?"

"I will be glad to see you."

In the reflection on the mirrored wall to my right, I saw I was holding the phone so tightly my knuckles were white. I concentrated on relaxing, of letting go of whatever tension had built up inside me.

"Yeah," I said. "Me, too."

A couple of minutes later I was staring out the window overlooking the pool when Kelly stepped out of the bathroom wearing a white terry-cloth robe with a towel wrapped around her head.

"Oh, that felt great," she said. "Whatcha looking at?"

"Come see," I said. She crossed the room and stood next to me. Outside, several floors below, steam was coming off the swimming pool next to a several-stories-high fake mountain painted to look like brown rock, with caves and fake animals and a waterfall cascading down from the center.

Kelly turned to me, smiled. "They built that a few years ago to hide the air-conditioning equipment."

"Amazing," I said. "Just amazing."

She turned her whole body around, facing me, and leaned against the glass. "What do you think?"

"About what?"

"Reno," she said. "What do you think about Reno?"

"Parts of it are like a movie set," I answered, then adding truthfully: "I love it."

Her face seemed to get serious for a second. "Did you find out where your girlfriend lives?"

I started to correct Kelly, to tell her the truth, that Marsha wasn't my girlfriend anymore, that whatever relationship we once had was gone and whatever existed now was tenuous and probably fleeting.

But I decided to hold my tongue.

"Up on Mount Rose," I said.

"That's very pretty up there," Kelly said. "Why don't I drive you?"

"You've already done too much," I said. "I'll just grab a cab."

"Nonsense, a cab'll cost you a fortune. Besides, it's a pretty drive. I may even go on up to Lake Tahoe. There're some really nice restaurants up there."

Kelly pulled the towel off her head and ringlets of damp red hair fell down over her shoulders. What little makeup she wore had been scrubbed off in the shower, revealing skin that was smooth and freckled and soft. I stood maybe two inches taller than her. Looking down at her, I suddenly felt this roiling in my stomach. The room seemed very quiet; I couldn't even hear either of us breathing.

"What?" she whispered.

I shook my head. "Nothing, I . . ."

"What?"

"Are you sure it's not too much trouble?"

"No, Harry, it's no trouble at—"

Then I leaned down and kissed her.

Chapter 8

The drive out of Reno and up Mount Rose started out flat and level, but by the time we got halfway up the mountain, the car was straining, Kelly was downshifting, and our ears were popping. The temperature dropped as well, and in a little while, we began seeing patches of snow that became thicker and more frequent.

I watched her as she navigated the curving, narrow road up the mountain. She'd dried her hair, pulled it behind her, and put on jeans and a turtleneck sweater with a white cotton shirt over it. Kelly and I were mostly silent. I studied the few road signs, searching for the landmark Marsha'd told me about. We passed a closed restaurant on our right and then, about another half-mile or so along, I saw a sign: LATHRAN RANCH ROAD.

"That's it," I said. "Turn here."

"Your friend's aunt must be really well off," Kelly commented. "This is prime real estate up here."

"I think Aunt Marty's pretty loaded. She's got an apartment in Reno if the snow gets too high here, plus places in L.A. and New York that I know of. Maybe others as well."

"Jeez, Harry, you sure it's such a good idea not to pursue this relationship as far as it'll go?" Kelly said, teasing.

She slowed and made the turn into a development of

houses with big lots, Range Rovers and the like parked in aggregate driveways, with sticker prices that I would estimate started in the high-six figures.

"I've always heard marrying money is the hardest way to earn it."

"Well, old buddy," she said, faking a slow cowboy drawl, "I wouldn't know one way or the other."

"Actually, that was one of the things that was always an issue with us," I said, not sure why I wanted Kelly to know that.

"What, money?"

"Yeah, it always seemed like there was never enough to do the things we wanted to do. Marsha made a lot of money, but she worked her tail off doing it. And my work was up and down and it was always tough making ends meet."

I watched the numbers on the mailboxes climb as we drove on. Marsha'd told me Aunt Marty's was the last house at the end of a dead-end street.

"I've always wondered if there was much money in being a detective."

"There can be, if you're either well connected or willing to take any case that comes along. I only took domestics when cash was really short. Hated that kind of work. For a while, I had a pretty good gig investigating workmen's comp fraud cases. But that all dried up."

"If it's such a tough business, why'd you stay in it? I mean, you look like a pretty smart guy." She turned, smiled at me. "You've got pretty good people skills."

"Thanks," I said, then pointed out the window. "Should be just around this next curve."

"So why'd you stay in the business?"

"Truth? Truth is, I like it. I like working my own hours, being my own boss. I never was very happy in corporate life. Too much bullshit, too many meetings."

Kelly negotiated the right curve and then we saw it: Aunt Marty's Little House on the Hill.

Kelly slowed, braking the car to a stop right before the driveway. We both stared out the windshield.

"Holy cow," she whispered.

"Yeah," I agreed.

Aunt Marty's house was a three-story redwood Alpine minimansion, beautifully and expensively landscaped, with windows that ran twenty, maybe twenty-five feet high across the front of the house. A long circular driveway ran off the cul-de-sac to the front of the place. Tall Ponderosa pines framed the house like something out of a movie. In fact, that's all I could think at the moment: *Another damn movie set.*

"Guess we're here," Kelly said after a moment. "The least I could do is pull down the driveway for you. That is, if that's okay."

"Why wouldn't it be?"

She shrugged, eased the car down a slight incline onto a driveway that ran a good thirty yards off the street before curving around to the front. She shifted the manual transmission of the car into neutral, switched the car off, and set the parking brake.

"Why don't you come in, meet Marsha?"

"Oh, I don't think so," Kelly said. "Something tells me you two are going to need some time alone."

"It'll be okay, really, we're—"

"No, Harry." She smiled. "You're on your own with this one, big guy."

"Okay. Look, Kelly, I—"

"No, you look, okay? I want you to understand that back there, back in the hotel room, it's not that I didn't want to. You see that? It's just that we've only known each other a short time and—"

"Believe me, I understand," I said. "I just hope you

don't think I was making any assumptions or coming on too strong or anything like that. It's just been a long time since I've enjoyed being around anybody so much."

She reached over, put her hand over mine. I turned my palm up and held on to her.

"It's been a long time for me, too," she said.

"Look, maybe I can call you sometime."

"You've got my number."

I patted my shirt pocket, where I'd stuck her business card with her office and home numbers on it.

"You better get on in there," Kelly said. "You've got work to do."

"What are you going to do?"

"Drive up the mountain," she said. "We're only about fifteen minutes away from the lake. Maybe I'll get dinner, play a little blackjack at the Cal-Neva."

"Good luck," I said.

"Yeah, you, too. And if and when you get your stuff straightened out, then maybe you'll give me a call. We can get together sometime."

"I'd like that," I said. Then she leaned over and kissed me, very softly and very sweetly, and I didn't want to pull away from her and didn't want her to leave, but then it was time. I got my bags and boxes out of the back of the Saturn and watched as she pulled away and was gone.

Then I turned and rang the doorbell. Why did I feel like a man who was, as they say, facing the music?

Estella pulled the door open, flushed and out of breath. She was a middle-aged woman, moving quickly toward plump, with dark skin and jet-black hair pulled up on her head in a tight bun. Her eyes were nearly as black as her hair and surrounded by whites that were clear, unsullied. She wore a flowered print dress that bunched slightly at the waist.

"You mus' be Señor Harry," she panted.

"And you must be Estella," I said, smiling at her.

"Sorry it take me a while to get down here," she said, holding the door open. "I was upstairs with Dr. Marsha."

I stepped in, set my bags in the foyer, then reached back outside and pulled the two boxes in behind me. Estella gave me a quizzical, almost funny look, as if she didn't quite know what to make of a man who arrived with his things in a mixture of mismatched luggage and cardboard boxes sealed with duct tape. She reached for one of the bags. I held out my arm to stop her.

"Please, Estella," I said. "Let me take care of those. If you'd just let me know where to put them."

"Señora Marty says you go in the other guest room upstairs, down the hall from Dr. Marsha."

I smiled, nodded. "Just show me the way."

She looked down at my shoes, which were an old pair of hiking boots I'd worn for years solely for comfort. They were threadbare, the fabric faded, but other than that they didn't look any shabbier than those you'd find on a million college kids and former yuppies these days.

"Should I take them off?" I asked. "I don't think there's any mud on them."

Estella nodded and I obliged her by leaving the boots in the foyer. I followed her up a flight of stairs to the second floor, all the while scoping out as much as I could of the main floor. On the far wall, there was a massive stone hearth around a fireplace that ran all the way up the wall. The sunken living room in front of it was furnished comfortably, with furniture that looked like it might have belonged in a second home or a summer place on the lake, only I suspected Marty had paid top dollar for it. A big-screen TV dominated one corner of the room to the left of the fireplace. A dining area with a table big enough to seat about ten people was off to the left behind the TV area and I figured there was a kitchen off somewhere behind that, although I couldn't see it.

The stairs led up to a second-story landing that looked out over the great room. I turned to the left, following Estella down the hall to a room at the end. She held the door open for me and I walked into a small bedroom, with a double bed pressed against one wall, a bureau against the opposite wall, and, tucked in the corner away from the door, a small writing desk under a large window that looked out over the woods. A beautiful antique quilt covered the bed, and the room, like much of the house, had the look and feel of a 1940s ski lodge.

"It's very nice, Estella," I said.

"*El cuarto de baño* is next door," she explained. "I sorry it no connect to room."

I turned, smiled at her. "I'll get by," I said. "Somehow."

Estella turned, started back down the hallway.

"Where's Dr. Marsha?" I asked.

Estella pointed. "The other end of hall. She said to bring you as soon as you settled."

We passed the stairway leading to the top floor. "What's up there?" I asked, pointing.

"My room," Estella answered. "And some storage space."

We retrieved my boxes from downstairs and carted those back up. I set them down on the floor, then turned to leave.

"You stay here," Estella said, holding an arm out to me, palm forward. "Clean up next door. I go tell Dr. Marsha you here."

I looked down at myself. Jeez, I thought I was pretty clean now. I'd shaved and showered this morning in anticipation of seeing Marsha again.

"Uh, Estella, is there something wrong with me?"

She frowned. "At leas' you no wear blue jeans first time you see Dr. Marsha," she instructed.

I figured what the hell, maybe she's right. I had a pair of khakis in my bag somewhere and a light blue button-down oxford shirt. That and running a comb through my hair might help me pass muster.

"Give me five minutes," I said. Estella shut the door behind her. I laughed quietly. I had a feeling that staying here at *Casa Marty* was going to be a real adventure.

Estella knocked on the door a few minutes later and I emerged in a clean pair of non-denim pants and a dress shirt I'd tucked extra hard into my trousers in an attempt to smooth out the wrinkles. I pasted my hair back across my head and made it behave as much as possible. Estella ran her eyes up and down the length of me, pursed her lips, and shook her head, trying in vain to rein in her obvious disgust.

"C'mon, Estella," I said in as placatory a fashion as I could. "I've been on the road for days."

"Dr. Marsha said bring you right down." She motioned for me to follow.

"How is she?" I asked, halfway down the long hallway. Estella grunted; that was as close to an answer as I was going to get.

She stopped in front of the last door. As far as I could tell, there must be at least four bedrooms on the second floor. I wondered why Marty'd bought such a huge house. She had been widowed years ago and never had any kids of her own—which was why, I supposed, she'd kind of adopted Marsha.

Estella raised a brown hand and rapped softly on the door. A muffled voice came from within and she pushed the door open quietly. My stomach did a quick tumble as I stepped into the doorway behind Estella and stopped.

A king-size bed dominated the room, and in the middle

of it, propped up on pillows, a comforter pulled up to her chest, bare arms lying outside it, was a woman I barely recognized.

Her hair was long, much longer than I'd remembered, and combed out formally over the pillow in a way that could only have been done by someone else. Estella'd obviously had a hand in this.

But as long as her hair was, it couldn't hide a face that was bloated and red and swollen. Her cheeks seemed to literally bulge out from a face that was layered in fat, with great purple bags under the eyes that showed even through skillfully applied makeup. And rising from the bed was a body under all those covers that seemed to be twice the size I remembered. Next to her, on a small nightstand, was a tray filled with brown plastic pill bottles. I stared at Marsha from the doorway as Estella stood at the foot of the bed. They both seemed to be staring at me, as if I'd missed a cue or something.

"Hi, stranger," she said. Her voice was tired and thick, almost slurred.

"Hi, you," I said softly.

Marsha shifted slightly and turned her head toward Estella.

"Leave us alone, Estella. Please," she said.

A look of shock raced across Estella's dark face and she almost opened her mouth. The thought of two unmarried people—one of them in nightclothes—being left alone in a bedroom was probably anathema to her. I imagined that what she really wanted to say to Marsha was, "Look, isn't that what got you into this mess in the first place?"

I glanced back at Marsha and wanted to say to Estella, "What do you think we're going to do? Rip off our clothes and chase each other around the bedroom?"

But I kept my mouth shut as Marsha smiled at me and gave a slight roll to her eyes. "It's okay, Estella. Really."

I stepped aside as Estella walked past me out of the room, mumbling something in Spanish as she went by.

"Shut the door," Marsha said.

I closed the door, crossed over to the bed, and stood next to her, looking down at her tired, bloated face.

"How are you?" I asked.

She sighed. "How do I look?"

I learned a long time ago that there's only one answer to that question, and reality has nothing to do with it.

"You look fine," I said.

"Liar. But it's sweet of you." She patted the side of the bed. "It's okay, you can sit down."

I eased down carefully on the bed. "Sorry I couldn't meet you downstairs," she said.

I stared at her for what seemed like the longest time. "Tell me what's wrong," I said finally.

"I have a condition called preeclampsia," she answered. "I'll spare you the doctor stuff on it, but basically about six weeks ago, after an otherwise normally miserable pregnancy, I began putting on weight like a son of a bitch and nobody knew why. My blood pressure shot up and I was retaining fluid like a sponge."

Marsha looked at me and studied the expression on my face. "Yeah, like you hadn't already guessed that."

"C'mon," I said. "Don't be tacky. Just tell me what that is."

"In and of itself, preeclampsia isn't dangerous as long as that's all you get. It's just damned unpleasant and you have to control it. The risk is that it can go into full eclampsia, which is also called toxemia."

"Oh, yeah, I've heard of that."

"I'll bet you have," she said. "Most people know it's some bad shit. And it is. Dangerously high blood pressure, convulsions, coma. It's a full-fledged medical emergency."

"So why aren't you in a hospital?"

"Harry, a hospital is the worst place to be if you're sick. My ob-gyn and I got together on this. He brought in another doctor on a consult, and we all agreed that for now we're just going to watch the diet, keep me completely in bed, and monitor everything. A nurse comes every day. And I watch for signs that it's getting worse."

"What does it mean for the baby?" I asked.

"I'm in my thirty-sixth week," she said. "Right now, as long as the preeclampsia doesn't progress, we're going to give it about two more weeks. If nothing happens, we'll induce."

"Jeez," I muttered. "How does that happen?"

"I have no idea," she said. "But it's nothing to get in a panic about yet. But I was scared and terribly lonely here, Harry. I don't know anybody. Nobody comes by here except for the hired help. Television sucks. I just missed you and couldn't stand it anymore."

"I'm glad you called." She reached over and took my hand in hers, which for the first time was larger than mine. The skin was stretched so tightly over the back of her hand that it was curved outward and shiny. Her fingers were as fat as sausages, and hot and moist.

"You running a fever?" I asked.

"No, it's just . . ." She hesitated. "I'm just a little tired."

"Maybe I should let you sleep for a while?"

Her chest moved and she let out a long breath that became a sigh as it escaped her lips. "Sorry, I'm no fun," she said.

"Not your fault. Look, do you need anything?"

"Just maybe wake me up in an hour or two," she said.

"I'm not normally this sleepy, except I was up all night with the baby kicking."

I smiled down at her. "Sure, I'll come back up in a bit. Is there a way for you to call downstairs if you need anything?"

She motioned with her head to a white plastic box on the nightstand. "I can buzz Estella on the intercom." Her voice was weaker all of a sudden and her eyelids sagged.

I stood up, careful not to jostle her. "I'll let you drop off to sleep now."

"I was hoping to show you around the place. It's really nice."

"It looks like it," I said. "I'll get Estella to show me around."

"There's a big TV down there," she said. "And a satellite with all the movie channels." Her voice was slurring now, drifting.

"Great." I had turned and taken a couple of steps toward the door when I heard her voice behind me once more.

"Hey," she whispered.

I turned back. "Yeah?"

"Aren't you even going to kiss me?"

I stepped back over to the bed and leaned down, placing one hand on the pillow to steady myself, then kissed her very softly, my lips just brushing against hers.

She moaned. "You always were a good kisser," she whispered. "I've missed your kisses."

"Hush," I said quietly, "before you get me all hot and bothered. Go to sleep. I'll see you later."

"Good night, sweetie."

"Good night, Marsha."

I was at the door when she spoke again, had just flicked off the overhead light.

"Harry?" Her voice was a whisper in the darkness.

"Yeah?"

"Thanks."

"De nada," I said. Then I stepped through the door and closed it behind me.

Down the hall, I went into the bathroom, closed and locked the door behind me. Then I turned on the water, pulled the lid down on the toilet, and sat down, my head in my hands.

God, I felt low. And guilty. God, so guilty. Because as soon as I saw her, I knew the truth that had been gnawing away at my guts for months, that had been burrowing away at my insides, through my insides, until now it was in front of me, clear as day and unshakable as hell.

As much as I wanted to, as much as I tried, as much as I denied it, there was no way around it.

I didn't love her anymore.

Chapter 9

Jesus, what was I talking about? Of course I loved her. I'd spent years with her; my daughter's inside her! I cared for her, about her. As Woody Allen once wrote: "My concerns are your concerns. We laugh a lot. We have great sex."

Wonderful, I thought. *Now I'm quoting Woody Allen as a relationship expert. Why don't I just pick up a phone and dial the Psychic Hot Line? They'll know what to do.*

I sat on the commode with the bathroom door locked and stared into the mirror, a blank look on my face and a thin layer of sweat on my forehead.

"What the hell am I going to do?" I whispered. And I thought back over the last year or so, of the times when Marsha and I'd begun—gradually at first, and then like a runaway locomotive—to drift apart. The evenings we spent together now seemed, in retrospect, to have a certain sameness about them. The silences between us were comfortable at first, the silences of two people who knew each other well, who didn't have to fill every moment with inane chatter, small talk. But then the silences had grown longer and heavier until they had hung between us first like a burden and then more like a chasm that grew wider and wider, the shifting tectonic plates of our hearts moving further and further apart until there was an empty emotional canyon that neither of us could cross any longer.

And I'd left my life behind, at least for the moment, and driven thousands of miles and nearly gotten myself killed all in answer to the plea of a person whom I hardly knew anymore. Marsha was a stranger to me, someone I used to know, used to be involved with, enmeshed with.

Now it was gone.

I leaned over, took my head in my hands, and rubbed my temples and then my eyes. I was suddenly very tired, as if all the air and fire had been taken out of me and there was nothing left but an empty blob. I stood, ran water in the sink as hot as I could stand it, soaked a washcloth and then plastered it, steaming, across my face. When I pulled it off, my face was red, flushed, bright with heat.

I stared into the mirror for a while longer, at eyes that seemed older and more tired than ever, and resolved to finish what I had come here for and then go back to my life. Marsha had been the one who left me, the one who left my life and shut me out of hers. And now that she wanted me back in—if that was, in fact, what she wanted—I could and would be the one to say that once a door was closed, it could never be opened again. I'd feel as guilty as I had to about that and then I'd go on with my life. I'd help raise the child, do my duty, give whatever support I was able—financially and otherwise—and be as big a part of her life as her mother would let me be.

But I had to go on. There was no other way.

Downstairs, Estella was setting the table for dinner, accompanied by some wonderful smells drifting out of the kitchen. Outside, through the plate-glass window that looked out over the pine forest that covered most of Mount Rose, the sun was setting below a line of trees.

The ground, I noticed, had little in the way of grass. It was mostly a thick bed of brown pine needles.

"Can I get you anything, Señor Harry?"

I thought for a second. It was a little early in the day, but what the hell.

"A *cerveza frío* would be nice," I said.

Estella smiled. "I thought you not speak Spanish."

"Just enough to get in trouble."

"Why doan you have a seat in the den, and I bring it out."

"Thanks, Estella," I said. "I appreciate it."

As I walked through the dining area into the large den, I wondered how I'd fill the time that lay ahead of me. As Marsha'd said, she was looking at a couple of weeks before the baby came. After that there'd be plenty to do for as long as I was going to be here. But for now I could be company for Marsha, catch up on my reading, maybe see a bit of Reno.

"Mind if I turn on the television?" I asked as Estella handed me a cold mug of dark beer.

She pointed to a remote control on a table next to a large brown leather sofa. "Make youself at home. Please. Señora Marty wants you to be comfortable."

"I noticed you were setting the table for several people."

"Sí, Señora Marty, Señor Barrone are getting in about six, and Jake will pick them up at the airport."

"Señor Barrone?" I asked. "Who's he?"

She smiled. "Ah, Señor Barrone, he is Señora Marty's—*¿cómo se dice?*—ah, *boyfriend?*"

"Yes, Estella, boyfriend. So Señora Marty's got a boyfriend?"

"Yes, Señor Barrone, he is *muy interesante*."

"I look forward to meeting him," I said. "Is there anything I can help you with?"

Estella shook her head. "No, but if you want to build a fire, there is the logs outside on the patio. Everything else is okay."

"Thanks." I turned on the TV as Estella turned and went back to her work. There were three remote controls: one for the television, one for the satellite, and one for the VCR. Figuring all that out took the better part of twenty minutes and then I found an old black-and-white film noir classic, *D.O.A.*, that was about to start on one of the movie channels. I had just enough time to haul in some logs and build a fire, then settle onto the couch and watch Edmond O'Brien play Frank Bigelow, an otherwise unremarkable accountant who suddenly finds out he's dying from iridium poisoning. A true victim of circumstance, he tracks down his killer in a film that was as dark and cynical as any I'd ever seen. Maybe it wasn't the kind of movie I should be watching right now, but somehow I was just not up for Julie Andrews bursting into song while flinging her arms up. I tried to forget the last few days and all the things I'd been through, was going through, and just fade into the dream-reality of a man who was being manipulated and doomed by forces he could neither control nor understand, but who fought on anyway.

I was just beginning to completely identify with Frank Bigelow when I heard the whirring of a garage-door motor from far behind the kitchen. I stood, looked out the front window as a dark blue Mercedes sedan eased forward toward the garage. Then I heard Estella saying something in the kitchen and the sound of a door opening and more voices. The voices grew louder and then I saw Marsha's aunt Marty in the doorway. I stood there awkwardly, not knowing whether I should walk toward them or just stay here.

The decision was quickly made as Marty burst into the

den. She was a woman best described as handsome, with a perfect coif of naturally silver hair perched atop features that were patrician, aristocratic. She emanated an aura of old money, although I remembered that Marsha had once told me that she'd made most of the money herself. She walked quickly, with a gait and posture that was self-assured, even a bit noblesse oblige.

"You must be Harry Denton," she announced in a strong voice with just a trace of upper-crust tidewater Virginia in it. It wasn't a southern accent, really, and certainly not a drawl. Just enough to give her a distinctive, impressive voice.

"Yes, ma'am," I said. "It's a pleasure—"

She offered her hand, then grabbed mine before I had a chance to finish my sentence. "Martha Bishop," she said. "But my friends call me Marty. I'm so glad you made it. How long have you been here?"

A short, gray-haired man in a gray suit and an open camel's-hair topcoat, walking with the aid of a cane, came in behind her, accompanied by a taller man in a black nylon windbreaker and jeans. Behind the two of them was Estella with a suitcase in each hand.

"I just got here a couple of hours ago."

"I thought Marsha said you were coming in Thursday," Marty said, unbuttoning her coat and sliding it off. She was dressed in a pair of light brown slacks and a silk blouse with an oddly feminine bow at the collar. She wore the clothes well. She was still slim and in good shape, even though, as Marsha had told me, she was approaching seventy.

"I got delayed," I said. "Had car trouble."

"Oh, well, I hope you got it fixed with no trouble," she said.

"Actually, I wound up selling it. Thought maybe I'd look around for something new here."

Marty turned. "Jacques, come meet Marsha's friend, Harry," she instructed.

The man in the suit approached, transferred his cane from his right hand to his left, and offered me a handshake. His grip was strong, though his hand was thin and blotched with brown liver spots.

"Harry Denton, Jacques Barrone," Marty said.

"Mr. Barrone," I said, shaking his hand and nodding slightly. "It's a pleasure."

He nodded back without saying anything.

"And this is Mr. Shalinsky," Marty continued, motioning toward the other man. He was at least as old as Barrone, if not older, and strangely scruffy. A long lock of thick salt-and-pepper hair hung down over a forehead crisscrossed with deep lines. He had a large nose with a bump about three-quarters of the way up and slightly off to the left. His posture wasn't good; he slouched, and his jeans were a couple of inches too large for him. He wore a pair of scuffed, worn Nikes, a T-shirt, and a wind-breaker with the words CIRCUS CIRCUS POKER ROOM emblazoned across the front.

Somehow, he didn't quite fit in with Aunt Marty and Jacques Barrone.

Shalinsky stepped forward, grabbed my hand, and pumped it. "Glad to meetcha, kid," he said. "Welcome to Reno."

"Thanks, Mr. Shalinsky."

"Jake," he said. "Everybody calls me Jake."

"So how is our mother-to-be today?" Marty asked.

I gave a slight shrug. "Hard to tell," I said. "She was really tired, wanted to take a nap, so I came down here to give her a chance to sleep."

I glanced over at the antique clock on the mantel. "In fact, she wanted me to wake her up about now."

"Such a shame she can't get out of bed," Marty said,

as Barrone removed his topcoat, folded it, then handed it and Marty's overcoat to Jake.

"Yes, I think it's pretty tough on her," I offered.

"Why don't you go wake her up, see if she's up for some company," Marty said. "In the meantime, I'll freshen up while Mr. Shalinsky makes us some drinks."

"The usual, Mrs. B?" Jake asked.

"Yes," she answered. "Jacques? Care to loosen that tie?"

Barrone smiled, nodded. "After you," he said. It was the first time he'd spoken. His voice was soft, cultured, well educated.

"You having a drink?" Jake asked, pointing at me.

"Just finished a beer a while ago," I said.

"Good." He grinned, revealing a perfect set of Hollywood-white teeth that were so uniform and pristine that they could only be dentures. "You're ready for another one."

"Need any help with the rest of your bags?" I asked.

"Estella's already got them in," Marty said, walking away.

I climbed the stairs and padded down the hallway, hoping that I could wake Marsha up without startling her. Darkness had settled in while I was watching the movie and the hallway light was off. I didn't know where the switch was, so I had to feel my way along. I got to Marsha's door and knocked softly a few times.

Marsha's voice answered from within, very softly: "Come on in."

I opened the door, peeked in. "You awake?"

She reached over, turned on the small lamp on her nightstand. "What are you doing in the dark?"

I smiled. "Couldn't find the light switch."

"Well, don't break your neck, dummy," she teased.

I walked in and sat on the edge of the bed. "How are you?"

She smiled at me from a face that still seemed strange and foreign. "Much better."

"Your aunt's home," I said. "With Mr. Barrone and Jake."

"Ah, Shaky Jake," Marsha said. "One of my favorites. He hasn't been around much this week, with Aunt Marty gone."

"Where was she, by the way?"

"She and Jacques went to Washington. Business, I think."

"What does Mr. Barrone do?"

"He's an attorney," Marsha said.

"Hmm, I'm not surprised. He has the look."

"He's quite famous around here, really," Marsha said. "A former prosecutor in Storey County, very successful law practice after that. He's very respected."

"He's retired?" I asked, curious.

"Partly," she answered. Then a quick grimace shot across her face and she jolted in bed.

"You okay?"

"Just a pain. Look, can we continue this later? I need to go to the bathroom."

I reached out and took one of her hands in mine, held it tightly. "C'mon, I'll help."

"No," she said. "There are certain things a lady needs to do either alone or with the help of another lady."

"I understand," I said. "I'll go get help."

"Don't bother." Marsha reached over, pushed the button on the intercom. "This'll be faster."

Behind me, the hallway light came on and I heard footsteps on the carpet. I turned just as Marty came to the doorway.

"Hello, sweetheart," she said. "How are you?"

"Right now I need to get to the bathroom," Marsha said.

"I offered to help, but—"

"Don't be silly, young man," Marty said, striding quickly into the room and over to the bed. She placed her palm against my shoulder and pushed me away. "Go downstairs and join the men, while Marsha and I take care of an urgent matter."

"I'll be downstairs if you need me," I said, backing away. There was no point in arguing with these two, I knew. I'd been dismissed.

Chapter 10

By the time I walked back downstairs, Jake had made drinks, switched off the television, and put a Paul Desmond CD on the stereo; the low, sweet tones of an alto sax on "My Funny Valentine" filled the room, warming it up. I felt a little odd, out of place, but even that was better than being all alone in the biggest room of the house. Not to exclude Estella, of course; she just wasn't much of a conversationalist.

"So, kid," Jake said in an accent that I tried to place and finally decided was either Brooklyn or Ninth Ward New Orleans. "Where ya from?"

He handed me a mug of dark beer with a thin head of foam floating on top. "Nashville," I said.

"No shit. So you, like, hang out with country music stars and shit, huh? Ya know Johnny Cash?"

"We don't exactly travel in the same circles," I answered. "And other than a couple of starving songwriters, I don't know a single person in the music business."

"Jeez, how can ya live in Nashville and not know anybody in the music business?"

"It's easy," I said. "We got a million people in greater Nashville now. Not everybody works in the music business."

I followed Jake into the den, where he set his drink

down on the mantel, grabbed a fireplace poker, and started rearranging the logs. Barrone was already eased down onto one end of the sofa with a martini glass held gingerly in his right hand.

"You'll have to excuse Jake," Barrone said. "He's lived in New York City, Miami, Las Vegas, and Reno. That's the extent of his exposure to America."

"What?" Jake asked defensively. "Like that ain't enough?"

"Marty tells me," Barrone said, "that you're a private investigator."

I sat down in a rocking chair next to the fire, the flames warming the left side of my body. "I used to be," I answered. "And I guess technically I still am. I've got a current Tennessee P.I.'s license. But I've sort of been on sabbatical the last few months."

"How long have you been in that line of work?"

I shrugged, took a long sip of the beer. Hell, at this point I'd have to sit down and figure it out. "I kind of slid into it slowly. I used to be a reporter and then I quit doing that."

"Yuk," Jake snapped, "reporters!" Then he mimicked spitting into the fireplace.

I smiled. "What have you got against reporters?"

"Bottom-feeding, scum-sucking, mother—"

"That's enough, Jake," Barrone said, cutting him off at the verbal knees. "Don't insult our guest."

"No problem," I said, raising my glass to Jake. "I largely agree with him. I went from the state legislature to hanging out in front of seedy motels with a video-camera in my lap and figured it was moving up in the world."

Jake pointed at me and looked at Barrone. "I think I'm going to like this guy."

We all turned as Marty came down the stairs and

entered the room. She walked over to a silver tray on a buffet and poured herself a martini from the glass pitcher.

"It can't be long," she said, toasting us. "Any day now. I can feel it."

"So can she," I said.

Jake broke out laughing and even Barrone cracked a smile.

We continued on with the cocktail hour and small talk and getting to know one another a bit and then the four of us moved into the dining room. Estella brought in some kind of chicken-based soup that was thick and spicy and great on a cold night with a fire burning in the next room. Then she brought in a salad and bread and a paella full of sausage and shrimp, with one ice-cold white wine after another. First a Chardonnay, then a Chablis Blanc. Damn, for a guy who forty-eight hours earlier was standing on the loneliest road in America without a nickel to his name or even a way to prove who he was, I was in pretty high cotton. We talked politics for a while and argued over which state had the most crooked politics, Nevada or Tennessee. Then we compromised and decided that it wasn't worth arguing since Louisiana had the stew beat out of all of us on that count anyway.

Marty also talked of her sister, Marsha's mother, who'd died of breast cancer ten years ago, and of Marsha's father, a retired surgeon living on the Costa del Sol. As an only child, Marsha had little family left except for Marty. There were a couple of other cousins out there somewhere, but no one really kept track of one another.

As for Marty, Mao Zedong made her a widow the day he ordered his troops across the 38th Parallel. She went to college on her husband's death benefits, never married again, and spent the next thirty-five years or so climbing the ladder at a brokerage house in New York. Ultimately she became one of the first women to ascend the ranks all the way into partnership back in the early seventies. She'd invested well and retired early, and now she managed her money and traveled and was on the boards of various charities and arts organizations. She and Jacques Barrone had met five years earlier at some kind of charity gig and had been a pair ever since, though if there were any plans to move their relationship to a higher level, neither spoke of them.

Barrone, I learned that night, was the descendant of a Basque sheepherder who all his life saved to climb out of the western Pyrenees and put his family on a schooner out of the Bay of Biscay, then sail halfway around the world so that his kids wouldn't have to herd sheep or pay taxes to a king. Barrone's great-grandfather had settled the northern cowboy country along with other Basques when Nevada had been a state for less than a decade. They'd bought land and sheep before they bought anything else and fought their share of battles with cattle ranchers for water and grazing rights. A couple of generations later they were sending their kids to med school and law school. For Barrone, it had been the University of Nevada Law School, then a career as a prosecutor and a state legislator. There had even been some talk early on that he might someday be governor, but that had never happened. A bit too liberal for cowboy country in the end, he'd withdrawn from public life and made a fortune in private practice. Now he was mostly retired, although he made some reference to a willingness to take on interesting cases if they were interesting enough.

There was good food and good wine and after that coffee with brandy in the den and more conversation. Marsha ate her meal upstairs and I went up a few times to check on her, but she was feeling so lousy that she basically wanted to be left alone, a sentiment she went to great lengths to apologize for. I understood, though, and was, candidly, relieved. We had a lot to talk about, but hell if I knew where to start.

Estella ate in the kitchen, then cleaned everything up and said good night to everyone. She checked on Marsha on her way up, then poked her head back downstairs to whisper that Marsha was already asleep. It was just after eleven when Marty and Barrone announced that it was past their bedtime as well and disappeared into the back of the house, where Marty's master bedroom, private office, and dressing room were located.

Jake polished off the last of his beer, then stood up in front of the fire and stretched.

"So, kid," he said. Over the course of the evening I'd almost managed to get used to being called "kid." "You like to gamble?"

"Never done much of it," I said.

"Good," he said, smiling. "They'll love you. Why don't I come by tomorrow morning; we'll hit a few casinos. I'll give you the grand tour."

"Might be a good idea for me to check with her first," I said, motioning upstairs. "Marsha might want me to hang around, keep her company."

"C'mon, kid," he said. "You can't baby-sit her. Estella and Marty's taking good care of her."

"Yeah, I kind of wonder what I'm doing here."

"You're here to help out your sweetheart," Jake said. "Give some moral support. Ain't nothing wrong with that. But there ain't much you can do either, at least not until you get in the room. Then you can say 'breathe, breathe' while she cusses you out for knocking her up."

I couldn't help smiling at him. "So that's the way it works."

He shrugged, held out his hands. "Well, couldn't tell it

by me. None of my wives ever had kids, you know. Just lucky, I guess."

"Wives?"

He shook his head. "Don't go there."

"Okay," I said, "let's do Reno tomorrow. Maybe I'll get lucky on the slots."

"Slots?" Jake said, his upper lip rising. "That the best you can do? Slots? Old ladies in curlers and drunk frat jocks play slots."

I remembered the crowd at the Peppermill. "Come to think of it, you're right. So what should I play?"

"I'll teach you blackjack, kid. The only game that ain't a sucker bet."

"Works for me," I said. And then he left, leaving me in a house full of sleeping people with me not the least damn little bit sleepy. I suddenly felt totally alone as I stirred the dying red embers of the fire and turned the television back on, the volume as low as I could get it and still hear. I searched for a movie or something even remotely worth watching and, after scanning 175 channels, didn't find a damn thing that met any of my standards, which were pretty low to begin with. So I flicked off the tube and put the Paul Desmond CD back on, then settled back on the sofa with one last drink, staring at the fire and listening again to that sweet, mellow alto sax, all the while wondering what Kelly was doing back at the Peppermill.

I sat in a wooden chair next to Marsha's bed as she finished her breakfast. She ate little, just a bit of cereal and toast, and a cup of hot herbal tea. Her back was sore, so she rolled over on her side and I gave her a backrub, or as much of one as I could. She couldn't lie on her stomach and she was so heavy that I couldn't move her as easily as

I once might have. Nothing seemed to help much and she appeared tired, depressed, ready to get this over with.

Not that I could blame her. It was hard to sit there knowing she was hurting and not be able to do anything about it. There was also an unspoken and awkward conversation that neither of us seemed to be interested in having. We made clumsy small talk. She asked me what was going on at the medical examiner's office in the months since it had been privatized and she had resigned from her job there. I told her what little I knew, which wasn't much since I didn't really keep up with the news anymore. Too many years of swimming in it, I guess.

I took her breakfast tray downstairs and asked Estella to go up and help Marsha into the bathroom. After she attended to that, Estella helped her back into bed and I went to her room again.

"Would you like me to read to you?" I asked.

She smiled wanly and shook her head. "No, I don't think so."

"Is there anything on television you want to watch?"

"No."

I must have sighed loudly without meaning to, for she suddenly looked hard at me and said, "Look, you don't have to sit here with me if you don't want to. I know I'm no fun and this is very boring."

"That's not it," I said. "This is less fun for you than anybody."

Then I became quiet for a few moments. "What?" she asked uncomfortably.

"I was just wondering which one of us is going to finally break down and really say something."

She folded her arms across her swollen belly. "This is a hell of a time to decide you really want to talk."

"I tried to talk to you a lot back home," I said. "And you—"

"First of all," she snapped, "that may be home for you, but it's not for me. And second, you were the one who checked out on me."

"Only for a while," I countered. "Only to do a little mending. Then I was back with you."

She turned her head away from me and stared out the window. "I shouldn't have asked you to come here."

"This is my child, too," I said. "Nothing you can do will change that. And I had a right to be here."

She rolled her head back over on the pillow slowly, painfully, and looked at me through eyes that were shiny with tears.

"We both know it isn't going to work," she said softly.

"I know."

"If you want to go," Marsha said, "that's okay. I'll understand."

"Can I stay until the baby's born?" I asked. "So that I can at least see her."

"Yes, of course you can, Harry."

"Where will you go?" I asked. "Where will you and the baby live?"

"Here for a while," Marsha answered. "Until I get back on my feet physically. Estella will help with the baby. After that, who knows? Reno's a nice place. I may stay here, go to work for the M.E.'s office."

"Maybe I can come visit sometime, or maybe the two of you could come to Nashville."

"Maybe," she said.

"You know," I said, "I'm not sorry. As hard as this has been, I'm not sorry. We had a lot of fun together."

"Yes," Marsha said. "We did."

"A lot of adventures."

"A lot of adventures," she agreed.

"And we'll always be in each other's lives," I said. "We'll have a kid."

Her eyes glistened. "Yeah, Harry. We will."

I didn't know what else to say after that. We sat there for what felt like a long while, only the silence was less uncomfortable and awkward now. It seemed that we were both going to be able to find some peace, some—as pop psychologists are so fond of saying—"closure" to all this.

When I opened my mouth to try to say something else, there was a soft knock at the door. "Come in," Marsha said.

Estella opened the door with a cordless phone in her hand. "It's for you, Señor Harry. It's Jake."

I looked at Marsha and rolled my eyes discreetly. "He wants to give me a tour of Reno," I said.

"I think you should let him," Marsha said, smiling. "You can't sit here in this dark room all day with me. We'll both go mad."

I took the phone from Estella. "You sure? You'll be all right?"

She nodded.

"Hello," I said.

"I'll be there in thirty minutes," Jake said. No intro, no small talk. Straight to the point.

"I'll be ready," I said. I turned the phone off, handed it back to Estella.

"I think I might nap for a while," Marsha said. "I didn't sleep well last night."

"Okay," I said. I stood, leaned over, and kissed her softly on the forehead. "Need anything from town?" I asked.

"No, but thanks."

I followed Estella out of Marsha's bedroom and downstairs. Outside, through the plate-glass windows, I saw that a light snow had begun to fall. Just a dusting, but sweet and idyllic, like a Currier & Ives painting, pristine and pure and untarnished. I walked over to a window and leaned my head against the glass, watching the fine white powder fall. When I straightened up, there was a smudge on the glass, and through it the snow seemed dirty, sullied and dingy. I pulled my shirtsleeve down over my hand and tried to wipe the glass clean, but my efforts only made it worse.

"Damn it," I muttered. This was getting to be the story of my life.

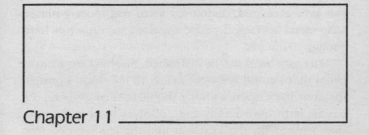

Chapter 11 _____

A few minutes later Shaky Jake Shalinsky pulled into Marty's driveway in a yellow and brown mid-Seventies AMC Pacer, which, let's face it, is just not something you see every day this close to the turn of the century. I hadn't known Pacers were made well enough to have survived this long, and when I got a good look at Jake's, I realized I was right.

The car was held together with body rust and coat hangers; the back window was a former dry-cleaning bag held in place by layers of duct tape. The tires were bald, which made me feel real good about climbing down Mount Rose just as it was starting to snow.

I threw on a sweater and my coat and went out the front door. Jake reached across and pushed on the passenger door to open it for me, only it was clear that something was wrong. The door wouldn't open. I watched through the window as he unbuckled his seat belt, threw his legs over the transmission hump, braced himself against the driver's-side door, then kick hard with both feet. The door gave way and shot open with a horrible squeal. I jumped out of the way just in time.

"Mercedes in the shop, huh, Jake?"

"Don't get smart, kid," he said, buckling himself back in. "C'mon, let's roll."

I slid onto what had once been a brown vinyl seat but

was now a ragged, discolored foam pad loosely placed atop metal springs. I pulled the door to, only not hard enough to latch it.

"Ya gotta slam it," he instructed, mashing on a brake pedal that I could see went nearly to the floor. I pushed the door back open with my shoulder, then grabbed the handle with both hands and pulled as hard as I could. Jake yanked on the gearshift and the car jumped into reverse.

"The seat belt, kid," he said. "Fasten it."

"Oh," I said, surprised. "You mean it actually works?"

"Of course it works!" he yelled. "Ya gotta have a seat belt. It's the law!"

He pulled out onto the street, sliding a few feet backward as he braked the car, then threw the gearshift into forward. As the car began moving, I looked around the ragged heap.

"You know, Jake, I'm a great believer in getting as much use as you can out of a car, but is this puppy actually going to make it down the mountain?"

"Oh, yeah," he said, laughing, "it'll make it *down* the mountain."

Jake made a right onto the Mount Rose highway, and we started down the slope. Despite my misgivings, Jake was a pretty good driver, and with the exception of a couple of hair-raising slides, we did okay. I kept quiet, not wanting to distract him, but about halfway down the mountain the snow stopped, the streets were dry, and I relaxed a little.

"So what's the plan, Stan?"

Jake turned, his grizzled face close to the steering wheel as he hunched over it. "We'll grab some lunch. I'm kinda hungry."

"Sure," I said.

"You didn't happen to notice if Mr. Barrone left this morning, did you?"

"Yeah, he and Marty drove off around ten."

Jake's head bobbed up and down as he negotiated a particularly sharp curve, braking as we started to drift across the center line.

"I figured he would," Jake said. "That was his Mercedes last night. I stopped by his place and picked it up on the way to the airport."

"You mean he and Marty didn't think they could get all their bags in the Pacer?"

Jake turned and saw that I was smiling. "Yeah, something like that."

"So Marty had to give him a ride down the mountain."

"They'll spend the day in Reno," Jake said. "Then Mr. Barrone has to go to work tomorrow."

"Yeah? Where's he working?"

A funny look crossed Jake's face, although truth is, it was hard to tell how much was look and how much was face. "We'll get into that later."

I wondered what the hell that meant.

"In the meantime," he said, "listen up. Blackjack basic strategy'll give you an edge over the house of about two-hundredths of a percent, and over the long run, that's enough to win. And win big, if you know what you're doing and the cards treat you right."

"Maybe I'll become a counter," I said. I was just kidding, only Jake didn't pick up on that.

"Fuck counting!" he yelled. "Nine out of ten counters only think they can count!"

I had to let that one sink in for a minute.

"And all it does is get 'em in trouble."

"Hey, Jake, I was just making a joke. I'm not going

to count cards. I don't want to get barred from the casinos."

Jake broke out laughing, little droplets of spit flying out over the top of the steering wheel. "I ain't had a real, honest-to-God rube come my way in a long time, kid. We're gonna have a good time together."

"What? What do you mean?"

He shook his head as his right foot began pumping the brake rhythmically. Ahead of us, down a slight incline and just past the cloverleaf under the freeway, was the stop sign at 395. As far as I could tell, the car wasn't slowing.

"Hell, kid, that's not the trouble you'll get in. The casinos love card-counting tourists. The trouble is, you'll wind up losing your ass."

He continued pumping the brakes, then reached up and jerked the transmission into low. A thunking sound came from the tunnel by my left knee.

"Speaking of losing my ass, you going to be able to make that stop sign?"

Jake cleared his throat while staring ahead intently. It was a long, wet, phlegmy, gravelly sound and under ordinary circumstances it would have bordered on disgusting. However, I was too busy bracing myself to worry about it.

Jake rolled down the window as we approached the intersection and hawked loudly out the window. I turned away, saw the intersection approaching rapidly, and decided that the best thing to do was hold on and close my eyes.

Jake must have timed it perfectly because we never really completely stopped. He just kind of coasted through the intersection during a convenient break in the traffic.

"Everything in blackjack depends on what the dealer's showing," Jake continued without missing a beat as I opened my eyes, looked around, and once again had the sensation I'd had a couple of days earlier: *Damn, I'm alive!*

"Of course, what you've got showing is important, too. Don't ever think it ain't. But if you know what the dealer's card means, then you'll know what to do. Wait, hold on a minute."

Jake jerked the transmission back into drive, stomped the gas pedal, switched lanes, and shot past an old truck full of fifty-gallon drums. The engine roared and I began to smell exhaust inside the car, but the damn thing had more pickup than I expected.

"Now the worst card a dealer can show is a six," Jake continued. "Dealer's got a six showing, chances are he's going to bust."

He went on like that nonstop for the next twenty minutes as we drove into town on South Virginia. I got a crash course in basic blackjack strategy, about ten percent of which I imagined would actually stay with me once I got out of the car. He was deep into the rules for splitting aces and sevens as we entered solidly into the flow of Reno traffic. A few minutes later we passed the Peppermill on the left and I faded away for a few moments, thinking of Kelly, and when I came back, Jake was rattling on about soft seventeens or some such. I realized I'd totally lost my seat on his train of thought.

"Where are we going?" I asked.

He turned to me, scowling at my interruption. "You said you were hungry."

"So?"

He braked to a stop at a red light. "We're going to the Awful-Awful."

"The what?"

"You can't come to Reno without hitting the Awful-Awful. You gotta have your first Awful-Awful."

I shifted in my seat, and a piece of metal spring jabbed me on the right side of my butt, which caused me to yelp and jump about two inches.

"Ya gotta watch that," Jake said, chuckling.

A few minutes farther on, we crossed the bridge over the Truckee River, then Jake made a left and pulled into a parking garage. Despite the snow up on Mount Rose, downtown Reno was cool and dry, with a brilliant blue sky above. It was a beautiful, crisp day and my spirits seemed to lift the farther into town we got.

We parked the car, took the elevator down two levels, and walked back out onto Virginia Street. The streets were crowded with tourists, strollers, locals out on bikes. A few blocks north was the famous Reno Arch and I made a point to ask Jake if we could walk up and take a closer look. I felt like a tourist and figured I may as well go with it.

"You should've seen this town a few years ago," Jake said as we walked.

"What?" I asked. "Was it different?"

"Different," he said, snorting. "Hell, it was great! All the action's moving out on South Virginia now. It's terrible."

"Seems pretty hectic down here to me." We stopped at a corner for a few moments, then, like a true New Yorker, Jake found an opening in the traffic and jay-walked, with me scurrying to keep up with him.

"Look around ya, kid!" he said. "Take a look."

I started looking closer and realized to my immediate left that the Woolworth's was closed, its windows papered over. That was no big deal; Woolworth's are pretty much closed everywhere. But then Jake pointed behind me and I saw the Mapes Hotel, all boarded up and closed.

"I can reel 'em off for you, kid," he said, walking

rapidly down the sidewalk with me in tow. He pointed
north along Virginia. "Harold's Club, down the toilet.
The old Nevada Club, it's kaput. The Riverboat's gone.
And it's not just the old clubs. The American Bandstand
went under. The King's Inn and Gil's. Jeez, I used to date
a poker dealer at Gil's. God, she knew how to use her
hands."

Jake stopped on the sidewalk, looked around to get his
bearings. "Yeah, here, over here," he instructed, and I
followed him into someplace called the Nugget.

"Oh, I've heard of this place," I said.

"No, you haven't," Jake shot back. "You've heard of
the Golden Nugget in Vegas or maybe Ascuaga's Nugget
over in Sparks. Those are classy places. This place is a
dump."

"What?" I asked. "It's a casino, right?"

"It's a slot bar," he snapped. "Kids and tourists playing slots and video poker. Ain't a real casino. No table
games."

"Then what are we doing here?" I don't know; I just
had to ask.

"The Awful-Awful," he answered.

What the hell? I shut up and followed him.

The Awful-Awful, it turned out, was the name of the
hamburger at the lunch counter in the Nugget. The lunch
counter was just that: a counter with a shelf and a bunch
of stools, with a row of stools on the wall opposite against
a huge floor-to-ceiling mirror. Customers—mainly kids,
all smoking, most with tattoos and body piercings—
jammed the place. A thin sheen of grease from the grill
had settled over everything upon cooling. Signs on the
wall proclaimed the health benefits of eating meat, with
one declaring: NINE OUT OF TEN VEGETARIANS DO NOT
EAT HERE!

Jake ordered for us: two large Cokes, two large fries,

two Awful-Awfuls with everything. We found two stools farthest down on the counter, away from the loudest parts of the crowd, and settled down to wait for food.

"Now, ya gotta understand," Jake said. "Ya can't do this every day. Not unless ya just want a heart attack."

"Every once in a while won't kill us," I agreed.

The food came a few minutes later and I bit into what was possibly the best hamburger I've ever had. We ate silently for a few minutes, just listening to the chatter of the men who worked behind the grill and watching the kids come and go.

"Mind if I ask you something personal?" I asked.

Jake set his burger down on the plate, turned to me with an eyebrow raised. "Shoot," he said. "If I don't want to answer, I don't gotta."

"Fair enough. I was just wondering where Shaky Jake came from. You don't appear to have any extraneous vibratory accouterments."

Jake put both elbows on the counter and reached for his soda. He took a long slurp off the straw and seemed to gaze across to the smoking grill for a moment. Then he turned to me and spoke in a low voice.

"Well, it's like this, kid. When I was younger, I used to be in the rackets. My specialty was debt collection, if you get my drift. Some deadbeat'd borrow money from my employers and then he'd fall behind on his payments and I'd have to go discuss his situation with him. And sometimes that discussion involved—what was it you called it?"

"Extraneous vibratory accouterments?"

"Yeah, what you said. Sometimes I'd have to turn 'em upside down and shake 'em a little bit. Eventually, the nickname caught on and I became Shaky Jake."

"I don't mean anything by this, Jake, but you don't

look like you've got the body weight to hold somebody upside down and shake him."

He took another bite of the burger. "Well, ya gotta understand," he said, his mouth full. "I was in a supervisory position. I had other gentlemen who actually did the physical labor."

"Oh," I said. "So you were, like, a gangster, right?"

He shrugged, took another bite while staring straight ahead. "Well, if ya gotta label everything."

I spun on the stool to face him and leaned against the counter, my left elbow on the counter and my head resting on my palm. "I've got to ask, Jake. What was it like, being a gangster?"

He shifted slightly to meet my gaze. "For one thing, you normally didn't have to take shit from people calling you gangster."

"I'm not giving you shit, Jake," I said. "I'm curious. Really."

"I grew up on the Lower East Side in New York in the late Thirties, early Forties. My old man worked for Mr. Lansky as an accountant. God, Mr. Lansky was a great money man. My old man learned a lot from him. It was just natural for me, only I didn't have the head for figures and I hated being cooped up in an office. So when I turned thirteen, I dropped out of school and my old man got me a job running numbers. Later he moved out to Vegas to work for Mr. Siegel, only as everybody knows, Mr. Siegel's employment contract ended kind of abruptly."

"So I'm told," I said.

"My old man went back to work for Mr. Lansky after that and I went out to Vegas and started working there. These days, it's all corporations and shit. You don't pay a gambling debt today, they just ruin your credit rating, write you dirty letters, et cetera. But back then it was different. Debt collection was a little more forceful."

I motioned to the grill man and asked for refills on the Cokes. He pointed to a ketchup-stained sign that said refills were fifty cents. I nodded; he came over and grabbed our glasses.

"So you worked in the debt-collection industry until you retired, and now you drive a '76 Pacer."

"It's a '77, smartass," he said. "And no, I didn't finish out my career in debt collection."

"Yeah, where did you finish it?" I said, grinning like I'd made some kind of joke, only Jake was stone-faced, staring at me.

"I finished out my career doing just under twenty at the federal penitentiary in Atlanta."

The grin disappeared from my face. "Oh," I said. "Sorry."

He shrugged. "No biggie," he said. "And it sure as hell ain't any big secret."

"So what'd you go down for?"

"Bad attitude, mostly," he said. "No, seriously," he added, seeing my reaction. "I was among a select group who were the first locals indicted under RICO back in 1972. And the feds decided my attitude of noncompliance was counterproductive to their efforts. I'd never done hard time before and I ain't real big, so when I got into the system some guy tried to punk me out and I had to kill him. I mean, it was that simple, only it added time on as well—"

That one got me. "Jeez, Jake, I'm . . . Maybe I should just shut up."

He took the Coke refill, lifted it to his lips, and took a long swallow. "Like I said, it ain't no big deal. I got paroled back in '92 and by then everything had changed. All the guys I used to work with had either gotten old or retired, some were dead. Some of 'em had just disappeared. I went back to Vegas for a while, but there was nothing there for me. I came up here three years ago just for the hell of it and decided I liked it. I met Mr. Barrone and he gave me a chance to do some part-time work for him, and then Marty let me house-sit for her every now and then. It's a few extra bucks here and there."

"You ever have any family, Jake? I mean, brothers or sisters?"

"Nah, nobody I'd have anything to do with. I got a brother who's back east, but I ain't even sure where. I had a sister who died when I was a kid. And my mom; jeez, she and the old man split up during the war and she ran off with some soldier. We never saw her again."

"And you told me you never had kids, right?"

He shook his head. "Yeah, and my last wife divorced me when I went down in '72. I ain't going that route again."

There was something about the way Jake had described his life that brought me right down. It's not that I ever expect to spend twenty years in the Atlanta federal penitentiary, but increasingly I could imagine myself old and broke and alone, and that was depressing as hell.

Jake must have read my face. "It ain't so bad," he said. "I've had a hell of a lot of fun in my life. And I've got a couple of girlfriends who cop me a meal every now and then, along with plenty of good, basic recreational sex."

I smiled. "Hey, ain't nothing wrong with that. So, you want to teach me some blackjack?"

Jake's face went blank and he sat there, staring at me. "No," he said after a few moments. "Mr. Barrone asked me to take you out, get a feel for you. Try to figure out what kind of guy you are. Mr. Barrone says I'm a good judge of character. Between last night and today, I think I've got you figured out."

"Yeah?" I asked. "Why would Mr. Barrone want you to—what'd you say?—take me out and feel me up?"

"Hey, that ain't funny, kid," Jake said sternly. Then his voice softened. "I'm serious here."

"Okay," I said. "Why would Mr. Barrone want you to evaluate my character?"

"Because," Jake answered. "Mr. Barrone's got a problem and he could use your help."

Chapter 12

Thirty minutes later the Reno skyline was behind us and we were in the foothills to the east, turning off a two-lane county road onto gravel that led to Jacques Barrone's ranch.

The house was a one-story beige stucco with a red tile roof. It looked like what movie set designers come up with when the script calls for a Mexican hacienda. Barrone's Mercedes was parked in a large parking area in front of the house. Jake pulled up next to the sedan and stopped the car.

I hadn't asked Jake what kind of problem Barrone had, despite my curiosity as to his dilemma and why either of them thought I could help with it. I got out of the car, my shoes crunching on the gravel and shells, and scanned the house. Barrone had let the landscape stay in its natural state, unlike many of the locals who insisted on golf course–caliber lawns. The ground was bare, packed earth with little patches of moss and scrub brush, interspersed with some rocks and cacti and other desert plants and bushes.

I followed Jake through a metal gate at the front of the house and then an arch outlined in brick over a tiled walkway. The house, I could see now, was four-sided, with a large courtyard and a swimming pool in the center.

We walked through what felt like a tunnel out into the courtyard.

Barrone exited the house from our right, dressed in khaki trousers and a starched white Mexican shirt and leaning on a cane topped with a white bone handle.

"Welcome, gentlemen," he said, nodding to us. "I appreciate your coming this afternoon. Is it warm enough to sit outside or would you rather go in?"

"What do you think, kid?" Jake asked.

"There's no wind," I offered. "It's warm enough for me."

"Excellent," Barrone said in a tone of voice that was firmer and more energetic than any he'd used at Marty's house the previous evening. "Jake, would you mind going in and making us some drinks while we get settled?"

"I'd be happy to, Mr. Barrone," Jake said, and then turning to me: "What can I get you?"

"Doesn't matter," I said. "Maybe a soda. Don't think I'm ready for a beer."

"Good deal," Jake said. "And for you?"

"There's an open Cab on the kitchen counter," Barrone answered. "I'd like a glass of that."

Jake disappeared through the same door Barrone had come through. Barrone motioned me over to a large table with a patio umbrella and four wooden chairs with a thick, brightly colored throw pillow on each. I sat down, looking out over the pool, which had a tall fountain in the center with a statue of a nude woman pouring water out of a pitcher.

"You've got quite a nice place here, Mr. Barrone," I said. "How much land have you got?"

"Thank you," he answered. "This place has been in my family for three generations. I'm the last one left. My kids have all grown and moved away. And I've sold off most of the land over the years. I'm down to about seven hundred acres."

I laughed. "Oh, gee, just a tiny little place by Nevada standards. Where I'm from, we'd throw in some streets and plumb the place for sewers, then put up about twelve hundred houses on it."

Barrone smiled. "There are developers around here who've made me just such an offer, but I won't take it."

We made more small talk until Jake brought our drinks out on a tray. I took the tall glass he offered and sipped while Jake settled down in a seat.

"So," I said, my curiosity getting the better of me. "Jake said you had a problem, Mr. Barrone, and that for some reason or other, you think maybe I could help with it."

Barrone slowly rubbed the palm of his hand across the bone handle of his cane, as if trying to subtly scratch an itch.

"Let me ask you a question, Harry."

I nodded. "Sure. Why not?"

"Have you ever heard of the Mustang Ranch?"

I looked at Jake and tried to suppress a grin. "This is a trick question, right? Sure, I've heard of it. World's most famous legal cathouse."

"That's right," Barrone said. "What else do you know about it?"

I sat there for a moment, wondering where the hell this was going. "Nothing, I guess."

Jake and Barrone glanced at each other as if sharing some private joke.

"Well, let me fill you in," Barrone said. "The Mustang Ranch goes back to the Sixties, I guess. Maybe even earlier."

He shifted in his chair and took another swallow of wine. "The man who started the Mustang Ranch and who, by the way, single-handedly built it into the county's largest business was a fellow named Joe Conforte. There is some evidence that Mr. Conforte's background might be suspect, but I'm not going to go there because it doesn't matter for the purposes of our discussion. But in short order Mr. Conforte had the entire Storey County government in the palm of his hand. He would register his girls as voters in Storey County and then tell them how to vote, which made his employees the single biggest voting block in the county."

I laughed at that one. "You mean there was a hooker caucus?"

"That's about it," Barrone said.

"Why not?" I asked. "God knows we've already got enough whores in Congress. May as well have them running local governments as well."

"Exactly, and over the years Mr. Conforte basically did run the government. He worked closely with local law enforcement, was the biggest political contributor in the county, and even influenced the state legislative races in Storey County. He also gave money to charitable causes and once a year opened up the Mustang to the entire county for the biggest party of the year."

"You mean . . ." I hesitated, not quite knowing how to ask this. "You mean he gave away free . . . ?"

"No, not exactly," Barrone said, smiling. "It was free beer and barbecue at the party. But he got his employees to dress up nicely and they mingled with the locals and it was just one big happy family."

I nodded. "Got you."

"Then four years ago the incumbent Storey County district attorney was voted out, to everyone's surprise. The winner of that race ran on a reform platform and his first political promise was to get Mr. Conforte. He was unsuccessful at that, but he raised enough hell that the U.S. attorney's office became interested. They'd, of course, been watching the Mustang Ranch operation for years, but what could they do? It was a legal business."

"Let me guess—that didn't stop the feds."

"Very good," Barrone said, nodding. "In time, the U.S. attorney's office was able to dig up enough on the financial dealings of Mr. Conforte to convince the Justice Department that they had a pretty good tax fraud and evasion case."

"Oh," I said. "They Capone'd him."

"Yes, only unlike Capone, Mr. Conforte knew that despite the protections afforded citizens by the constitution, once the government decides to come after you, you're basically a lost cause."

"Yeah, you're screwed. Can't argue with that."

As we talked, Jake sat there silently, taking occasional sips from a bottle of Dos Equis. But Barrone did virtually all of the talking.

"In any case, Mr. Conforte disappeared."

"He rabbitted?" I asked, surprised. "Or did somebody use him for construction material in a football stadium?"

"Reports have him in hiding in Costa Rica," Barrone answered. "Although he's also turned up in Mexico, Bonaire, Argentina, and a few other places, all with extradition policies that are not as friendly as our government would like."

"So," I said after a moment, "what happened to the Mustang Ranch?"

"The government seized it in a tax lien two years ago," Barrone answered. "All this has been widely reported in the newspapers. What has not been as widely reported is that the federal government has continued to run the Mustang Ranch as a profit-making enterprise."

I sat up, my jaw dropping. "You're serious?"

Barrone nodded. "Very."

"The feds own a whorehouse?" I said, trying hard to stifle a belly laugh.

"A very successful one," Barrone said.

I started howling, laughing so hard that Coke was threatening to shoot out of my nostrils. "Well," I said between bursts of laughter, "it kind of puts a whole new slant on getting screwed by Uncle Sam, doesn't it?"

Jake was laughing now, too. "You ain't heard nothing yet," he said.

"Oh, please," I cackled, pulling myself up from where I'd almost doubled over in the chair, "no more. I can't take it."

"Oh, no," Barrone said, "there's more. Guess who's running the Mustang Ranch for the government?"

I sat up straighter, trying to get myself under control. I don't know why that struck me as so damn funny, but I hadn't had a laugh like that in years. My eyes watered and my jaw hurt. I was just glad I hadn't had a mouthful of soda.

"Okay," I said, more or less in control. "I give up. Who's running the Mustang Ranch now?"

Barrone looked me straight in the eye. "Me."

That sobered me up quick enough. I looked back at Barrone as he stared at me, the deep lines in his face more severe than I had noticed before.

"You're serious," I said.

"Completely."

I shook my head. "Wow," I muttered. "I never met anybody who ran a whorehouse—excuse me, brothel—before."

"For what it's worth," Barrone said, "it's a new experience for me. I've been involved in a variety of business ventures before, but never anything like this."

I leaned back in the chair, thinking. "So," I asked,

"what's your problem and what makes you think I can help you with it?"

"First of all, Harry, let me ask you a question. What is the number one crime in America? In the world, in fact."

I shrugged. "Well, war and plague come to mind, but technically they're not crimes. I guess I'd have to say drugs."

Jake looked down at his drink as Barrone slowly shook his head.

"Okay, murder."

Barrone continued shaking his head, pursing his lips into a tight smile.

"Drugs, murder. Let's see, what else is left? Robbery, arson, rape. But something tells me I'm wasting my time on those. How about fraud? Yeah, that's it. White-collar crime."

Barrone's tight smile broadened. "Very good. Not exactly correct, but closer than most people get."

"Okay, I give up. What's the biggest crime in the world?"

Barrone swirled his wine around in the bottom of his wineglass, then held it up and studied it for a moment. "Contrary to the old saying, Harry, crime does pay. And it pays very well. If I were a young man coming up today, especially if I were a young man of diminished circumstances or little educational background, or perhaps had the misfortune to be born into an ethnic or racial minority, I very much imagine I would turn to crime as the way to a better life."

"There is a downside," I said. "Prison, for instance, or worse. Death, maybe."

"There are risks in any occupation, and even though the prisons are jammed, we don't come anywhere near close to incarcerating all the criminals."

"It's enough to make one cynical," I commented.

"A smart man is always cynical," Barrone said. "Because to be cynical is to be realistic. A cynic is, above all else, a disappointed idealist. And in the real world, ideals are always crushed."

"Jeez, as if I wasn't already depressed enough. But what's this got to do with the Mustang Ranch and me? After all, in the state of Nevada, we're not talking about a crime."

"Oh, yes, we are," Barrone said forcefully, shifting his weight forward in the chair. "We're talking about the world's largest crime in terms of gross dollars: money laundering."

"What?" I asked.

Barrone and Jake exchanged a look that probably meant they couldn't believe what a dumb shit I was, or at least that's the way it felt to me.

"Did you know that the federal government has done studies," Barrone said, "that consist of random samplings of currency now in circulation? And that virtually every bill in circulation in America today, right now, including whatever you have in your pocket, has microscopic traces of cocaine dust on it?"

"That's a new one on me."

"And that's only the money currently in circulation," Barrone said. "There are reports of huge warehouses in Colombia that are full of American dollars. Packed floor to ceiling, so many that they can't be counted, only weighed. If it were all introduced back into the economy at once, the U.S. would suffer a disastrous hyperinflation."

"You know what cocaine importers call American singles and five-dollar bills?" Jake asked.

I shook my head. "I call them rent and utilities, but that's just me."

"They call the small denominations *trash*, and they either throw 'em away or use 'em to pay smurfs."

"Smurfs?" I asked. "Little blue cartoon guys? You sure you two haven't been sniffing bills?"

"Smurfs," Barrone explained, "are the money-laundering equivalent of mules in the drug trade. They're the lowest rung of the ladder, the foot soldiers who scurry around all day exchanging cash in small enough amounts not to be noticed, at least theoretically."

"And they get to keep the trash?" I asked.

"Within limits," Barrone said.

I stood up and walked around to the back of my chair, then leaned my forearms across it. "So the problem is not making the money in crime. That's the easy part."

"Yes," Barrone said. "The hard part is spending it without getting caught. If you don't have a legitimate job, or if you have a low-paying cover job, how are you going to explain that Jaguar and the expensive house and the diamonds around your wife's neck or, more likely, your mistress's? And if you can't spend the money without getting caught, if you can't enjoy your so-called ill-gotten gains, what's the point?"

"So you clean the cash," Jake said. "You have to make it look legitimate."

"How?" I demanded. "Some druggie's got a hundred grand lying around. How does he make it look legit?"

"Hah!" Barrone snapped. "A hundred grand is pocket change for these guys. Your friendly neighborhood crack dealer, even a low-level distributor, makes that much in a week. It's not the hundred grand you worry about. That won't get anyone's attention. It's running a million, or ten million, or twenty, or a hundred that's the challenge."

"Okay," I said, getting into the game, "I'm Joe Pot Grower from east Tennessee. I grow a good-quality pot, I don't sell it to kids. I'm careful. And I've got one million dollars in hundred-dollar bills. What do I do with it?"

"Easy," Barrone said. "A million dollars in hundreds will fit in a suitcase. You pack it with your underwear and your bathing suit. You cut your hair, dress like a tourist, take one of those long weekend excursions to Freeport. Buy a cheap package, one where the plane will be full of working-class, blue-collar folks.

"Then you get to Freeport, check into a hotel, go back to the airport, take a flight to the Caymans. In the Caymans, along with Panama and a number of other countries in the Caribbean, you can buy an off-the-shelf corporation for a few hundred dollars on up to a couple grand. Or if you want, take Luxembourg, Liechtenstein, or even Nauru or Vanuatu in the South Pacific. In any case, you open a bank account, deposit your million in cash. Then you fly back to Freeport and have a good time."

"Okay, then you fly home and all you've got is a bank account in the Caymans. Then what?"

Barrone held out his empty wineglass to Jake, who took it and went back to the kitchen without saying a word.

"Then you go back to your hometown, where you 'borrow' fifty grand, a hundred grand, whatever, from the Cayman Islands corporation, and you open up a nice little restaurant, preferably with a bar. If it's in a blue-collar part of town or near a campus where people will pay in cash, that's even better. Then at the end of every month, you deposit fifty to a hundred grand in the bank as profits from your successful bar. Now you have clean money. You pay taxes on it so you won't go to jail and you buy that Jaguar."

"It's that easy," I said.

Jake came back out and handed Barrone a fresh glass

of wine. "Basically," Barrone said. "There are details, as always, and it's not as easy as it used to be. But that's the process. And the more money you've got, the more complicated the details. There are variations on the theme, of course, but the model and the theory work."

"And the only real danger is the point when you get the money back into the system," I said. "A Cayman bank officer calls the cops and reports that there's a guy in his office with a suitcase full of cash—"

"Ah," Barrone interrupted, "but you make sure you're dealing with a place where that won't happen. You see, it's a three-step process. The first step is, you place the money somewhere; that is, as you said, you inject it back into the system. Then there's the layering component, where little by little you distance the funds from the original source. You weave as complex a network of corporations, businesses, and any other ways to legitimately generate large amounts of cash as possible. Then finally comes the integration component, where you regain control and use of the money, only now it has a legitimate paper trail to explain where it came from."

"Mr. Barrone," I said, "this is fascinating, but I still don't get the connection to the Mustang Ranch and any problem that I can help you with."

Barrone looked up at me. "I have enemies in this state, political enemies. You can't live your life here and work in the arena I've worked in without making them. When I was appointed by the Justice Department to administer the affairs, so to speak, of the Mustang, my enemies saw it as an opportunity to cause me harm."

"How can they harm you?" I asked. "I don't mean to sound naive, but if the government got you into this, can't they protect you?"

"Harry, I believe that the Mustang Ranch has become

a central, focal operation for money laundering in this part of the country."

I looked from Barrone to Jake. "How? What's makes you think that?"

"Money laundering moves all around, kid," Jake said. "A few years ago Miami was the center of money laundering for the whole country. Then the feds cracked down, started using GTOs."

"What?"

"Geographical targeting orders," Barrone said. "Bank reporting laws already require that any cash transaction over ten thousand dollars be reported to the IRS. The smurfs got around that by doing all their transactions in nine-thousand-nine-hundred-dollar chunks."

"Then the feds wised up," Jake added, "and made a rule that said that in areas where money laundering is a problem, say like Miami or Queens, any transaction over seven hundred and fifty dollars has to be reported."

"Holy shit," I said. "Aren't they drowning in paperwork?"

"They're bureaucrats," Jake cracked. "They breathe best in paper."

"But the government's efforts had the effect of moving these laundering operations elsewhere. For the past few years, Los Angeles has been the main arena for money laundering. Now that's changing and the activity is moving north, to San Francisco and Seattle. And with the passage of Proposition 5 in California, which authorizes Native American gaming in Northern California, we'll see a lot of the activity move there."

"Casinos are perfect for laundering large amounts of cash, but here in Reno you didn't hear me say that," Jake said.

"So as the center of operations has moved north, more and more of the day-to-day activity has moved here," Barrone continued. "And that's my problem. I've been appointed by the U.S. attorney, but the U.S. attorney has political enemies here as well, many of them within the federal bureaucracy. The local FINCEN field investigators—"

"The what?" I asked.

"The Financial Crimes Enforcement Network, the government agency whose mission is to eradicate illegal money laundering. Their field investigators in this part of the state don't get along with the U.S. attorney. And I've heard from my own sources that they're investigating the Mustang and, by association, me. My local enemies are, needless to say, cooperating fully."

I sat back down across from Barrone. "You know, we got a saying back home: You get down in the mud and wrestle with the pigs, you got to expect to get a little stink on you."

Jake grinned.

"At least that's the way I think it goes," I added. "So why don't you just quit?"

Barrone's eyes narrowed. "I don't quit, Harry. I never quit. If I let those bastards make me quit, then I'm through."

"So what do you think's going on there? Do you believe the operation is dirty?"

"I'm not sure," Barrone answered. "You have to understand, I'm the administrator of the Mustang, but it's not like I have an office there or anything. Basically, I oversee the financial affairs, but I have to depend on the numbers they give me. I'm not at the front door counting customers."

"And you think they're reporting receiving more money than they're actually taking in so that they can run a laundry for somebody?"

"Exactly," Barrone said.

"But it's a legal brothel," I said. "How the hell could you ever tell, short of taking down names and numbers?"

"Jake has already helped me some in that regard," Barrone said.

I turned to Jake. "I've been doing some casual checking the place out," he said. "Hanging around, you know. Truth is, Harry, the whorehouse business ain't what it used to be."

"Oh, really," I said, suppressing a grin. After all, this was supposed to be a serious discussion.

"No, seriously," Jake said. "Back in the Seventies, you used to have adult theaters in every town. You could go sit in a legitimate movie theater and eat popcorn with your girlfriend and watch Harry Reems get a blow job. Then we got videotapes. Now you can buy porns for ten bucks and watch 'em over and over. Ba-boom, ba-boom, no more triple-X movie houses. Today you got free porn all over the Internet and the videos are getting cheaper."

"Yeah, but this ain't porn, Jake. It's real sex."

"Hey," Jake insisted, "porn's real sex, but let's don't go there. The point is that thirty, forty years ago a place like the Mustang had a waiting list on Saturday night. Then the sexual revolution came along and then feminism. Now nobody has to pay for it anymore, ya understand, kid? The broads'll hit on you."

"Yeah. Happens to me all the time. It's a real inconvenience."

"Don't laugh, kid. The only guys who come to legal bordellos nowadays are guys who can't get it anywhere else. We don't even get the thrillseekers anymore. How much thrill is in it when it's legal, the place takes credit cards and makes you wear a condom? You looking to take some risks, you go to New York and pick up some crack-addicted, HIV-positive whore outside the Lincoln Tunnel."

I nodded. "Point well taken."

"Yeah, old farts like me and losers. That's all they get at the Mustang anymore. Ain't like the old days."

"So you guys have taken informal surveys," I said. "And you're seeing X amount of money reported and you can't figure out how the hell it got there given the number of customers."

"Right," said Barrone. "I believe you understand the situation fully."

"What I still don't understand is how I can help you."

Barrone and Jake looked at each other, as if sharing some private, proprietary information. I sat there quietly, an uneasy knot of tension growing somewhere in my middle. Then Barrone turned to me.

"I've been, for lack of a better word, checking up on you, Harry. Marsha spoke so highly of you that when I found out you were coming out here, I made a few phone calls. I've worked with a couple of attorneys in Nashville on various matters. It wasn't hard to find references."

My eyes narrowed. I tried not to be too surprised by Marsha's praise. But I was growing increasingly suspicious of what Barrone had in mind.

"And?" I asked.

"Your references are excellent. You're intelligent, determined to the point of obsessive, and very good at what you do. The only bad things that anyone said about you were that you had a certain disrespect for authority, which I believe one person referred to as an 'attitude problem,' and that you have what another person called 'a smartass mouth.' "

"Quit," I said. "You're going to make me blush. Besides, I think you're just buttering me up for the kill."

Barrone's lips barely moved as he said: "I need someone on the inside, Harry. I want you to work for me."

"Me?" I said, pointing at my chest. "You want me to work for you? Doing what?"

"Like I said, I need someone on the inside."

I shook my head. "Oh, no. I came out here to help Marsha with the birth of our daughter. That's all the work I'm looking for."

"I'll pay you well," he said. "Name your price. And you'll be protected. I won't ask you to do anything that will put you at risk. I quite literally only want you to keep an eye out and count customers."

"Yeah, kid," Jake said. "I'd do it, but they know I ain't got any money. I'm too old to work there, and if I came out as a customer, they'd know somebody was fronting me the dough."

"Look, guys," I said, "if I could help you, I would. But I don't know anything about managing a whorehouse."

Barrone cleared his throat, looked away. "Actually, Harry, we have a manager. Not someone I trust, but a manager. And if I got rid of him and brought you in, that would raise entirely too much suspicion and put you at risk."

"Okay," I said. "I'm not going to be the manager. So what do you want me to be?"

"What we had in mind for you, Harry, was a position that's been open for a few weeks."

"Yeah? What?" I asked.

Barrone's eyes met mine. "Maintenance man," he said quietly.

I stared at him for about two seconds and then broke out in hysterics—the kind of laughter that comes from so deep within that you're totally out of control, helpless, completely at the mercy of it as it rolls through your body in waves, like being out of your head at the height of a fever. A full minute passed before I regained control.

"What is it, kid?" Jake asked. "What's so goddamn funny?"

"Oh, nothing, Jake," I said. "It's just that five years ago I was a respected political reporter. Now . . ."

I leaned back against the chair, shaking my head, tears rolling down my face. "Oh, shit. Now I'm going to be a janitor in a whorehouse."

Chapter 13

I reached for my third glass of wine as Barrone ladled more beef stew into a large ceramic bowl and handed it to me. I'd polished off one bowl already and discovered to my surprise that I had to have more of this hearty, rich, fragrant, thick concoction. Damn, it was maybe the best meal I'd ever had.

"What'd you say this was called?" I asked Barrone.

"It's my variation of a boeuf Bourguignon," he answered. "I take the traditional Bourguignon and then add a few Basque touches."

"Man, it's incredible," I mumbled, my mouth full.

"So you're straight on how this is going to work," Jake said to me.

"Yeah," I answered, tearing off another hunk of French bread. I raised my hand up and counted on my fingers. "I just got out the joint last month. I was at—what'd we say?—Middle Tennessee Reception Center, where I was doing three to five for possession with intent, and I got paroled after twenty months under the safety cap."

"And you met my buddy Woody Baxter, who's pulling a bitch as a habitual criminal."

"Right," I said, "and Woody was my rabbi in the joint. And you guys knew each other when you were both in the same unit in Atlanta. I lost my job in Nashville, my family wouldn't have anything to do with me

138

after I got sent up, and my wife left me. I didn't have nothing there, and Woody suggested I look you up in Reno. So I jumped on the dog and I'm staying in your apartment."

"And you were gonna work the casinos." Jake picked up the story. "Only nobody told you that you can't get a casino license with a felony record. So now you're broke and stuck in Reno."

"And you got a line on this job at the Mustang and I can use the dough and I'll work hard and keep my mouth shut," I said. "I don't see nothing; I don't hear nothing; and if they want to pay me in cash, so much the better."

Jake turned to Barrone. "What do you think, Mr. Barrone? Think he can pull it off?"

Barrone eyed me. "As long as nobody looks too closely. You don't seem like a guy who's done hard time."

"He's not claiming to," Jake said. "That's the beauty of it. He's a regular guy who was in the wrong place at the wrong time and didn't pay off the right people when he got nailed."

"Before that," I said, "I sold insurance or something. Whatever."

"It better be better than whatever," Barrone said. "And you understand, Harry, that in no way are you to do anything that puts you at risk. I want you to observe and take mental notes. I don't even want you to put anything on paper when you're there."

"I'm counting cars in the parking lot, watching traffic patterns, and doing a—if you'll pardon the expression—head count."

"That's it," Barrone said. "And if there's a problem getting you hired, I'll call the manager. I can do it casually, like I'm just helping you do a favor for a casual friend."

"But we won't call on you unless we have to," I said.

"Right. And I want the two of you to sit down and put together some kind of contingency plan or code system or something. So that if something happens and Harry needs help, there'll be a way for him to get the message to you. Do you understand what I'm telling you?"

"Sure," I said, smiling. "Okay, Jake? If you pick up the phone and hear somebody whispering 'the yellow mushroom has fallen under the table lamp,' you'll know to send in the cavalry ASAP."

"This is nothing to joke about," Barrone said sternly. "Keep in mind that according to the figures I'm being given, and if my suspicions are correct, approximately a half-million dollars a month is being laundered through the Mustang Ranch. People have been hurt—or worse— for less."

That one sobered me up a bit. "Okay, Mr. Barrone. Gotcha."

Barrone loaned me one of the pickup trucks from his ranch, a battered fifteen-year-old GMC, and I followed Jake to his apartment in town. I trailed him as we snaked through the residential streets of Reno, which seemed, at this time of night, away from the glitter and the blazing lights of the casinos, just like any other small town in America. The tiny yards were well kept, with late-model cars parked neatly along the curbs. Signs warned of children playing and pedestrians crossing, and it all seemed very quiet and peaceful. The left rear blinker on Jake's Pacer started flashing and then one dim brake light fired up. I followed him as we eased off the street and parked at the curb.

"This your house?" I asked quietly as I approached him on the sidewalk.

"Yeah, right, like I could afford a house," he said. "I

rent an apartment in the basement. It ain't too bad, though."

I followed him down the short driveway and around back of a modest frame cottage that didn't look big enough to have a basement. Sure enough, though, we rounded the driveway and found the cement staircase leading down below ground level at the back of the house. At the foot of the stairs, Jake unlocked a mildewed, partially rotten wooden door.

"C'mon in," he said. He reached in, flicked a wall switch, and the overhead light illuminated a tiny, one-room efficiency with painted cinderblock walls and no windows. A door to the right led to a tiny bathroom with a shower. Along the far wall, a small sink and counter stood over a dorm-room-size refrigerator. All in all, it seemed firmly entrenched somewhere between cozy and depressing.

Jake plopped down on a rattan chair next to the bed, then motioned to a metal folding chair leaning against one wall. "Have a seat, kid, and welcome to your new home."

"Jake, I can't stay here," I said. "There's not enough room."

There was barely room enough for the bed and the small television wedged into a corner by the door. On the wall opposite the refrigerator, a crudely made bookcase of unpainted pine boards held row after row of paperbacks interspersed with an occasional hardcover. I already figured that Jake was smarter than he was willing to let on, and his choice of reading confirmed it.

"Dostoevsky," I commented, pointing to a copy of *Crime and Punishment*.

"Appropriate, ain't it?" he said. "I read a lot during the time I was removed from society."

"And Faulkner, Joyce," I said. "Jeez, Jake, I should try to keep up with you."

"Don't bother. You couldn't. And as for you staying here, okay. You don't have to if you don't want to. But you at least gotta know where the place is."

"And what if somebody comes looking for me?"

Jake leaned back in the rattan chair, then planted one foot on the bed. "You got some babe somewhere," he said. "Let's say some poker dealer over at Ascuaga's Nugget. She works second shift, gets home about ten. You crash with her a lot. And no, I don't know who she is or where she is, but I'll be glad to give you a message when you get back."

"Not bad, Jake," I said. "That's nearly the truth."

"Nearly the truth is always easier to remember, kid."

"I'll keep that in mind," I said. "What's the plan for tomorrow?"

"You show up here around ten," he instructed. "We'll drive out to the Mustang and I'll show you around, introduce you to the manager, tell him what you're looking for."

"You got it. Who is the manager, by the way?"

"The girls call him Goumba Joey," Jake said. "Only not to his face. That peg him for you?"

I nodded. "Enough to get started."

"Okay, kid, take off. You know where you are?"

"I think so," I said, pointing to the wall opposite Jake. "Virginia's about three blocks that way. When I get there, go right, head out of town to the Mount Rose highway. From there I'm okay."

"Good. You're gonna do fine. Just keep a cool head. And watch those curves in the dark." Jake reached behind him, opened a compartment in the headboard, and extracted a small metal box. He opened it and pulled out a skinny hand-rolled joint.

"Wanna burn one before you leave, kid?" He held it out to me.

I raised one eyebrow. "That what I think it is?"

"The best anywhere," he answered.

I shook my head. "Take a raincheck, pal. I'm driving."

"Suit yourself, kid. Have a good trip home."

I took that as my cue. "Good night, Jake. Sleep well."

Jake made a circle with his lips, poked the joint into his mouth, and drew it slowly back out.

"Always, kid. Always."

The Sunday-night traffic on Virginia had thinned. Even the blaze of flashing lights at the Peppermill and, farther down, the Atlantis seemed almost desperate. I thought of pulling into the Peppermill and seeing if Kelly was still there, but it was almost certain she'd checked out and gone back to Eureka. And if she hadn't, then what?

I needed to keep my mind on where I was and who I was, even though I found myself missing her more than I thought possible. It was as if I'd been walking around sleeplogged for months, which was not far from the truth, and then for a brief few hours found myself fully awake again, fully alive again.

I don't have any idea why I agreed to go along with this scheme of Barrone's. Maybe I was bored; maybe I needed something to keep me busy and take my mind off Marsha and Kelly and the mystery of finding some level of personal happiness in the world. Or maybe he got me when he'd said Marsha had spoken highly of me, maybe there was something inside me that needed to prove her right, if not to her, then to me.

Or maybe—and I was beginning to wonder if this wasn't the case—I was just an adrenaline junkie. It had been months since I'd really worked. I'd spent the last few months renovating a house, learning to plaster walls and paint trim, fix plumbing. I thought I'd been satisfied to do that, was even considering letting my P.I. license expire when it came time to renew it in January.

And now I was going to work in a legal brothel to find out if the cathouse was a front for a money-laundering operation. It was all I could do to keep from laughing all over again.

Thirty minutes after leaving Jake's apartment, I was pulling into Aunt Marty's driveway. I backed in—the nose of the truck didn't look quite as tired and worn out as the rear—and pulled in close to the house in an attempt to be as inconspicuous as possible. I didn't think that if I got the job at the Mustang, anybody would bother to look for me up here on the mountain, but it seemed a good idea to be as low profile as possible from the get-go.

I went around back, knocked on the glass door leading out to the patio. Estella appeared in a few moments, wiping her hands with a dishcloth.

"Señor Harry," she said. "Where you been all day?"

Something in my gut cramped. "Why? Is she okay? Is something wrong with Marsha?"

"No, Dr. Marsha, she fine. But she was wanting to know where you been today."

"Jake took me out to Señor Barrone's ranch and I wound up spending the day out there."

"You are hungry?" she asked, turning back to the kitchen. The clock on the wall in front of her read 8:30.

"No, thanks, Estella. Señor Barrone fed us," I said.

"Oh," came a voice from behind me. "Did you like the Bourguignon?" I turned as Marty raised her head above the sofa and looked at me.

I walked across the room, sat in the rocking chair

across from Marty. "It was great," I said. "I've never had anything like it. How does he do it?"

Marty was dressed in a pair of creme-colored silk pants and a sheer blouse that revealed some kind of lacy teddy underneath. She had one leg curled under the other and was leaning against the armrest of the leather sofa. In her lap, she held a copy of *Money* magazine, although the way she looked, it should have been something like *Town & Country*.

"Good God, Harry, he'd never tell me and I wouldn't want to know. He might expect me to actually make it for him someday, and that would be the end of us right there."

Marty smiled at me, a warm and easy smile that made me feel at home and comfortable and almost, within limits, safe. I smiled back at her.

"Is there anything you'd like, Harry? If you're not hungry, perhaps Estella could fix you a beer or a glass of wine."

"Maybe in a bit, Marty. I really appreciate it. I thought I'd better run up and see Marsha right now. If she's awake and feeling up for company, that is."

"I was up there about fifteen minutes ago," Marty said. "She's awake, watching a movie on television. She's had a pretty good day, I think."

"Good." I shifted my weight to stand up.

"Harry," she said. "Do you mind if I ask you something?"

I settled back down. "No, I don't think so. I'll answer it if I can."

"I care very much about Marsha, Harry, but I have no illusions about her. She's an intelligent, caring, sensitive person with a lot of good points. But she's also tough and driven and there's a part of her that's angry and often cold. I don't expect she'll ever be easy for any man to handle. But I don't want to see her get hurt any more than she has to be."

Marty paused for a second, eyeing me from her perch on the couch. "Neither do I, Marty," I said uncomfortably.

"She won't talk to me about what happened back in Nashville," Marty said. "I was hoping you could tell me. What happened between you two?"

I leaned back in the rocking chair, the legs squeaking softly as they moved on the rug. "I don't know if I understand it myself. I went through a bad time, got involved in the case of a missing teenager, a young girl. I found her, but the guy who'd kidnapped her killed her before I could free her. And in the process of trying, I killed him."

If Marty was shocked, she didn't show it. She sat there calmly and waited for me to go on.

"Nothing like that had ever happened to me before and I guess for a while I kind of checked out. Didn't go to work, practically never left my apartment. I didn't know this at the time, but Marsha was having a rough time as well. Things were falling apart at work, through no fault of her own, but she suffered the consequences all the same. Then she hit forty and I think the biological clock quit ticking for her and started clanging like church bells.

"Anyway, I couldn't be there for her. We only saw each other a couple of times during those few months, but at one of those times, she got pregnant. I came out of whatever funk I'd fallen into and decided to get back in the world. Only by then Marsha'd decided that maybe I wasn't the right man for her. I didn't understand it at the time, but I figured it out later. When she lost her job—"

"She told me she resigned," Marty interrupted.

"She did, but the handwriting was on the wall. She resigned, but if she hadn't, it would have gotten ugly."

"Oh," Marty said, looking down into her lap for a moment. Then she looked back up, her eyes clear and shiny.

"Anyway, when I found out she was pregnant, I was actually quite excited. I wanted to marry her, but by then I think she'd already started to have doubts about us. By the time my head cleared and I was ready to move ahead, she'd already bailed on me."

Marty folded her hands in her lap. "That's incredibly sad, Harry."

"Well," I said, becoming even more uncomfortable, "I mean, like the bumper sticker says, effluent occurs. Things happen the way they happen and sometimes we don't like it. But you go on anyway."

"Yes, but I also believe that any gap can be bridged, that any differences between two people can be settled if they both want it to."

I took a deep breath, fought the urge to hold it in until I passed out, then let it loose in a long sigh.

"Yeah, Marty," I said, fumbling for words, "but I don't know. We may be past that. I know Marsha doesn't want that, and I'm not even sure I do anymore."

"Well, if the gap is unbridgeable," she said. "I've just never been one to give up on anything."

I smiled. "Yeah, that's what Marsha always told me," I said. "I think that's one of the reasons that when it all fell in for her, she headed in your direction."

"I can help her," Marty said. "I can take care of her and I can make her well again. And the baby, my great-niece. I've got the resources and the will to take care of them, to help. I could do the same for you, if you'd let me."

I stood up. She raised her head, looking directly at me. "I appreciate that, Marty. I really do. I'll be around for a while. Marsha and I are talking. We'll just have to see what happens."

Marty smiled. "If that's the best deal I can get, I'll take it. Now go on upstairs and see Marsha. She's waiting for you."

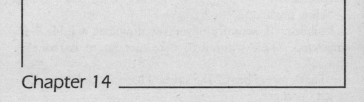

Chapter 14

Marsha was sitting up in bed, a couple of thick foam pillows propped between her back and the headboard with a thick, fluffy comforter wrapped around her. The room was cold, almost frigid, and I realized that her bedroom window was cracked.

"Aren't you freezing?" I asked.

She turned, shook her head sleepily. "No, the fresh air feels great. I'm so tired of being cooped up in here. I wish I could get this over with."

I pulled a chair over to the bed and sat down. "Marty said you'd had a pretty good day."

"Okay," she said, her voice steady but low. "I mean, as days go, it was all right. The baby's been moving around a little bit, but not as much as usual."

"You got a little bit of a break," I said. "So what are you watching?"

"Oh, nothing," she said, raising the remote control and muting the sound. "There's nothing on worth watching. I'm just too tired to hold up a book."

I studied her as she lay there in bed. Her skin was pale, splotchy, and stretched tight. She looked weak, pasty.

"It'll all be over soon," I said.

She shifted her weight in bed, turning a bit to face me. "So what have you been up to?"

"Jake gave me a quickie tour of downtown. We ate at

the Awful-Awful and did a quick run-through of a couple of casinos."

"How'd you do?"

I smiled. "I actually never sat down at a table," I answered. "Jake wanted to take me out to Barrone's ranch."

"That's nice, I hear," she said. "I haven't had a chance to get out there."

"Yeah," I said. "Real nice. I spent several hours out there talking to Barrone and Jake. It seems Barrone had a little proposition for me."

"Yeah?" she asked. "Last week he was asking me all kinds of questions about you. I figured he had something up his sleeve."

"He's got an interesting situation going on. I'm going to help him out with it."

"Tell me about it."

So I did, in the two-minutes-or-less encapsulated version. Her facial expression went from blank to scowling in the process.

"God, Harry," she snapped. "How could you?"

"It's a chance for me to make some extra dough," I said. "And it'll give me something to do. If I just sit around this house until you go into labor, we'll both go nuts."

"Oh, great," she said. "When my water breaks, I'll call you at the whorehouse."

"No, you won't," I said. "As part of the deal, Barrone loaned me a pager." I lifted my sweater to reveal a candy-apple-red translucent plastic box hooked onto my belt.

"But, Harry, the idea of—"

"Marsha," I said. "To begin with, I'm going to be working undercover there."

"That's what I'm afraid of," she interjected.

"You know me better than that," I said. "That isn't

my style and you know it. Second, you've already made it incredibly clear that you and I are finished as a couple. So even if I did want to take advantage of the situation, what difference could it possibly make to you?"

"I'm beginning to be sorry I asked you out here," she said meanly.

"Why *did* you ask me out here?" I demanded, trying to hold my voice down without much success.

She fidgeted on the bed, shifting her weight from side to side in an attempt to find some position that was less uncomfortable.

"I don't know," she said irritably. "I was lonely and scared and there was no one else I could ask. Serves me right."

I leaned over, put my hand on hers. "Marsha, I'll do anything I can for you. You know that. Things aren't the way they used to be between us, yeah, but that doesn't mean that I can't still care for you. Can't still want what's good and best for you. But you have to help me here. You've got to give me some idea of what I can do."

She settled her head back on the pillows and stared at the ceiling. A single tear ran down the left side of her cheek and formed a tiny wet spot on the top pillow.

"Harry," she said softly. "There's nothing anyone can do. I just have to get through this."

I squeezed her hand. "Don't say that. There has to be some way for us to connect here, Marsha. Some way for us to touch each other again."

Her eyelids drifted downward. "Harry, I'm tired," she said. "And I'm sorry if I've hurt you. I never meant to."

"I never meant to hurt you, either."

She squeezed my hand back. "I think I could drop off to sleep for a while. Why don't you go back downstairs? It can't be any fun sitting up here with me."

"That's not the problem."

"Well, I can't fix the problem right now, baby. Just go on, let me sleep for a while."

"Are you sure your doctor knows how bad you feel?"

She nodded weakly. "This will all be over soon."

"You're beginning to make me nervous," I said.

"Go on. Relax. I'm okay."

I stood. "I wish I was as sure as you are."

"Trust me," Marsha said. "I'm a doctor."

"You really didn't have to come up here and get me," I said the next morning as I eased into the Pacer next to Jake. "Especially given that every time this car comes up the mountain it loses another week or two off its life expectancy."

Jake grumbled something, but I didn't hear it as he'd craned his neck away from me backing out of Marty's driveway. Monday morning had dawned bright and blue and a good fifteen, twenty degrees warmer than it had been during the weekend. All traces of snow were gone and the roads were dry and clear.

Jake had phoned me about eight and told me to wear clean jeans, a pair of running shoes if I had them, and a clean, casual, pressed but not too dressy shirt.

"This ain't like a job interview at a bank, kid," he'd said. "You gotta look like somebody what just came out of the joint, and that ain't Brooks Brothers."

"So," I said, holding out my arms as Jake started down the mountain. "Do I pass muster?"

Jake turned to me, scowling. "You'll do," he said. "I just hope you can pull this off."

Jake wore faded jeans, a scuffed, dirty pair of Nike knockoffs, and his Circus Circus windbreaker. A pair of black plastic aviator shades covered his eyes.

"How long does it take to get there?"

"About a half hour, forty minutes," Jake answered.

"And you better be taking notes. The Mustang ain't got a street address. You just have to know where it is."

"Okay," I said, beginning to make mental notes. We drove down the Mount Rose highway and connected back onto South Virginia, drove through town to the nearest I-80 interchange, then got on the highway. Truck traffic zoomed past us at breathtaking speeds as Jake hammered down on the Pacer to get us up to the flow.

"So who am I going to be talking to?" I asked.

"Goumba Joey," Jake said, "only you be careful not to call him that to his face. Not unless you want your hands slapped."

"Goumba Joey slaps hands?"

Jake switched lanes to pass a powder-blue Cadillac that had slowed in front of us. "Goumba Joey'll probably break your fingers," he said. "Guy's name is Joey Fennelly. He's originally from New Orleans."

"He a made guy?" I asked.

Jake grinned. "*Made guy?* What are you, fuckin' Mario Puzo or something? Where'd you learn that expression?"

"Mob culture has infiltrated popular culture to the extent that the two are virtually synonymous."

Jake turned, pulled his shades down his nose with his right index finger, and eyed me over the top of the black plastic. "Excuse the fuck outta me," he said. "Make that *Perfesser* fuckin' Mario Puzo."

"So answer the question. He with the mob in New Orleans?"

Jake turned back to the traffic. "Probably," he answered.

"How old is he?"

Jake shrugged. "Beats me. Forty-five maybe. Young guy."

"Would that make him old enough to be part of Carlos Marcello's operation?"

"How tha' fuck should I know?" Jake said. "Besides, what difference does it make?"

"Not much," I said. "I just like to know who I'm up against."

"You're up against Goumba Joey," Jake said. "That oughta tell you enough right there."

The traffic thinned as we headed east on I-80 away from Reno. The hills on either side of the freeway were high, their edges soft and rolling against that brilliant blue Nevada sky. The land became even more brown, the desert earth providing barely enough sustenance for the low brushes and wildflowers that hugged the ground, as if to grow any higher would put them out of reach of everything needed to survive. Occasionally we'd pass a low-slung ranch house in the distance or some fenced-off land with a few cows grazing or perhaps horses. It all seemed barren and lifeless, but I knew somehow that appearances were misleading, that beneath the apparent superficial naked desolation of the desert was life in continual, unending motion.

Shaky Jake slowed the Pacer, its engine rattling and knocking, and pointed us toward exit 23, which was marked with a green and white highway sign that contained only one word beneath the exit number: MUSTANG.

We coasted off the freeway and down the off-ramp. Jake braked at a stop sign at the end of the ramp and turned to me. "Listen, kid, I'm gonna show you what the lay of the land is like here. One quick stop before we hit the Mustang."

He turned right and drove maybe a quarter-mile down a deteriorating, barely paved road that was a lane-and-a-half wide, then stopped at another four-way.

"The Mustang's about a mile down there," he said, pointing ahead. "But I want to show you something."

He eased the car through the intersection, turning right again, back toward Reno on the frontage road that paralleled the interstate. About a half-mile down, we came to what looked like a junkyard, with acres of rusting cars, machinery, and junk baking in the sun. A little ways past that a narrow gravel road ran to our left at a ninety-degree angle from the road we were on.

Jake turned onto the gravel road and stopped. "See that?" he asked.

Just off the gravel road, a large boulder maybe three feet high sat in a thatch of yellow wildflowers. The boulder's edges were sharp, jagged, and the rock had been painted white. And on the rock, in crude block letters a foot high, someone had painted in black:

NO THROUGH TRAFFIC!
PRIVATE PROPERTY!
DO NOT GO ANY FURTHER!

"So take a wild guess what'll happen if we go any farther."

I turned to Jake. "Beats me. Guard dogs, maybe? Shotgun blast over our heads?"

Jake smiled. "You get the point," he said. "And the point is, people around here keep to themselves, mind their own business. The sooner you get into that mindset, the better off you'll be."

I stared at the boulder for a few seconds and then down the road that led away from it. I squinted, looking down as far as I could see. There were no houses or buildings visible from where we sat.

"C'mon," I said. "Let's get out of here."

Jake backed the car onto the frontage road, then

headed out toward the Mustang Ranch. At the intersection, he turned right onto a narrow road that went for about a quarter-mile, then went under a railroad trestle. Past that, the road crossed a narrow bridge over the Truckee River and dead-ended at the Mustang Ranch parking lot.

Cinders and loose gravel crunched under my feet as I stepped out of the car. In front of us sat an ordinary house that would have fit right into any suburb in Southern California. Only this house was surrounded by a black wrought-iron fence maybe eight or nine feet high. Over the gate was perched a large, hot-pink sign with a black pen-and-ink representation of a woman's face with long flowing black hair. And below that alluring face were the words: WORLD FAMOUS MUSTANG RANCH.

At ten o'clock on a Monday morning there were three other vehicles in the parking lot besides ours: two pickups and an old Ford station wagon. Not a BMW or Lexus in sight. The Mustang might be world-famous, but it sure drew a down-home clientele.

Across the parking lot from the gate was a souvenir trailer with another Mustang Ranch sign. I walked over to the front of the trailer and looked in. A young blond sat behind a counter with a cash register in front of her.

"Hi," I said.

She looked up from a copy of the *National Enquirer*. "Hey," she said, bored. "What can I get you?"

"Just looking," I answered. There were racy postcards and T-shirts for sale, along with coffee mugs, matchbooks, and other souvenirs. I wondered how many customers stopped off here for a little memento of their visit to paradise.

Jake stepped up next to me. "There're actually three places here," he said, pointing behind us. "There's the

Mustang right there and then down there"—he pointed
to a building maybe seventy-five yards to the left—"is
the Mustang Ranch II."

I smiled. "What, like, they take the overflow?"

"I guess so," Jake said. "I never been in there." Then
he turned, pointed to a side road that led through an arch
of trees into a thick grove. "Down that little road is the
Old Bridge Ranch, which is another cathouse. Word on
the street is that Joe Conforte's son owns it, but nobody
really knows. That's all public-domain misinformation."

I smiled. "Public-domain misinformation," I said. "As
a former newspaperman, I like that term. I'll have to remember it."

"I didn't make it up," Jake said, walking away from
the concession trailer toward the front gate of the
Mustang.

"You want anything?" the blond asked.

"No, not right now. Maybe later."

She sighed, went back to her tabloid. "Whatever."

I followed Jake to the gate, where a sign instructed us
to ring the bell and push the gate. Jake punched the
button and we heard a high-pitched bell ringing, followed by another ringing sound right in front of us and
the *thunk*ing sound of a relay unlatching the gate. Jake
pushed it open, walked through with me in tow; we
sauntered up the concrete walk to the front door.

"Why am I suddenly nervous?" I asked.

"Everybody's nervous their first time in a whorehouse,"
Jake said.

"Yeah, but we're not going in as customers."

"Doesn't make any difference. Everybody's nervous
their first time."

The door swung open in front of us and we stepped
into a dark entrance foyer. A large open room adjoined
the foyer and beyond that I could see a mirror covering

the wall behind a bar. Row after row of liquor bottles sat on shelves beneath the mirror.

As we entered the room, from a hallway to our right paraded a line of as many different varieties of women as one could imagine. A tall, muscular black woman with serious biceps in a shiny red one-piece bathing suit covered in sequins led the procession. Next to the body-builder a pale blond in a diaphanous baby-doll night-gown smiled at me, her blue eyes so bright she had to be wearing contacts. After that a Sixties-era, presurgical Cher look-alike (or perhaps, I thought, it really *is* Cher) came to a stop in front of us and planted her hands on her hips, as if she was ready to pull some *Mod Squad* kind of confrontational kick-ass thing.

I don't know, maybe I'm just not ready for this. My head started to buzz a little bit and I swear I started to get dizzy. I'm no prude, but the thought of walking into a room, pointing to a woman, and saying: "Okay, I'll take *you* this time," and then walking into a room and having sex just struck me as something so foreign to my experience that I'd probably fail miserably at it. I'd be the guy who winds up paying the hooker a hundred bucks to sit and talk for a half hour.

A short, almost stumpy woman in black polyester pants, a white shirt, and a black bow tie stepped out from behind the door and eyed us. A small ripple of fat encircled her waist and her eyes were beady and a little bloodshot. Her salt-and-pepper hair looked as if it hadn't been styled in months, and I used all my skills as a trained investigator to infer that she wasn't one of the working girls.

When she saw Jake, her upper lip curled into a sneer.

"Hi ya, Mabel," Jake said.

The woman turned to the line of girls still parading into the room and, with a wave of her hand, dismissed them. Immediately, without missing a beat, they reversed direction and disappeared back down the hallway.

"C'mon, Mabel, how do you know we ain't here as customers?"

Mabel shut the door behind us. "Because it's near the end of the month and your check hasn't come in yet."

Jake laughed. "God, baby, you know me too well. Listen, we got an appointment with Joey. This's my buddy, Harry Denton, from Music City, U.S.A. He just got off a twenty-month vacation, courtesy of the Tennessee Department of Corrections."

"Congratulations," Mabel said, her voice a flat, bland monotone. "I'm happy for you."

"Glad to meet you, Mabel," I said quietly.

Jake turned to me. "Mabel's the first-shift floor manager. She's in charge of the girls, is the head cashier, and in general makes sure everything works smoothly."

"Great," I said.

"Yeah," Mabel said, turning and motioning us to follow her. "It's a living."

If Mabel was in charge of the money, I figured she must be a key player in any money-laundering operation at the Mustang. I made a mental note to keep an eye on her as Jake and I followed her down the carpeted hall to the left. Closed doors ticked by on either side of us and I briefly wondered what all went on behind those doors, then decided I was probably better off not knowing.

At the end of the hall was another closed door, this one with an intercom panel. Mabel pressed the button, which made a buzzing sound, followed by the static of a voice on a cheap loudspeaker.

"Yeah," the voice crackled.

"Mr. Fennelly," Mabel said into the intercom, "your ten o'clock's here."

The door buzzer went off after that. Mabel pushed the

door open and held it for us. Jake went in first, calling out, "Hey, Joey!" as he went in.

I followed Jake into a large room, paneled in dark wood, air-conditioned like a meat locker, with thick red carpet on the floor and a massive desk in the center. On the wall to the right of the desk, to our left, a floor-to-ceiling oak cabinet sat with its doors closed. At the desk sat Joey Fennelly, and as soon as I spotted him, I understood the nickname. He looked like a Hollywood version of a Seventies mob guy. A shiny, striped polyester shirt was stretched across his hefty stomach. He was clean shaven, wore dark sunglasses even in the dimly lit office; his hair was slicked back and blow-dried, probably held in place with hairspray. To top it off, as he stood and reached across the desk to shake Jake's hand, I saw a gold pinkie ring with a diamond about the size of a pea on his finger.

Jeez, it's going to be tough not to slip up and use his nickname.

"Shaky Jake," Fennelly cried out in answer. *"Buon giorno, amico!"*

The two shook hands heartily, like two old war buddies who hadn't seen each other since the last reunion.

"How are ya, Joey?" Jake asked, his voice still excited, animated. I stood off to one side, trying to look invisible. Fennelly placed his hands on either side of his stomach and rubbed his shirt with great relish.

"Prosperity's fucking killing me, Jake. Times are just too good," he said, grinning, then motioning to the two visitor's chairs in front of the desk. *"Prego, si accomodi!"*

Jake sat down in the chair on Fennelly's right. I took the one next to him. Behind us, Mabel closed the door to Goumba Joey's office, leaving the three of us alone.

"Joey, this is my buddy Harry Denton from Nashville."

"Harry Denton from Nashville!" Fennelly yelled, sticking a meaty hand across the desk. I took his hand, shook it. "How about that country music!"

"Glad to meet you, Mr. Fennelly. Yeah, that country music—"

"Love that country music!" Fennelly said. "Yeah, can't get enough of that . . . that . . ." He snapped his fingers. "Oh, hell, what's his name?"

I looked at Jake, an edge of panic on my face. *Okay, is this some kind of test here? Do I not get the job if I can't read Goumba Joey's mind?*

"Oh, yeah," Jake said, snapping his fingers as well, "that guy, what's his name?"

"Yeah, what the fuck's his name? Grant? Garp?"

"Garth," I ventured. "Garth Brooks?"

"Yeah, that's him!" Fennelly yelled, slapping the desk. "That guy. I fucking love that guy."

"Me, too, Mr. Fennelly," I said. "You're right, he's one of the best."

Jake leaned back in his chair and crossed his legs at the knees. "Listen, Joey, my pal here's in kind of a spot. He just got paroled out of the joint in Nashville and got permission from his P.O. to come to Reno. Didn't tell him, of course, that he was coming to see old Shaky Jake."

Fennelly burst out laughing. "Good thing, you old knee breaker, you! Ain't there a law against associating with known bad guys?"

Jake laughed at that one, too, and I cracked what I hoped would be interpreted as a shy smile.

"So what'd you get popped for, Harry?"

"I got set up, Mr. Fennelly," I said, which made him laugh even harder. "They popped me for possession with intent to distribute, but it was just a little recreational doobie. You know, nothing serious."

"Yeah," Fennelly said. "Those mothers."

"I mean, I didn't even smoke much back then and I

don't touch the shit now, but the local D.A. went after my ass because I wouldn't tell the cops who my supplier was."

Fennelly nodded approvingly. Nobody likes a snitch.

"So I got three to five but was cut loose under the safety cap after twenty months."

Fennelly grinned, folded his hands together over his stomach, and leaned back in his high-back leather chair. "Yeah, them prosecutors is fucking crazy. I take it you couldn't afford a hired gun."

I shook my head. "No, man, didn't have the scratch. The P.D.'s office represented me."

"Tough break," Fennelly said. "I feel for you. You ever been up before?"

"My first time," I said.

"Oh, man, I do feel for you."

I shrugged. "It wasn't so bad, really. I did my time at MTRC in Nashville, minimum security. I got trusty status after six months and it was practically work release. Plus"—I shifted my weight in the chair and motioned to Jake—"I had me a rabbi."

Fennelly pursed his lips, nodded approvingly.

"Yeah, that's how we got hooked up," Jake said. "My buddy Woody's doing a bitch as a career criminal, but he's got a clean record, so he's on minimum as well. He and Harry here got to be good buddies."

"And when I was on the inside," I said, continuing the story, "my wife dumped me and my family'd had enough of me. You know how that goes, or maybe you don't. Anyway, when I got cut loose, Woody suggested I head to Reno, find out what's shaking out here."

"You mean besides Jake?" Fennelly barked, breaking into a howl at his own joke. "Smart move. Reno's a wonderful place. Lots of chances for a guy to start over."

"Right now, Harry's just looking for a job. Anything.

As you know, Joey, a lot of places won't hire an ex-con, even if he is clean. And my man Harry here is clean. Right, Harry?"

"I'll go pee in a cup right now if you want."

"Not necessary," Fennelly said. "So what're you thinking, Jake?"

"Harry's got some good mechanical skills," Jake said. "And I know you been looking for a maintenance guy. I was thinking maybe you could put him to work out here."

Fennelly shifted in his chair, turned to me. "So what can you do?"

"Well, I'm no HVAC guy," I said. "But I can do PMs, replace a light switch, rebuild a toilet so it don't leak anymore. Busted light fixtures. Stuff like that."

All of which, I didn't bother to tell him, I learned while renovating my house back in Nashville.

Fennelly stared across the table at me and grunted. "You do landscaping work, cutting grass, shit like that?"

"You name it, Mr. Fennelly," I said, "I'll do it."

"You clean, huh?"

"As a whistle," I answered. "Like I said, you want blood, urine, I got 'em both."

He smiled. "Nah, no need for that."

He shifted in his chair, pulled his full bulk forward, leaned his elbows on the desk, and pointed a fat, sausage-like right index finger at me.

"You don't drink on the job, you don't smoke no doobie, you don't put nothing up your nose," he said. "You show up on time, you don't talk to the customers, you don't hit on the girls. You want an employee discount, we got one. But no freebies, you understand?"

I nodded. "Yessir."

"Job don't pay much. Five bucks an hour, but at the end of every month you'll get a piece of the toke. Not much, but a little. It'll help. You work ten hours a day, six days a week. You okay with that?"

"No problem, Mr. Fennelly. I appreciate the chance to work for you."

He studied me for a few moments. "Yeah, right. Whatever. You start tomorrow. Be here at eight in the morning. You leave at six-thirty at night. You got it? Half hour for lunch in the employee break room."

"Got it."

"Okay, see you tomorrow. I'll have Mabel draw up some paperwork for you, turn in the W-2. We play by the rules around here. Don't want no problem with the feds."

"I understand."

"Good. Go on, take off. And you, Jake," Fennelly said, "when the fuck you coming back around? I ain't seen your ass in a month of Sundays."

"I been a little short lately, Joey. You know how it—"

Fennelly leaned back and let loose with a belly laugh. "I don't care about the size of your dick. That's between you and the girls."

Jake grinned. "Aw, c'mon, Joey. Gimme a break."

Fennelly reached down, pulled a drawer open, and extracted a small metal box. "I'll do better than that, Jake." He pulled a business card–size piece of paper out of the box, turned it over, and scribbled something on the back. "Here," he said, handing it across to Jake. "Be my guest."

Jake stuffed the piece of paper inside his shirt pocket. "Gee, thanks, Joey. I appreciate it."

Jake stood up; I followed his lead. "Thanks for your time, Mr. Fennelly," I said. "See you tomorrow."

"Yeah, go on, get out of here. And if you see that fucking Mabel out there, tell her to bring me a cup of coffee."

Jake grinned. "Will do."

Outside, in the hallway, with Goumba Joey safely behind us, Jake leaned toward me. "God, what an asshole," he whispered.

"Yeah. What was that he slipped you as we were leaving?"

Jake pulled the card out of his pocket and flashed it at me. There was a picture of the front entrance of the Mustang Ranch, and across that, in bold white letters: MUSTANG RANCH—PLEASURE PASS.

"Know what I'd do?" I said as we stepped out into the warm sun.

"What?" Jake said.

"Save it for a double-coupon day."

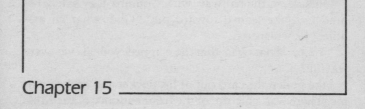

Chapter 15

The fog was still thick as fur on Mount Rose as I pulled the GMC rust bucket out onto the highway and pointed it down the slope. It was barely ten minutes past seven and I'd been up for almost an hour. Estella had knocked on my door at a quarter past six and I'd shot up out of bed like somebody'd thrown a snake on top of me. I was dazed, exhausted, still half-asleep after having trouble dropping off the night before.

Truth is, I'm not used to being up this early. Since I gave up regular office hours six months ago, I've taken to sleeping in late and then staying up all hours of the night either reading or working on my house. I spent a lot of time alone and nobody was waiting for me to check in anywhere. It just didn't matter what my sleeping habits were.

The return of day-job reality was abrupt and painful. It was little help that in addition to the five bucks an hour I'd be making from the Mustang, I was also getting fifty bucks an hour from the Justice Department, by way of Jacques Barrone. He didn't exactly come out and say that was who'd be paying me, but I figured he wouldn't spend his own money on me. We'd talked last night and both agreed that ten days to two weeks ought to be plenty for me to survey the traffic flow at the Mustang. I'd turn my results over to Barrone, then he and his auditors would use it to do whatever they had to do. Maybe, I warned him, the Mustang did a better business than he thought.

Still, I remembered, there'd only been a few filled slots in the parking lot yesterday.

I maneuvered off the mountain and onto Virginia, then over to I-80 eastbound. In about forty minutes I was at the Mustang Ranch's front gate, pressing the buzzer to get in. I gazed around at the parking lot and all I saw were two battered old wrecks and a Volkswagen minibus that looked remarkably good for its age.

Inside, Mabel had already waved the girls off their approach. She wore a pair of khaki cargo pants, a white sweatshirt, no makeup. Her hair was pulled back in a ponytail, her eyes bloodshot; in general, she looked like she'd had a rough night.

"Morning, Mabel," I said, as pleasantly as I could muster through the fatigue.

"Look, the first thing you got to know is employees buzz in like this." Mabel held up her right index finger and mimicked pushing a button, made a buzzing sound followed by a break, then another buzzing sound. "You got that? One long, pause, one long. That way you don't disturb the girls. Understand?"

"Yes," I said, nodding.

"This way," she said, heading down the hallway to the left of the entrance. To our immediate left, Mabel stopped and pointed into a small alcove. "That's the computer room," she explained. "The girls all log in their customers. You'll have a code, too. That's how you'll punch in and record your time. I'll show you how later."

We walked on, then turned left into a smaller room just before we got to Fennelly's office. The tiny room was crowded and bare, with a metal surplus desk and chair and a bookcase and filing cabinet jammed in behind the desk against the wall. Across from it, a recessed cabinet similar to the one in Goumba Joey's office was built into the wall. The cabinet was closed and locked; I couldn't tell what was inside.

"The shift managers work out of this office," Mabel said. "First thing we do is get your tax forms out of the way. I need your address and phone number as well as your Social Security number."

She handed me several papers. "I'm just crashing with Jake Shalinsky right now," I said. "Can I put down his address and phone number?"

"If that's all you got, it's all you got," she said. "But let me know when you find your own place."

I leaned down and filled out the tax forms standing up, then Mabel took me on a guided tour. Out in the hallway, she turned and locked the door to the office.

"You'll have keys to the maintenance shed, the supply rooms, the hot-tub rooms, and a couple of others. But you won't have keys to this office or Mr. Fennelly's, understand?"

I nodded.

"You *never* go in this office without knocking first. This door is *always* locked. You need to see me, call me on the house phone or knock first. Got it?"

I nodded. "Yes, ma'am," I said. "And what about Mr. Fennelly?"

She glared at me. "You don't bother Mr. Fennelly for any reason, understand? You have no reason to even talk to Mr. Fennelly unless he talks to you first. You need anything, you go through me or Gary."

"Gary?"

"Gary's my son," she explained. "He manages the place at night."

"Okay," I said as she walked past me.

Back at the entrance, Mabel pointed out the two hall-ways that branched off at right angles to the front door. We'd already been down the left hallway; she stopped and motioned.

"Those are all the girls' rooms," she said. "Some of them actually live here. The ones that don't rent trailers at the mobile-home park about a half-mile away. We encourage them to stay out of Reno and Sparks as much as possible, but we can't make 'em. They work about three-week shifts, then have a week off, for obvious reasons."

Mabel stopped and pointed at the bar, where a middle-aged guy wearing a white shirt, vest, and narrow black bow tie stood polishing glasses. "We got a day bartender, then another guy that comes on at six. We got one security guy per shift. Smiley Gilstrap's the chief. He works days. Just do what he says and be ready to back him up if there's trouble. But there ain't much trouble here."

"Okay," I said again, following her.

"If it looks like we're going to be busy on Friday and Saturday nights, we get an extra security guy. Just in case," Mabel continued, motioning me to follow her. We walked around to the right of the bar and entered another hallway. Closed doors on the right, she explained, led into more of the girls' rooms.

"How many, uh, employees actually work here?" I asked awkwardly.

"We can handle up to about twenty. Day shift during the week, though, we only keep eight, sometimes ten. A dozen or fifteen during night shift. Weekends, we can accommodate up to twenty-five."

"Wow," I said quietly. "I'm impressed."

Mabel opened a door to our left and stuck her head in. I looked over her shoulder. "Hi, Pat!" she yelled. "You and Susie having a good time?"

I spotted a shriveled-up, little, old bald man in a

Speedo sitting on the edge of a large, six-person hot tub smoking a short, smelly green cigar next to a nude blond of truly gargantuan proportions. I looked away quickly as the man, in a high, cracked voice, said: "Hi ya, Mabel. Why don't you join us?"

Mabel laughed. "Sorry, big guy. Too much paperwork. Susie, this is Harry. He's the new maintenance man."

The blond looked up from where she was massaging her customer's shoulders. "Hi, Harry. Welcome to the Mustang."

I cleared my throat, tried to be cool and not stare. "Hi, Susie."

Mabel backed out, shutting the door. "See you guys later."

"So long, Mabel!" Pat yelled.

Mabel must have caught the look on my face. "Thank God for Viagra."

"Yeah, but even if he could, it looks like the effort would kill him."

Mabel snickered, the first time I'd seen her do anything that approached a laugh. "Pat's a tough old cowboy. He can handle her. C'mon, let's go."

She led me down the hall to a long room that extended the width of the building. A full-size restaurant kitchen and a hot buffet line were at the back wall, with four large tables covered in green and white oilcloths filling most of the rest of the space. In the corner to our right, though, four provocatively dressed women were relaxing on a large sofa and matching chairs watching the *Jerry Springer Show*. Jerry was standing in the middle of the studio audience, his arms folded, the microphone in one hand and an exasperated look on his face. Onstage, Jerry's beefy security guards were trying to pull apart two women engaged in a serious hair-pulling contest.

"You go, girl!" yelled the large black woman I'd seen earlier. The other women giggled like a bunch of teenage girls at a slumber party.

Mabel clapped her hands together. "Hey, ladies. Your attention for just a moment."

The four women turned around instantly.

"Ladies, this is Harry Denton, our new maintenance man."

"Hi, Harry!" they said in unison.

Mabel pointed to the black woman. "Harry, meet Aphrodite Jones," she said.

"Hi, Aphrodite," I said, cracking a nervous smile.

"Yo, Harry, welcome to the Mustang," she said.

"And this is Serena," Mabel said. She motioned to the thin woman I'd seen before in the wispy, translucent, flowing nightie. Then she pointed to the Cher look-alike. "Julie."

The fourth woman turned around and sat on the edge of the sofa when Mabel pointed to her. This one wore white makeup, black lipstick, and heavy eye makeup; long black hair with crimson and burgundy streaks cascading over her pale shoulders; and a sheer black nightgown. I tried not to stare too blatantly, but I couldn't help it. I'd never seen a Goth hooker before.

"And this is Raven," Mabel said. "She's the house dom."

"The what?" I asked.

Mabel subtly rolled her eyes as the other girls grinned. "The house dominatrix. She doesn't get as many customers as the other girls, but the ones she does get pay top dollar."

Raven glowered at me. "You got a problem with that, worm?" she demanded.

"No," I said defensively. "Not at all. I've always had a thing for women who sleep hanging upside down."

"I could arrange a private demonstration for you some-time," Raven hissed, as the other girls broke out laughing. Even Mabel was grinning widely at the thought.

"Asshole," Raven muttered, turning back to Jerry Springer. I turned and followed Mabel across the room. She stopped in front of the hot buffet table.

"That's Miss Mary over there," Mabel said, pointing to a black woman in a white starched dress standing in front of a Garland stove. The woman turned, looked over her shoulder as she continued stirring something in a big pot.

"Hi, Miss Mary," I said.

"This is Harry," Mabel said, "the new maintenance guy."

Miss Mary nodded as Mabel continued. "Staff and the girls can eat here for free, but you're expected to toke Mary good. Customers are not allowed back here without permission of the shift manager or Mr. Fennelly. Got it?"

I nodded. "I understand."

"And through that doorway"—Mabel pointed to a door at the far end of the cafeteria—"is the examining room. We got a doctor what comes in here three times a week. The girls are required to be examined and tested at least once a week. We rarely have any problems. Customers are required to use condoms."

"Okay," I said, my amazement growing at the efficiency of the operation.

"Let's go." She crossed to the other side of the cafeteria and down another hallway, which ran parallel to the one we'd just been in and would take us out to the main room on the other side of the bar. It was a mirror image of the other side of the house, with a second hot-tub room on the left and rooms for the girls on the right.

"The girls are all ICs," Mabel said. She saw the look on my face. "Independent contractors," she explained.

"They pay to work here, take care of their own taxes—all that stuff. But we got an accountant who comes in once a quarter to help them with their books."

She stopped at another door on the right, knocked softly, and when no one answered, pushed the door open. It was a big room, the walls painted a pastel rose, the floor covered with what looked like a hot-pink wrestling mat.

"This is the party room," Mabel explained. "Sometimes groups of customers come in, want to hire several of the girls, have a party."

"You mean . . . ?" I asked. "Like an orgy?"

Mabel nodded. "That's the business we're in, Harry. You got any problems with that, get over 'em quick."

"No problems," I said. "No problems at all. I'm with the program."

She led the way back out to the front room. The whole time we'd been on the tour, I hadn't heard the buzzer ring once. There was no one in the reception area, no one in the bar, no one behind the bar. The place looked empty. Then Mabel took me into the computer room and set me up with a time account. I would log in with my screen name, HARRY1, and a password that only she and I would know.

Ten minutes later she led me back down the hallway past her office and through a door leading to the backyard.

Out there was a maintenance shed with tools, a riding lawn mower, a workbench, and a small desk with a battered vinyl office chair.

"This is where you'll be when you're not working." Mabel stepped back, eyed me for a second. "You look like a medium," she said.

"Yeah, usually."

She opened a locker in the corner and pulled out a blue

work shirt with a white patch over the pocket that said
MUSTANG RANCH — MAINTENANCE.

"You stay here ninety days, I'll get you one with your
name on it."

"Boy," I said. "Something to look forward to."

"You getting smart with me?" she demanded, her
voice low and gravelly.

"No, ma'am."

"Good. I don't allow no getting smart with me, not
from you, not from the girls. You do what I tell you, we'll
get along just fine."

"Yes, ma'am."

"Now change into your shirt. On that clipboard is
a couple of work orders. I know one of the drains is
stopped up in the number two hot tub. Get that taken
care of first."

"Okay, Mabel. Thanks," I said, smiling at her.

Her face was a complete blank as she stared back at
me. "Again, you need anything, you come to me. And remember, under *no* circumstances do you bother Mr. Fennelly with anything. Don't even speak to him unless he
speaks to you first. Got it?"

I nodded silently. Then she turned and was gone. I
looked around the shed, checking out the place where I
now worked as the maintenance man at the most famous
whorehouse in the world.

"Jeez," I whispered. "For this I went to college."

The first couple of days were pretty rough and completely messy. That first day I had to siphon the water out
of the hot tub, then partially disassemble the drain to pull
out a clump of hair that certainly put me off my Wheaties
for the rest of the morning. I finally got the plug cleared
out, though, then put the parts back together. When I got
the tub filled up, I was delighted to see that it was leak-

free and in good working order. After that I changed the air filters on the three heating and cooling systems that kept the Mustang comfortable. Around two, I broke for lunch and went back to the cafeteria. Raven, Serena, and a couple of other girls I hadn't met were parked in front of the tube watching Oprah. Julie, the Cher look-alike, and Aphrodite Jones were absent. A mental picture of Aphrodite Jones with the little wizened Viagra guy in the Speedo jumped into my head before I could cut it off at the pass.

I shuddered as I stood at the buffet table.

"What's the matter, Harry?" Miss Mary asked.

"Nothing," I said. "Just had a sudden chill."

"What can I get you today, darlin'?"

I surveyed the chow line. The food looked surprisingly good. "Piece of that fried fish, please," I said. "Maybe some green beans, mashed potatoes, and that corn bread looks pretty good, too."

"My corn bread's better'n pretty good," Miss Mary said, grabbing a plate off a stack and going to work. "I got the best corn bread this side of the Mississippi."

I smiled. "Where you from, Miss Mary?"

"Tupelo, Mississippi," she said. "Born and bred there."

She scooped a huge pile of mashed potatoes onto the loaded plate and handed it across to me.

"Thought I recognized the accent," I said. "Nashville, Tennessee, here."

Miss Mary broke out in a laugh that startled me. "I knowed there was something I liked about you, boy! I got me a brother what lives in Nashville right now. Drives a truck, lives over in East Nashville, across the river."

"Hey, that's where I live," I said. "I mean, that's where I used to live before I moved out here."

"Well, welcome to the Mustang, Harry. You going to like it here just fine." She handed me a second plate with three huge hunks of corn bread and enough butter pats to cause an arterial traffic jam.

I dropped five bucks into Miss Mary's tip jar, then took my lunch over to a table farthest from the television and sat with my back to the wall, facing the center of the room. The food was good and I'd worked up an appetite wrestling with the hot-tub drain. But I also wanted to see what kind of traffic flow came and went in the Mustang. While I did my first set of chores, I heard the buzzer go off a couple of times, and once while I was carrying some tools down the hallway, a line of girls ran past me to parade out front. But the place was even more quiet than I expected.

Then again, I thought, this was Tuesday morning. Probably one of the slowest days of the week.

Just as I finished the last of Miss Mary's corn bread, a large man in gray trousers and a navy-blue blazer came into the cafeteria and sat down at the table across from me. He stared at me a few moments without saying anything.

"Hi," I said, suddenly nervous under his gaze. His face was pockmarked, his cheeks a ruddy red and lined with broken veins. His bulbous nose had been broken at least once and badly set. "I'm Harry, the new maintenance guy."

"Yeah," he said. "I know who you are. I'm Gilstrap. Smiley Gilstrap, chief of security."

"Glad to meet you, Mr. Gilstrap."

"Joey tells me you did time in Tennessee," he said.

"Little bit," I said. "Nothing heavy." Tension formed a knot in my stomach, pushing the food upward uncomfortably. I realized that if this guy decided to make a few calls and check me out, I was screwed.

"Possession with intent," he said. "That's what Joey said."

"Yeah, well, that's what it was officially, but truth is—"

"Drop it," he interrupted. "I don't want to hear it. I'm retired Reno PD, so I don't want no bullshit about how the cops railroaded you. There's just one thing I want to say to you. You keep your nose clean, don't cause me no problems, and we'll get along fine. You fuck up, punk, and I have any trouble out of you at all . . ."

"Yessir?" I said after a few moments.

"I'll fucking bury you so deep, they'll never find you. *Capisce?*" he growled.

I nodded. "Yessir."

He looked at me like I was something he needed to scrape off his shoes. Then he eased his two-hundred-fifty-pounds-plus out of the chair and walked off.

Miss Mary came up to the table, leaned down, and started gathering up my dirty dishes.

"Now," she whispered, "you know why they call him Smiley."

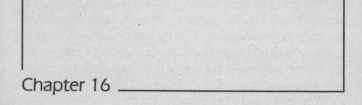

Chapter 16

My house-renovation skills came in handy that first day as the next job was a large drywall repair in a room off the one with the number two hot tub. Seemed a cowboy in from south of Carson City last Saturday night had gone a little too long without adequate time off for good psychological health. Blowing off a little steam for him had involved drinking a quart of tequila and bouncing one of the girls off the far wall of her room. It had taken both Smiley and the bartender to hold the guy down, while the girl had decided to take a few days off, just until that pesky lump on her head went down a bit. In the meantime, a couple of Storey County deputies had taken the cowboy away for a serious attitude-adjustment seminar.

All that was left was a two-inch-deep indentation in the sheet of drywall roughly the size of the girl's head and shoulders, a web of cracks and broken paint splaying out from it. Mabel asked if I could fix it and I told her I'd never done a repair quite that big, but given enough time I could probably do a passable job.

It was late in the afternoon and I was already on my way to being burned out when I got the materials together to tackle the job. I took a box opener and cut out a rectangle about two feet by four feet in the wall and peeled the broken drywall away. Then I cut a piece that fit the hole as close as I could make it, tacked it onto the studs, and mixed up some drywall mud. I was smoothing the drywall mud over the seam paper when the door behind me flew open and slammed against the wall.

Startled, I jumped back, dragging the trowel across the wet mud and digging a trench in it, and so screwing up about a half hour's work. I turned, aggravated, and faced the guy in the doorway.

"How much longer's this gonna take?" he demanded. He wore a white tuxedo shirt under a green polyester jacket. The shirt bulged open at the waistline. His hair was slicked back and shiny, and his face was clean shaven yet puffy and laced with spidery red veins. He looked to be about thirty-five with a lot of mileage on him.

"About a half hour longer than it would have if you hadn't slammed that door open like that," I said. "And by the way, who the hell are you?"

My shirt was covered in a white, powderlike dust and splattered with white drywall mud. I held the trowel in my right hand like a pistol.

The guy's face reddened and he crossed the room, then stopped about two inches from me. "I'm your boss, friend," he said, his voice low and threatening. "And if you want to keep your job here, you'll watch your language."

"Where's Mabel?"

"Mabel goes home at six. I'm Gary Weyrich, the night boss."

"Oh," I said. "Sorry. It's been a long day and"—I motioned to the botched drywall job behind me—"now I'll have to redo this."

"How long will it take?"

"Not long," I answered, going into good-soldier mode.

"When can I move a girl back in here?"

"Late tomorrow," I answered. "The mud's got to set up, then I have to sand it and paint it."

Gary leaned in even closer. "When I come on tomorrow night, I expect this room to be ready to go. You got it? This is costing Mr. Fennelly money and he don't like that."

"Yeah," I said. "I got it."

He turned and left. I had a feeling that Gary Weyrich and I were not going to bond.

Over the next ten days I unstopped more toilets, fixed more loose shingles, moved more furniture, mopped more floors, and painted more fence ironwork than I ever imagined possible. And as I did so, I watched and counted and made mental notes that were later transcribed onto paper. I worked overtime so that I could stay late and count customers. I volunteered for double shifts. Girls moved out and I painted their rooms to make way for the next batch. After all that time and all that work, I finally reached an opinion about the Mustang Ranch's ability to pull in the kind of dollars they were reporting to Jacques Barrone and the feds.

Ain't no way.

"What?" Barrone asked as I sat in his home office sipping a beer one night after getting off work at nearly nine o'clock. I was grimy and dirty, needed a shower and a backrub, but I'd stopped by his ranch on the way home.

"That's it," I said, opening my notebook and showing him the figures. I'd kept it in code, strictly numbers, and had two separate sets of data: cars in the parking lot and actual customers. "There ain't no way in hell the Mustang Ranch is pulling in the kind of money you've been talking about."

Barrone had pulled up the Mustang Ranch file on his computerized accounting program. On the spreadsheet, a row of numbers ran across the bottom, with some compiled statistics displayed in the boxes below. The Mustang Ranch was reporting an average monthly income of just over $525,000, and that's after splitting the gross income with the employees. Barrone had explained to me that each girl split her take with the house, the house getting fifty percent and ten percent of the girl's half held back for tips and expenses. Cab drivers, for instance, were toked by the house for driving customers out to the Mustang from Reno. Whatever was left was split by the rest of the staff.

"Do you realize how much frigging money that is?" I asked. "That means more than a million a month is coming in from customers."

I glanced down at my notes, studying them. "As best I can tell, during a typical week, there are about an even dozen girls working each shift. That's ninety-six, uh, what would you call them? Bed hours?"

Barrone smiled in that aloof, patrician manner of his and nodded. "I guess you could call them man hours, although it would certainly be a different take on the term."

"Okay, ninety-six man hours per shift," I said. "Here, let me borrow your calculator." I reached over and started tapping numbers on it. "Ninety-six hours a shift times, let's say, a hundred fifty an hour is fourteen thousand four hundred a shift times three is forty-three thousand two hundred. That's the maximum gross per day if every girl works every hour of every shift. Times thirty days is . . ."

I pecked out another series of numbers on the calculator. "A million, two hundred ninety-six thousand, split fifty-fifty with the girls is . . ."

Another series of numbers. "Six hundred forty-eight thousand. That's if every girl works every hour of every shift seven days a week."

"But you can see, can't you?" Barrone asked. "What they've done is come up with a number that's mathematically possible. It's mathematically possible to make that much money, so they took that number and reported a little less."

"Only look at my numbers," I said, opening my notebook. "I can type this up and make it look pretty for you, but the bottom line is, there ain't no way. They might be grossing a fifth that much, and that's giving them the benefit of the doubt. Last Wednesday the day shift had two customers. There was a third who came in, but he had two beers at the bar then either lost his nerve or his erection and left."

"Maybe both." Barrone leaned back and massaged his temples. "That's not quite two weeks' data," he said. "You've only been there a little less than two weeks."

"You think it was much different before I started?" I asked. "What, you think I'm driving off business?"

"No, I don't think that," he said. "It's just that we're going to need more information before we know for sure. Before we have what we need to go to FINCEN and get them off our backs."

Our backs? I wanted to say. What's this *our* shit? But I held my tongue.

"Another few weeks and we'll know for sure," he said.

I folded up my notebook, stuck it back in my shirt pocket. "The only problem, Mr. Barrone, is I don't have a few weeks. Marsha went to the doctor yesterday. Today's Thursday, and if she hasn't gone into labor by

Sunday, then he's going to induce. And I'm going to be there for the birth, and then after that I'm staying to help with the baby."

He leaned back in his chair and glared at me. "You mean you're leaving?"

I nodded. "I told you this was a short-term proposition. I've done what you hired me to do. There was never any mention of my staying on at the Mustang indefinitely."

"Nobody said anything about indefinitely," he said, his voice stern.

"Besides," I interjected, rubbing my left shoulder hard with my right wrist, "they're working my butt off out there. I'm too old for this."

"Harry," he said, motioning to my handwritten notes, "this is simply not enough for me to go to the U.S. attorney's office and say 'Look, guys, just to show you I wasn't in on this little scheme, here's the proof you need to shut it down.' I've got to have more, Harry, and I need your willingness not only to get it for me, but to back it up with your own deposition and possible courtroom testimony."

I leaned back and polished off the last inch of beer. "Look, this is what I'll do. I'll commit to staying as long as I can, but if Marsha's really ill or needs me, I'll have to start calling in sick at the Mustang. That's the best I can do. My first priority's got to be Marsha and the baby."

"Harry—"

"Besides," I said, standing, "you'll have enough to go to the feds. You've got the books, you've got my notes, and you'll have my sworn testimony that the books are padded. I don't know what else you'll need. The feds can go in there and seize the joint."

"They have seized it," Barrone insisted. "The money laundering is still going on!"

"Then they can close the fucking place down!" I said. Maybe it was fatigue, maybe it was the beer, but I suddenly started chuckling. "Get it? Close the *fucking* place down."

Barrone shook his head from side to side wearily. "Yes, I get it."

"They can just shut it down and indict everyone who works there."

"Yes," Barrone said. "I just hope they don't indict me."

Marsha was already asleep by the time I got home. Aunt Marty'd flown out the day before for the opening of an art gallery she'd bought into in San Francisco. Except for Estella, who was getting ready for bed, the house was empty.

Marsha'd had a bad day, Estella said, following an equally bad night. By this point in the pregnancy, she wasn't sleeping much at all and any napping she could get was on an absolute no-interruptions basis.

I showered at the other end of the hall while Estella warmed up a plate of leftovers for me. The water wasn't quite the same as a back rub, but turned up hot it felt great. Despite the fatigue, I'd noticed during the past week or so that the worst of the soreness was passing and that my pants were a little looser. What the hell, maybe I was getting in shape.

Estella set the plate in front of me with orders to put my dirty dish in the sink, then went off to bed herself. I grabbed another beer out of the refrigerator and sat down at the dining room table and ate dinner alone. Over the years since my divorce, I'd gradually gotten used to eating alone, although I usually had the television or the stereo on to make it a little less depressing. I was afraid of waking Marsha, though, so I sat and ate quietly, trying to ignore the sense I had of being absolutely alone in the world.

I put the dish away and grabbed another bottle of beer, then sat down on the couch with the cordless phone. My calling-card number was stored somewhere in my brain so was the one card that Greasy Blond and the Wolf couldn't get back in the desert. I fished through my new wallet and found the business card I was looking for, then punched in about twenty numbers to get through to the carrier, the number, and then the account information. A couple of seconds later a computerized voice thanked me for using the telephone, followed by a ringing on the line.

"Hello," her voice said.

"Hi, Kelly."

"Who is this? Wait, is that you, Harry?"

"Yeah, it's me. How are you?"

"Fine. I'm great, although I was beginning to think I was never going to hear from you again."

I kept my voice low as I talked. "You've been on my mind."

"I've thought about you, too. So, are you a dad yet or what?"

"Any day now."

Kelly hesitated a moment. "Well," she said. "How are things going for you?"

"Okay," I said. "Truth is, I've been busy. Believe it or not, I'm working a case."

"Yeah? A real private-detective thing?"

I smiled. Her voice sounded wonderful. "Yeah, the real thing. I wasn't looking to find any work up here, but it's a favor for a friend of Marsha's aunt."

"Oh," she said. "Great. And speaking of Marsha, how are things going?"

"They're not," I said. "We haven't been able to put things back together. We really haven't even tried. It's like there's this gulf between us that's never going to be closed. I guess I'm not surprised."

"That's too bad, Harry," she said. "I'm sorry."

"Me, too. I just have to get on with my life, you know? So how are you?"

"Just working. I mean, life's pretty quiet here."

"Right now, that sounds wonderful. No exciting helicopter rescues or anything like that?"

"Even that's routine after a while."

A silence followed; it got uncomfortable after a few moments. I cleared my throat awkwardly. "I was just thinking about you. Wondering how you were. Wondering if you were planning on coming to Reno anytime soon."

She laughed softly. "So are you, like, asking me or something?"

"Well," I said, "if you just happened to be coming to Reno anytime soon, I'd sure like to see you. We could get dinner, maybe you could teach me a little blackjack. Maybe that . . . what was it? Caribbean poker?"

"Yeah, Caribbean poker," she said. "So you'd like to get together."

"Yeah, Kelly," I said after a moment. "I would."

"And you're being straight with me," she said. "You're really not involved with her anymore."

"I'm not involved with anybody," I said. "And I don't know that I'm looking to get involved with anybody. I just know that the couple of days with you was the first time in a long time that I've enjoyed hanging out with someone."

"So you just want to hang out for a while, right?"

"Look, I'd like to see you. If it happens, it happens. If it doesn't, then take care of yourself and goodbye."

"Hey," she said, "don't get defensive on me. I'd like to see you, too."

"So let's stay in touch, okay?"

"Give me a number where I can call you."

I gave her the number at Aunt Marty's and told her Estella would take a message. Then I gave her my pager number, just in case.

"Okay," she said. "If I can get in some weekend soon, I'll call."

"Great, but not this weekend, okay? My daughter's being born this weekend."

Kelly broke out laughing. "Right, I forgot."

"Listen, it's great to hear your voice."

"Yours, too, Harry," she said. "I enjoyed spending time with you. In fact, I've been thinking about you."

"Yeah?" I asked, grinning. "Good stuff, I hope."

"Yes, Harry. Good stuff. Take care of yourself, okay?"

"I will. And you, too."

We hung up after that, and I sat there for a few moments, thinking about Kelly, wondering why I had called her when there wasn't much chance of anything happening between us. As soon as I finished my work here, I was headed home.

Or, I thought with a smile, maybe I'd take a side trip on my way back.

Twenty minutes later I was headed upstairs to bed when my pager went off. *Strange,* I thought, then pressed the button to check the number.

It was the Mustang. *Damn it.*

My second day there Mabel had spotted the pager on

my belt and demanded the number. I'd given it to her because I hadn't been fast enough on my feet to figure a way out of telling her. After a few days of not being paged, I'd forgotten all about it.

I pondered whether or not to ignore the page. After all, it was nearly eleven. I could reasonably claim that I was asleep, that I'd never even heard the beeper go off.

But some nagging, perhaps neurotic sense of something—certainly not responsibility—made me go back to the kitchen, pick up the cordless phone, and make the call.

"Mustang," a voice said when I answered. It was Gary.

"Gary, this is Harry Denton," I said. "You beeped?"

"We need you down here quick. The number two hot tub has sprung a leak where you fixed the drain last week. It's making a hell of a mess."

I sighed. "Listen, Gary, I've had a ton of overtime in the last few days. Can't it wait until tomorrow?"

"If it could wait, I wouldn't have called you," Gary said. "And you're the one that screwed it up in the first place with your crappy repair. We don't get this fixed tonight, it'll damage the subflooring and then we're talking a serious bill. It'll come out of your check."

"But, Gary, I—"

"You coming down here or not, Harry? You don't come tonight, then don't come back at all."

I held my hand over the phone and let loose with a whispered *Damn it*. Then I uncovered the handset.

"All right, Gary," I said wearily. "I'm on my way. In the meantime, cut the water off at the valve behind that panel next to the door and be sure to kill the power at the circuit breaker."

"Already done," he said. "Just get down here."

I hung up the phone, my head spinning at the thought of driving forty-five minutes down the side of Mount

Rose and out into the Nevada desert to fix a leaky drain in a whorehouse hot tub.

"Barrone," I muttered, heading upstairs for my work-boots, "I'm getting time-and-a-half on this one."

Chapter 17

As I drove out I-80 east into the black hole of the night desert, the lights of Reno burned behind me so brightly, I had to skew the rearview mirror.

There was no moon. I almost missed the turnoff. Gravel and dirt sprayed out behind the truck as I slid onto the exit ramp and down the access road, the lights of the Mustang Ranch parking lot the only guiding beacon. At the lot, there were maybe a dozen cars, which, given that it was nearly midnight on a weeknight, wasn't too bad.

I stepped out of the warm truck and into the frigid, dry Nevada night air. Just as the myth about the dry heat not being so hard on you was partially true, so it was also true that the desert cold could be equally misleading. One could go hypothermic without even knowing it.

I stepped up to the gate and hit the doorbell button twice in the employee code that would gain me access and not bother the girls. A moment later the door buzzed and I pushed it open. Gary was at the front door waiting for me.

" 'Bout time," he grumbled.

"Hey, I was at my girlfriend's house. It's forty-five minutes away from here."

I practically bit my lip to keep from going off on him. Gary Weyrich wouldn't even have this gig if Mabel wasn't

190

the day boss. Job or no job, I was in no mood to take crap from a guy who depended on nepotism to be the night-shift manager in a brothel.

He motioned with his head toward the back of the house. "Get busy," he ordered. Gary, like his mother, was a person of few words.

In the bar there were four guys laughing and downing longnecks at one table, with a couple of the girls sitting on laps. Trying to drum up business, I guess. I walked past them and down the left hallway, then stopped at the door to the number two hot-tub room. A hand-lettered sign read: OUT OF ORDER. I tried to open the door, but it wouldn't budge. Something was blocking it.

Nervously, I put my shoulder to the door and pushed hard. It gave maybe a half-inch or so but was still blocked by something. I braced myself, then put my shoulder to the door again, harder, and managed to shove it open a foot or so. I stuck my head inside.

A pile of soggy wet towels was wedged under the door. "Damn," I muttered. There was water everywhere, with more leaking out from the base of the tub in a steady stream. If I couldn't tighten the drain connection quickly, I'd have to rig a siphon with a couple of garden hoses and run them out the door in the kitchen. Gary wasn't going to like that, not to mention Goumba Joey, if he was around anywhere.

I pulled the door to and rushed outside for my toolbox. I wasn't entirely sure what the hell I was doing, but it seemed like a good idea to try something, anything, even if it was wrong.

An hour later I got the leak stopped. I had to pull off the redwood access panel on the hot tub, rig up a flashlight so that I could see what I was doing, and crawl under the tub until I found where the PVC pipe was coming apart. I'd been afraid that the pipe had cracked, which meant a major repair/replacement job, but I'd been lucky; a connector had just loosened from the vibration of the motor.

The downside was that I was soaking wet. I'd been lying on my back in a pool of water for nearly an hour, and I didn't have a change of clothes with me. I got the hot tub put back together, mopped up as much of the water as I could, and then gathered up all of the wet towels that had been thrown down to hold back the flood.

The temperature outside was now about twenty-five degrees, and I don't care how dry the damn cold is, when you're soaking wet you feel it. By the time I ran out to the maintenance shed to put up the tools, then ran back through the kitchen, I was shaking like a Chihuahua on methamphetamines. I ran behind the counter to Miss Mary's big restaurant stove and turned on one of the gas burners.

I leaned over it, rubbing my hands back and forth, trying to stop the shaking. I hadn't been this cold since the night my Mustang broke down on the other side of Eureka, and now it all came back to me as one bad memory.

"What happened to you?" a voice behind me asked.

I turned. Raven, the Goth hooker and resident dominatrix, had walked into the lounge and was standing behind me looking like she'd caught me with my hand in the cookie jar.

She wore a black leather bustier, black lace garter belt, fishnet stockings, and patent leather spiked heels. Today her long hair was streaked with white and hung draped over her shoulders. She had skillfully applied theatrical makeup so that her cheekbones were highlighted in rose just below the deep black pockets under her eyes.

"Had to fix a leak on the number two hot tub," I said, turning back to the stove. I was almost embarrassed to be standing in front of her like this.

"You're drenched," she said. "You'll catch your death."

"I'll be okay."

Her heels clicked staccato on the linoleum floor as she stepped around the buffet table and over to the stove. She stood next to me, reached out, and touched my shirt just below my right shoulder.

"I'm serious," Raven said. "You need to get out of those clothes. C'mon, I've got a bathrobe in my room. You can put it on while I throw these in the dryer for you."

"Look," I said, "Gary's giving me a hard-enough time as it is. I'm not even supposed to be talking to you."

She curled her upper lip. "I'm not afraid of Gary," she said. "He doesn't scare me."

"No, really, I'm fine—"

"Quiet, worm!" she barked, in dominatrix mode now. "To my room, mister! March!"

I turned. "Aren't you busy tonight?" I asked.

Her face softened and her voice lowered. "Slow night for ghouls, I guess." Then I swear to God she did something I'd never seen her do before. She almost cracked a smile.

"C'mon, Harry. Let's get you dry."

I followed her down the hall, past rooms with closed doors through which came the faint sounds of laughter, moaning, and a few intonations I'd never heard before.

She held a door open for me and I stepped into a room decorated with Victorian furniture. An ornately carved, heavy wooden four-poster bed dominated the room, while tarnished brass torchiere lamps topped with cranberry-glass globes perched in each corner. A thick rug covered the floor and the walls were painted a pastel rose. In the corner sat a wooden chair with cushions of red velvet.

"Nice," I commented, looking around.

"Thanks," she said, closing the door behind her. "I decorated it myself."

I felt suddenly apprehensive as she closed the door. "So this is where you live?" I asked awkwardly.

"If you want to call it living," she said coldly. "Get out of those clothes now."

I looked around. "You mind letting me have the bathrobe?"

Raven shook her head and opened the door to a large walk-in closet opposite the bed. "God, Harry, it's not like I haven't seen it all before."

"I know," I said. "I'm just freezing."

That was about half true—I *was* freezing—but I couldn't help feeling a sudden attack of shyness. I don't know why; after all, she'd see as many naked men as any practicing doctor, maybe more. Maybe that was why I felt so shy.

She handed me a black terry-cloth robe with a hood. The robe looked like it belonged to a monk, or perhaps to one of her assistant's in a more bizarre S&M scenario. But it was thick and warm and I didn't care what else it had been used for. I stripped off my shirt and T-shirt, then stepped out of my jeans and put on the robe. I turned my back to her and stepped out of my boxers and socks, then tied the robe around me and turned back to her.

"Here, let me take those down to the laundry room and pop them in the dryer," she offered.

I bent down, gathering the soggy wet clothes. "No, Raven, I can do it." It felt strange to be actually calling someone Raven.

"You just sit down," she ordered, motioning toward the chair. "I'll take these."

"I can wait in the lounge," I said.

She took the bundle of wet clothes out of my hands. "If Gary sees you wandering around the halls like that, he might accuse you of something you don't want to be accused of, and he's too stupid to buy the truth."

"What if you, uh, need this room?" I asked.

She walked to the door, opened it, then looked back at me. "Like I said, slow night for ghouls."

Five minutes later the door opened and Raven stepped back in, quickly closing the door behind her.

"You warming up?" she asked.

"Yeah," I answered. "It's much better now." I stood. "Here, you want to sit down?"

She laughed. "Don't be such a gentleman. Don't worry. If I want your chair, I'll let you know."

I smiled back at her. "Fair enough."

"Look, it's deader'n shit out there. I'd be really surprised if I had any more business tonight. Mind if I change out of the work clothes?"

"Sure, I'll wait outside."

She held her hand out. "Jeez, Harry, chill, okay? Sit down. If you don't want to look, you don't have to. But I don't care one way or the other."

Raven opened the closet door, took out another bathrobe, then sat on the edge of the bed away from me. She lifted first one leg, then the other, and dropped the spiked heels on the floor.

"My feet are killing me." She sighed, rubbing them. Then she backed farther onto the bed, lay down on her back, lifted her hips in the air, and shed the fishnet stockings in one smooth motion. The garter belt followed and then she sat up on the bed, her back still to me. I saw her arms rocking back and forth as she undid the snaps on the leather bustier, then it fell off behind her onto the bed. She hopped off the bed and turned to face me.

The bed was high enough so that I could only see her from the waist up. Raven was thin, almost anorexic, with pale skin and ribs that showed through below small breasts that rode high on her torso. Her nipples were bright red, almost as crimson as her lipstick, and I wondered if she used makeup for that effect as well.

"God, it feels good to have that damn thing off, too." She spread her arms above her head and stretched, then reached for the bathrobe and put it on. She bent over, picked up her things, and started putting them away.

I'd tried not to stare as she undressed in front of me but with very little success. She wasn't beautiful, unless you're heavily into heroin chic, but there was something about her that was attractive, even compelling. I'd never been able to take women at face value. I'd always assumed that there was something underneath that was hidden from the rest of the world, and for some reason or other with some women I had this compulsion to find out what it was. With Marsha, I'd discovered anger and resentment and a layer of deep-seated pain that was almost agony beneath her drive and intellect and sarcastic, often brutal humor. And now here I was in the private boudoir of a real pro, wondering if beneath the leather and the facade and the toughness and the makeup and the scar tissue there wasn't a little girl who never got held enough.

God, I'm a fool.

"Thanks for the help," I said as Raven fluffed a couple of pillows, then settled down on the bed in a half-reclining position. On the night table next to her was a portable CD player. She leaned over and pressed a button and the low, sweet tones of a tenor sax wafted out.

"I guess I didn't realize how cold I was," I continued. "I'd never have made it home."

"No problem, Harry," she said, eyeing me. "And where is that?"

"Where's what?"

"Home."

"I'm just crashing around right now," I answered. "Part of the time with Shaky Jake, the rest of the time with some other friends. I'm saving up enough change for my own place."

"I heard you were from back east, that you just got finished doing some time."

"A little bit," I said, wondering why she was suddenly so curious. "Nothing serious."

She chuckled. "I got popped a couple times in L.A. Did ninety days in county once. Ain't no such thing as non-serious time."

"Okay," I agreed. "Given a choice, I'd have passed on the experience, but it could have been worse."

"Anything could be worse," Raven said.

"Mind if I ask you something?"

She narrowed her eyes. "Long as it's not 'How'd a nice girl like you wind up in a place like this?' "

"We'll forgo that one," I said. "I was just wondering what your real name was."

"Why do you want to know?" she asked. She laid her left arm across the pillows next to her and crossed her legs at the ankles.

"Call it curiosity," I said. "Your parents didn't name you Raven, did they?"

"Would have been like them," she said, her voice low.

I stood up, walked over to the foot of the bed, and leaned against one of the posts. "Didn't mean to pry," I said. "I guess I'm sorry we started off on the wrong foot when I first got here. I don't exactly have a lot of friends.

Anybody who's kind enough to dry my wet clothes deserves better from me."

"Annie," she said after a moment. "My real name's Annie."

"So where're you from, Annie?"

She rolled her lower lip out slightly. "Harlan, Kentucky."

"Coal-mining country," I said.

"You're the first person here I've ever told that to."

"Really?"

"Of course, you're the first one to ask."

"How'd you wind up out here?"

"I told you not to ask," she said, her voice softening, all traces of the black-leather-clad dominatrix gone.

"I didn't mean how'd you wind up in this business," I said. "I just meant how'd you wind up in Nevada."

"It's a long story," Raven said. She scooted over slightly in bed and patted the comforter on her right side. "Why don't you climb up here? I'll tell you all about it."

For a few long moments I stood there in silence, the two of us staring at each other as the music continued to fill the room softly. Her mouth opened slightly, her lips pursed, her breathing slow and rhythmic.

"I'll probably hate myself in the morning for saying this," I said. "But I'd better take a pass, Raven."

The angle of her jaw shifted, as if the muscles in her face had tightened. "I don't let just anybody up here without the meter running."

"I appreciate the offer," I said. "But I probably ought to be thinking about getting home soon."

"Your clothes won't be dry for another half hour."

"Look, Raven—"

"Annie," she said. "It's Annie."

"Annie," I said. "Don't think I'm not tempted, but

you know how it is. Two people working for the same place get involved, things just tend to get complicated.

She let out a deep sigh and her head seemed to settle heavily onto the pillow. "I understand. Maybe you should just wait down in the lounge," she said wearily.

"Annie, I don't mean anything by it. It's just not a good idea."

"Whatever. Go on, Harry. You can leave the bathrobe in the laundry room. I'll get it tomorrow."

I walked around to the edge of the bed. Annie's head slowly turned, her eyes following me. When I got next to the night table, I leaned down.

"Good night, Annie," I said, kissing her softly on the cheek.

I managed to stay awake long enough to make it back to the Mount Rose house, but it was tough. I left a note for Mabel telling her I'd be late. I had to catch up on some sleep. It was nearly nine the next morning before I got up. I showered and shaved, then Estella made breakfast for me and I took it up to Marsha's room. Marsha seemed to have grown measurably larger in the past few days and her center of gravity had shifted downward. Clearly, the baby was due at any moment. I offered to stay home that day just in case, but Marsha waved me off, telling me that Estella was ready to drive her to the hospital as soon as it all started and that Aunt Marty would be back in Reno that afternoon. I left only after extracting a promise from her to page me the moment she felt anything.

"After all," I said, "that's why I came out here. Can't miss the big show."

Outside, a light dusting of snow had fallen overnight and the wind had died, leaving the whole landscape quiet and still, the air clean and sharp. I climbed back into the pickup and headed down the mountain and back out in the valley, going east on I-80. I turned off the Mustang exit and turned down the narrow road toward the ranch. I could see in the distance that the parking lot of the Mustang was nearly full.

Weird, I thought. I hadn't seen that before, even on the busiest nights.

But as I drove under the railroad trestle and emerged on the other side at the entrance to the Mustang Ranch, I saw that the lot was full, all right, but not full of customers.

The Mustang Ranch parking lot was jammed with squad cars, a paramedic van, and a whole herd of TV news trucks.

Chapter 18

"What the hell?" I whispered as a knot formed in my stomach. I'd seen Storey County Sheriff's Department cars in front of the Mustang a couple of times before, usually when one of the customers got a little too rowdy or drunk. But I'd never seen anything like this. It looked like the whole sheriff's department had shown up for this one, along with Reno P.D. as well.

I parked the truck over by the souvenir van and wove my way through the squad cars toward the gate. A well-dressed man with a microphone in one hand and behind him a guy with a large videocamera on his shoulder headed for me, calling, "Sir! Excuse me, sir! Do you work here? Are you a customer?"

I pushed past him without saying a word, my head cocked down away from the camera. A crowd of about ten guys, some in uniforms, others in suits, a couple in jeans, was gathered around the front gate. I dove into them and made my way over to a large man in the uniform of the Storey County Sheriff's Department.

"What's going on?" I asked.

"You can't go in today, buddy. The place is closed," he said. Then he spotted the Mustang Ranch label on my workshirt.

"That's right," I said. "I work here."

That seemed to get his attention. He held up a clip-board. "Name?"

"Denton," I answered. "Harry Denton. What's going on, Deputy?"

He checked my name off on the list. "They're waiting for you inside. See Sheriff Hinkle." He pushed the gate open and held it for me, waving me through with his free hand. "Check in with the officer at the front door," he instructed.

I walked quickly up the walk and through the front door. Another deputy, this one short and dark with a bandito mustache, stopped me.

"I was told to find Sheriff Hinkle," I said. "I'm Harry Denton. I work here. What's going on, Deputy?"

He shrugged. "Had a little problem last night," he said. "If you work here, you'll need to make a statement. Go down the hall on the left."

"Yeah, okay," I said, turning and heading down the hall. At the end of it, Goumba Joey's door was open and I could see a crowd gathered around his desk. I was about halfway down when the door to Mabel's office opened to my left and she stepped out into the hallway.

"Hey," she yelled, turning toward Joey's office. "Here he is!"

I stopped. "What's going on, Mabel?"

She turned to me. "Where the hell you been?"

"I left you a note last night," I said. "I got called in middle of the night to fix a hot tub."

Behind Mabel, Gary stepped out, still dressed in the same clothes he'd worn the night before. He grinned meanly—reminding me of the expression on a cat's face when it corners a mouse—and pointed at me, too.

"That's him, Officers!" he called. "He was here last night!"

"What the hell is going on?" I demanded.

Gary turned to me. "Just shut up, Harry," he snapped. "Just shut the fuck up. You're in deep shit now, buddy."

Two men in suits were already at the door to Joey's office, eyeing me as I stopped next to Mabel.

"Mabel," I said, almost pleading, "what's going on?"

"It's Raven," she said. "Somebody killed her last night. The cops want to talk to you."

The next few minutes were kind of a blur. There were hands on me and everybody was talking at once and shouts and someone was pushing me into Joey's office. Somebody started yelling at me—it might have been Gary again, but in the crowd it was hard to tell—and then this older man in a fringed buckskin jacket and a cowboy hat was shouting at everybody else to get out. Goumba Joey got in the sheriff's face and then a couple of uniforms were on him, pushing him out of the office, and then everybody else was gone, too, except for me and the two guys in suits and the fringed-buckskin man.

In this cacophony of voices and noises, I kept hearing Raven's—Annie's—voice talking to me as she had lain on the bed last night. She had seemed so frail and blanched, weary and worn down. And she had wanted me to lie down next to her and I wouldn't do it because I have this stupid hang-up about having sex with a hooker, but maybe it hadn't been sex she was after. Maybe she'd just wanted somebody next to her.

And I'd said no. I got up and left and drove home in the middle of the night and left her alone, and now she was dead. Now there was just yelling and screaming and shoving and news cameras and microphones.

"Mr. Denton," said the man in the cowboy hat and buckskin. He was in his early sixties, I supposed, with great bushy salt-and-pepper eyebrows. "Would you like to sit down?"

I looked around. "Where?"

"Over there," he said, motioning to the sofa against the wall in Goumba Joey's office. I stepped over, settled down onto the cool, dry leather.

The two men in suits pulled up chairs in front of the sofa, offered one to the older man, and then all three sat down.

"Mr. Denton, I'm Sheriff Barton Hinkle, Storey County Sheriff's Department. These two gentlemen with me are Detective Sergeant Mike Anderson and Detective Lenny Bouvier of the Reno Police Department."

I nodded to them, still numb all over, settling into that place nature gives us to fall into in the middle of a trauma, that place that protects us from the worst sharp edges.

Sheriff Hinkle looked over as one of the policemen pulled out a reporter's notebook and cocked his pen.

"Would you mind telling me your full name, Mr. Denton?"

"Sure," I said. "Harry James Denton."

"And what is your current address, Harry? By the way, you mind if I call you Harry?"

"No," I answered. "Harry's fine. I'm staying in Reno with my girlfriend's aunt. She lives up on Mount Rose."

I gave them the address and the two detectives looked at each other. "That's a nice address, Harry," one of the detectives said. "What, you just crashing up there?"

"My girlfriend . . . well, really, she's my ex-girlfriend. She's going to have a baby and she asked me to come out and stay with her until the baby's born."

"Come out here?" Sheriff Hinkle asked. "From where?"

"Nashville," I said. "Nashville, Tennessee."

"You got an address there?"

I reeled off my address and phone number. "You got

an employer?" the detective asked. His blond hair was cropped short; he was maybe in his late twenties—looked like he worked out a lot.

"I'm self-employed," I said.

"What line of work are you in, Harry?" the sheriff asked.

"I'm a private detective."

The three men looked at one another. After a few seconds, the older of the two detectives turned to me. "You mind telling us what you're doing working maintenance at the Mustang Ranch?"

I let my gaze drift down the line, moving from one to the other, as I wondered how much to say. "I'm working for a client," I said finally. What the hell, I thought. It was a safe bet my days at the Mustang were nearly at an end. Might as well come clean with these guys. I'd learned the hard way during the past few years that when there's a murder involved, it's best not to cop too big an attitude with guys in uniforms who have guns.

Unless you have to, that is.

Sheriff Hinkle furrowed his brow and frowned at me. "Let me see if I understand this," he said. "You're a private detective from Tennessee working a case here in Storey County, Nevada. You got a Nevada P.I. license?"

I shook my head.

"Well, boys," Hinkle said, turning to the other two, "seems like we got us a problem with that right off the bat."

The older guy in the suit nodded. "Maybe," he said. "Depends on what kind of work Harry was doing. But before we get into that, let me ask you, Harry. Where were you last night, say between midnight and three in the morning?"

"I was home, at my girlfriend's aunt's house, that is,

and I got paged about ten-thirty, maybe a little later. I answered the page, and Gary Weyrich, the night manager, told me they had a busted hot tub that was making a big mess and I had to get back here to work on it immediately. I didn't want to, since I'd already pulled about twelve hours yesterday, but he said he'd fire me if I didn't come. I didn't much care one way or the other, but I didn't think my client would be too happy about it because I haven't finished what he hired me to do. Anyway, I got here a little before midnight, I guess, and then took about an hour to fix the hot tub."

"That would make it around one in the morning," the younger detective said.

"Sure." I nodded. "Only I got soaking wet and I was trying to dry off in the kitchen when Annie—"

"Annie?" Sheriff Hinkle interrupted.

"Her, uh, professional name was Raven."

"But you knew her real name?" he asked.

"First name," I said. "I knew her first name."

Hinkle turned, looked at the other two detectives, and raised a furry eyebrow.

"Go on," the lead detective said.

"Anyway, Annie . . . Raven . . . whatever, saw me in the kitchen and offered—hell, she ordered me to go to her room and put on a bathrobe so that she could dry my clothes in the laundry room."

He looked straight at me. "So you were in Raven's room after one o'clock in the morning?"

"Yes," I answered. "By the way, which one are you? Bouvier or Anderson?"

"I'm Detective Sergeant Anderson," he said, and then pointing to his left, "this is Detective Bouvier."

"Thanks. It's a little disconcerting not to know who you're talking to."

"So how long were you in Raven's room?" Anderson asked.

"Not long," I said. "Twenty minutes maybe. We talked. It was late. I decided to wait in the laundry room for my clothes to dry. That took another fifteen, twenty minutes after I left her room. Then I drove home, went to bed. I didn't pay any attention to the clock, but it must have been pushing three by then."

"Where was Raven then?" Hinkle asked.

"When I left her room, she was lying in bed," I answered. "She'd changed out of her clothes into a bathrobe and was getting ready for bed, I guess. I never saw her after that."

Bouvier crossed his legs and propped his pad on his knee. "So you were in a working girl's room in a bathrobe and she was in a bathrobe, and . . ."

"And what?" I asked.

"And what happened between you?" Bouvier asked.

"Nothing."

The three men paused, looked at one another for a few moments, then Hinkle looked back at me.

"You were alone in a hooker's room in the middle of the night, and you expect us to believe that nothing happened?"

I stared back at them for a few moments. "Yes," I said finally. "I expect you to believe it because it's true."

Hinkle chuckled and shook his head. "Well, boys, we already know he's got him a pregnant girlfriend, so he ain't no fairy."

"Yeah," Bouvier added, laughing, "but he didn't say nothing about it being his kid."

The two men laughed and shifted their weight around in their seats. Anderson, the detective in the middle, sat stone-faced, staring at me. I stared back at him wordlessly.

"How did she die?" I asked quietly.

"You tell us," Hinkle said.

I ignored him. *Asshole.*

"You don't know?" Anderson asked.

"No," I answered. "I don't. How could I?"

"That's what we're trying to figure out," Hinkle said loudly.

Anderson turned, shot him a glance that shut him up for the time being. Then Anderson turned back to me. "You really don't know," he said.

"No, I don't."

"She was found facedown in the hot tub about four o'clock this morning," he said. "Coroner says preliminary cause of death is strangulation, but she was beaten pretty badly as well. Somebody went to town on her, Harry. Whoever did it, it'll go a lot easier on him if he'll just be straight with us."

A cramp shot through my gut from one side to the other. "Which hot tub?" I asked.

"The one closest to this side of the house," he answered, pointing.

"Number two," I said slowly. "That's the one I fixed."

Anderson seemed to relax as I said that, easing his weight back into the chair and stretching his legs out in front of him.

"Mr. Fennelly, the manager, told us you were an ex-convict on parole from Tennessee," he said. "I gather that was some kind of cover story."

I nodded.

"You've never done time?"

I shook my head.

"You have no criminal record of any kind?"

"How could I and have a P.I. license?" I asked.

"Mind if I see your license?" Anderson asked.

I looked away for a moment, drew a deep breath.

"Well," I said, "that's problematic. You see, on the way out here, I was sort of . . . well, mugged. They got my wallet, license, credit cards, the whole works."

"So you have no form of ID at all?" Anderson asked.

Just a trace of a smile came to my face. "My girlfriend might identify me. Depends on what kind of mood she's in."

Anderson continued the interview. "Do you understand the position that puts us in, Mr. Denton? You have no form of ID, no way to prove that what you're telling us is true. On the other hand, we have a murdered prostitute and a duty to investigate the homicide just like that of any other citizen. And you've admitted to being alone with the woman in her room shortly before she was killed, yet you claim that nothing transpired between you."

"Just conversation," I said.

"And you were seen leaving her room wearing only a bathrobe by at least two witnesses," Anderson continued. "No one else saw the woman alive after that."

"Annie," I said. "Her name was Annie, not 'the woman.' And you're wrong. One other person did see her alive after I did."

"Yeah?" Bouvier said. "Who?"

"Whoever killed her," I said.

Bouvier snorted derisively. "Yeah, right."

"I think we're going to need to head to the office and take a more extensive statement," Anderson said.

"You guys mind if I ask you something?"

Anderson nodded. "Sure, go ahead."

"Why is Reno P.D. in on this? I mean, the Mustang's in Storey County. Isn't this out of your jurisdiction?"

Hinkle reddened. "Listen, boy—" he started.

"No, that's okay," Anderson interrupted. "It's a perfectly reasonable question. Most counties in Nevada are so sparsely populated that they can't afford a fully staffed police department. There are only a half-dozen officers in all of Storey County. Under state law, any one county can request the help of any other in criminal investigations. They can also call in the NDI."

"NDI?" I asked.

"Nevada Division of Investigation," Anderson said. "And in this case, Sheriff Hinkle has chosen to bring us in. It's not unusual."

"Just wondering," I said.

"No problem," Anderson said, standing. "Now, if you'll just come along with us. We'll need to collect some forensic evidence, get a statement."

"Forensic evidence?" I asked.

"Blood sample, fingernail scrapings, hair and saliva samples. All routine stuff."

"Routine stuff to collect off a murder suspect," I said.

The three men stared at me, then Hinkle and Bouvier stood up next to Anderson. They towered over me, looking down at me on the couch.

"Yes, Mr. Denton," Anderson said. "Routine stuff."

I noticed that in the last couple of exchanges I'd gone from being Harry to Mr. Denton. That, more than anything else, worried me. The more formal they got, the deeper the effluent became for me.

"Okay," I said, "I'll be happy to go with you. But I want my lawyer present before I give a statement or provide you with any of the other things you need."

"Fair enough." Anderson said. "You can call him from here if you like. Who is your lawyer?"

"Barrone," I said. "Jacques Barrone."

That seemed to stop them all stone cold in their tracks. Anderson's eyes actually got a little bigger, then he cleared his throat.

"Barrone," he said, pointing to the telephone. I picked it up and dialed Barrone's number as Anderson turned to his buddies. "Now I know we need to go downtown."

Chapter 19

Sometimes the stupidest little mistakes or the slightest, most imperceptible shifts in the karmic winds can cause the worst disasters and catastrophes imaginable. I mean, some yutz decides that if you push the boat a little harder, you'll get to New York a few hours sooner, and hey, *icebergs*? *What icebergs?* . . . And the next thing you know, eighty-five years later, some male blond ditz named Leo is getting rich off your screwup. It's all chance and stupid mistakes.

Like last night, when I just happened to answer a page from the night manager of a whorehouse, and just happened to be manipulated into fixing a hot tub, and just happened to get soaked on a cold night, and a hooker just happened to offer to dry my clothes so that I didn't catch pneumonia. And then she gets murdered and now I'm in the backseat of a Ford Crown Victoria in handcuffs on my way to the Reno, Nevada, police department as a murder suspect.

All over a leaky hot tub . . . Damn, ain't life a bitch?

"C'mon, guys," I said as they pulled out the handcuffs and asked me to hold my hands behind me. "Is this really necessary?"

"Just routine, Mr. Denton," Anderson announced as he clicked the cuffs on me. At least he had the decency to leave them loose.

Then he pulled a card out from his wallet with his left hand and with his right grabbed my left arm just above the elbow and steered me toward the door. "You have the right to remain silent . . ." he began.

Jesus, I'm thinking. *Where have I heard this before?*

The crowd outside Goumba Joey's office seemed to part like the Red Sea as Hinkle, ten-gallon hat pulled low over his face, led us out like a cowpunching Moses. His chest puffed up even bigger as Anderson allowed him to continue the charade that he was actually in charge of anything. Behind the sheriff, Anderson walked sideways, leading me through the throng of people, with Bouvier behind us just in case, I supposed, I decided to make a break for it.

I kept my head down, let my eyes drift off into soft focus, like a kid playing the game of pretending that if I can't see you, you can't see me. Warm bodies bounced off me in the crowd and then we stepped out into the sun. A gentle heat warmed the back of my head as the cold air iced everything else over. Voices came at me from every direction in an unintelligible scramble of noise. Everything in me seemed to go numb except for this growing, gnawing lump of fear in my gut that seemed to radiate outward in every direction. And then there was a hand on top of my head pushing me down and I bent over and found myself in the backseat of a large car. The door closed, and Anderson and Bouvier got into the front seat and closed their doors, and then, thankfully, the voices and shouting and noises became muted and I could straighten up and finally look ahead.

That's when reality hit. I was in the back of an un-marked Reno P.D. car on my way to be questioned about a murder that, I realized when I thought about it, I really couldn't prove I didn't commit.

* * *

The city of Reno technically doesn't even have a jail. The police department building on Second Street, which borders a neighborhood that could be called marginal on its best days, had had several floors with cells, but they'd been proved totally inadequate years ago. So the cells had been turned into windowless offices for police department staffers who spent their days getting a slight feel of what incarceration there must have been like, the only difference being that they could go home at the end of their shift. Now Washoe County maintains the jail for Reno, along with Sparks and the rest of the county. Prisoners aren't even booked at the police department anymore; they're shuttled out to Washoe lockup for the process.

When Anderson explained it to me after I asked him if they were going to book me, I relaxed enough that it didn't hurt to breathe anymore. As soon as we pulled up to the main entrance of the building, Anderson and Bouvier took the handcuffs off and led me in for questioning.

"Sergeant," the receptionist said as we entered the lobby, "a Mr. Barrone called." She handed Anderson a pink slip of paper across the counter. "He's on his way down here and asks that you refrain from asking Mr. Denton any questions until he arrives."

Anderson turned, glanced at me with an expression that was hard to read. "Okay," he said. "Fair enough. Let's go get some coffee."

The receptionist buzzed us in. I followed the two detectives down a hallway and through a door into a maze of cubicles and offices. The crowded floor buzzed with uniforms and plainclothes cops as well as anonymous bureaucrats running around with stacks of paper and computer printouts. I was still unfocused, fuzzy around the edges, like I'd awakened from a deep sleep and found myself in the middle of the Reno Police Department without knowing how I'd gotten there.

Bouvier and Anderson came to a halt in front of a door and stepped in closer to each other, each tilting at just enough of an angle so as to be turned away from me. Anderson whispered something to his underling and then motioned with a subtle move of his jaw in the direction of a hallway. Bouvier nodded and walked off. Anderson turned to me.

"How about that coffee?" he asked pleasantly.

"I could use it," I said. For some reason or other, I felt a little better with Bouvier at least temporarily out of the scene. I'd been around young cops and prosecuting attorneys like him before; young, testosterone-driven, intense guys out to prove something and willing to do just about anything to do it. Anderson was older, more settled, maybe *mature* was even the right word. I relaxed, knowing he'd seen more of life than his younger partner and was less willing to accept surface appearances.

Or maybe I was just fooling myself, maybe putting suspects at ease before bringing the hammer down on them was Anderson's special gift. Maybe he was the guy the rest of the detectives called on when they wanted to get suspects to drop their guard just before nailing them with the big setup.

I followed Anderson into a break room and doctored up the Styrofoam cup of coffee he handed me. The coffee was no better and no worse than all the other cups of cop coffee I'd had during the course of my life and career. It all tended to taste the same, like nobody'd bothered to really clean the pot in a long time and the most recent batch had been sitting on the burner since before the last congressional impeachment hearings.

"I know I'm not supposed to be asking you any questions about the case before Barrone gets here," Anderson said as we stood there sipping. "But I was wondering how he became your lawyer."

He grinned over the top of his cup. "I mean, Jacques Barrone's a pretty well-connected guy in these parts. He doesn't take on just anybody as a client, and here you come out of nowhere and get right to him. I figure there's got to be a story there somewhere."

"There is," I said. "Maybe he'll tell it to you."

Anderson's smile disappeared. "You can wait in my office," he said.

A half hour later Jacques Barrone, Anderson, Bouvier, and I settled into a small conference room. There was a circular table in the center of the room, with Barrone and me on one side, the two Reno P.D. detectives on the other. Barrone had shown up just as I finished the coffee and we'd been given a few minutes alone in one of the tiny interrogation rooms. Barrone had quickly asked me what had happened and I had just as quickly summarized what I knew for him. After that, he'd given me instructions that consisted of two words: *Keep quiet.*

Happy to oblige, I sat to his left with my legs crossed and my hands folded in my lap, trying as hard as I could to keep a completely blank expression pasted on my face. Just for drill, Anderson and Bouvier formally Mirandized me again in Barrone's presence and, with a nod from Barrone, I'd agreed to answer questions with my attorney's input and approval. We went back over the same stuff I'd given them out at the Mustang, the two officers asking me the same questions worded slightly differently in the usual cop attempt to trip me up, catch me in a lie. But like my father used to tell me, it's easier to tell the truth because that way you don't have to keep your story straight.

"Are you in a position to tell us," Barrone asked,

"what evidence you might have against my client in this homicide?"

Anderson nodded. "Not right now, although obviously if Mr. Denton is charged with the homicide, there'll be disclosure at the arraignment and later before trial."

"You gentlemen know you don't have enough to even arraign Mr. Denton right now. You don't even have enough on him to hold him right now."

Bouvier locked his jaw. "Yeah?" he said irritably. "Well, how about—"

Anderson turned, waved a hand to cut his partner off. "Easy," he said. Bouvier reddened slightly as his mouth closed.

Anderson turned, put his elbows on the table. "Why do I have the feeling that we're working at cross purposes here, that we're talking at each other but not to each other?"

"What do you mean, Sergeant?" Barrone asked. "We've answered every one of the questions you've asked within the limits of my client's knowledge and his constitutional rights."

Anderson stared at us for a moment. "Would you gentlemen excuse me for just a second?" he asked, standing up.

Barrone looked down at his watch. "My calendar is quite full today," he said.

"This'll only take a second," Anderson said. "Lenny, get these guys some more coffee if they want it."

Bouvier's face had just gone back to an almost normal color. Too bad, I thought, as the red came back.

"I'm fine," I said. "None for me."

"Me either," Barrone said.

Anderson stepped out, closing the door behind him. The three of us sat there uncomfortably for a few minutes. Barrone retrieved a cell phone from his briefcase and called his secretary, pushing two appointments back further into the day. Just as Barrone clicked off the phone, the door to the conference room opened and Anderson stepped back in, followed by a gray-haired man in a tailored, light gray suit.

"Mr. Barrone, this is Lieutenant Brickman, my supervisor."

Brickman nodded to us and Barrone nodded back, both wordlessly, as the two men sat down.

"I've asked Lieutenant Brickman to sit in on our conference," Anderson said, "because I think that there's more involved here than just a homicide, and I want to see if we can't open things up a bit here."

"I'm not sure I follow you," Barrone said.

"This will become clearer in a bit," he answered. "As you no doubt know, Mr. Barrone, Reno is one of the centers of a variety of white-collar crimes in the west. Money laundering, counterfeiting, computer crime—we got it all here. The Reno Police Department has a financial-crimes investigation unit, which consists primarily of me working part-time in addition to my other duties. For some time now, I've been working with the two local Secret Service field men and two other field officers of FINCEN."

At the mention of FINCEN, I felt Barrone stiffen ever so slightly next to me. If the other men in the room noticed it, their faces didn't give them away.

"We've become convinced," Anderson said, "that the original owners of the Mustang Ranch have been using it more as the base of an immense money-laundering operation than as a legal brothel. FINCEN has been actively involved in this investigation for almost a year now. Local law enforcement has been involved for about two months. Surely, Mr. Barrone, you're aware of this."

"I'm aware that I've become a target of that investigation, that my reputation may be besmirched, my livelihood threatened," Barrone said firmly.

"Our investigation is continuing," Anderson said, "and I realize that I'm taking a risk by saying this, but so far there has been no indication of any involvement or wrongdoing on your part. Obviously, this inquiry will continue, but so far we have nothing that leads us to believe you're a part of this."

If Barrone felt any great sense of relief, that didn't show as well, I had to give that much to him; he kept his cool.

"I think the thing I'm most interested in, Sergeant," Barrone said, "is why you've chosen to tell me this."

Anderson turned to the lieutenant and the two made eye contact for a moment. Then Lieutenant Brickman gave the most subtle, almost imperceptible nod I'd ever seen and Anderson turned back to us.

"We have a situation, Mr. Barrone, in which a private detective licensed in the state of Tennessee shows up here out of nowhere, gets a job as a maintenance man at a brothel, and then winds up being the last man to see a murdered hooker alive."

"Next to last man," I interrupted.

"Excuse me," Anderson corrected himself. "Next to last man. And then this private detective—whom we are convinced did not come to Nevada to work because he's done nothing toward affiliating himself with a local licensed detective—"

"Thereby breaking the law," Lieutenant Brickman inserted.

"Thereby breaking the law," Anderson continued, "winds up getting one of the most high-powered attorneys in the state on his side when there is nothing to indicate this out-of-state detective is so well connected. And not only is his attorney prominent and high powered, he's also the man appointed by the Justice Department to oversee the financial affairs of the brothel where our mystery boy detective got his job in the first place. And this lawyer has himself become the subject of an investigation into possible illegal financial transactions at the brothel."

Anderson stopped, smiled at us across the table. "Now we have to ask ourselves some questions. Is this the most amazing set of coincidences since Sacco and Vanzetti, or is there something else at work here?"

"Like what?" Barrone asked after a few moments.

"Like the attorney has decided to conduct his own investigation—whether to find out the truth, cover his ass, or mislead us is yet to be determined—and has hired the mystery detective from back east to be his infiltrator into the operation of the Mustang Ranch."

All five of us sat there silently. I found myself biting my lower lip without even realizing it. It was only when I hit a nerve and a sharp pain shot through to my cheek that I relaxed.

"So far," Barrone said, "all you have is some interesting speculations."

"Well," Anderson said, glancing again at the lieutenant, "there is one other slight complication that muddies the situation even further."

"What might that be?" Barrone asked.

Anderson settled back in his chair and placed his hands on the table palms down.

"The prostitute at the Mustang Ranch, the murdered one who went by the name of Raven . . ."

"Yes?" Barrone asked again.

"She was *our* person on the inside," Anderson said flatly. "And now she's dead."

Chapter 20

Even Barrone seemed shocked by that one. As for me, I tried not to look too much like roadkill just before a truck slams into it, but I doubt I did a very good job of it.

"She worked for you?" Barrone asked.

Anderson nodded. "Yes, so you see, Mr. Barrone, this takes an interesting little homicide case in a Nevada whorehouse and turns it into something entirely different."

Barrone inhaled deeply and silently and held it for a few seconds, then exhaled slowly. "And I would guess the kinds of questions you're asking yourself are along the lines of: Did Barrone hire Denton to kill the girl because he knew she was working for us? Or perhaps: Did someone else at the Mustang discover what the girl was up to and murder her, then set Denton up for the fall? Am I anywhere near tracking with you on this, gentlemen?"

Anderson smiled. "Amazingly close," he said. "This leaves us with a real dilemma."

"How?" I asked.

"How what?"

"How did you recruit her?" I demanded. "What did you have on her? She was a hooker, for Chrissakes, not a white-collar crime expert!"

"Yes, you're right," Lieutenant Brickman said. It was the first time he'd spoken, and his voice was low, even, polished, one-hundred-percent stone professional. "But the woman, Annie Rogers, had more than a passing familiarity with white-collar crime. In addition to charges of prostitution in several other states, she'd also been arrested for credit-card fraud, passing bad checks, and had even done eleven-twenty-nine in the workhouse back in Arkansas, I think it was."

"During which time"—Anderson picked up where his boss left off—"Ms. Rogers took advantage of the local inmate-education program. Know what courses she took?"

"Let me take a scientific, wild-assed guess," I said. "Computer courses."

"Give the man a *cee-gar*," Anderson said.

"So you found all this out," Barrone said, "and then you recruited her."

"Recruited is a nice word," Anderson said. "I like it. It sounds like some kind of executive-placement thing."

I turned to Barrone. "What Anderson means is that they had something on her," I said. "They brought her in here and put her tits in a wringer. Right, guys?"

"Given Ms. Rogers's sexual proclivities," Anderson said, "putting her tits in a wringer would hardly be a major inducement. However, when we ran background checks on all the employees at the Mustang, we discovered that Ms. Rogers had an outstanding warrant for felony check fraud in Arkansas. And with her previous record, both in and out of state, Ms. Rogers would have faced some serious time if somehow word had gotten back east and she was faced with extradition."

"So you guys were happy to use that in the recruiting package," I offered.

Anderson nodded. "Delighted, in fact. We thought we'd found the secret handshake."

"Yeah," I said. "The secret handshake that got her killed."

Anderson tried to stare me down. To hell with him, I thought.

"The bitch was a hooker," he said. "A sexual deviant and a petty, punk criminal. We were using her to get to something much bigger than she could ever be. She was expendable."

"She was a human being," I said angrily. "An intelligent, living, breathing human being who deserved better than she got."

Barrone stepped in. "Can we take this in another direction?" he asked. "How long had she worked for you?"

"Not long," Anderson said. "Certainly not long enough."

"So," Brickman said, "we've been upfront and square with you. Now we expect the same courtesy. Were you or were you not, Mr. Denton, hired by Mr. Barrone to work for him on the inside of the Mustang Ranch?"

I glanced at Barrone. He turned my way, raised an eyebrow, then nodded. I turned back to the three men across the table from me.

"Yes," I answered. "But on a very limited scale. Mr. Barrone was convinced that the way to discover the truth about any possible money laundering at the Mustang was to compare the numbers reported by Joey Fennelly every month with my survey of the number of customers."

"How far had you gotten with this?" Anderson asked.

"Not very," I answered. "I'd put some numbers together. As best we can figure, there's some significant washing going on there. But keep in mind that all I was doing was counting heads, so to speak, and cars. And I was about to finish up. When I told you guys I came out here to attend the birth of my daughter, I was telling you the truth. It's very easy to check out. Just go visit the expectant mother."

Anderson put his elbows on the table and folded his hands together. He wiggled his fingers loosely, then turned to Brickman. Brickman seemed to tilt his head slightly, as if the two were reading each other's minds. They continued their eye contact for another couple of seconds, then Anderson dropped his hands to the table with a loud whack.

"Okay," he announced. "We believe you. For now."

"Does that mean I can go?" I asked.

"Yes, certainly, Mr. Denton," he said. "On one condition."

Barrone's eyes narrowed. "And what is that?"

"That you go back to your job at the Mustang Ranch and take up where Annie Rogers left off."

For a moment I thought I could hear my own heartbeat. I stared at Anderson for a couple of seconds; his facial expression never changed.

"You're serious," I said.

"As a heart attack."

"You're out of your mind. There's no way I can go back there now."

"Why not?" Anderson asked.

"Because you guys pulled me in here. I've been questioned about a murder! I can't go back. What good could I do? They'll be watching me like a hawk."

"Those are all weak excuses, Harry," Anderson said. "You're in a very good position to find out what the hooker had. The last time we communicated with her, she told us she'd discovered two sets of books maintained on the computers at the Mustang. She'd made backups of the real set of books. We want those files."

I shook my head. "I don't even know what I'd be looking for."

"A black three-and-a-half-inch disk," Anderson said. "Probably just one, maybe two at the most. She probably hid it somewhere at the Mustang. As the maintenance man, you'd have access to the whole place."

I shook my head even harder. "My ex-girlfriend is having a baby in a couple of days. That's where I have to be, not at the Mustang Ranch."

Anderson smiled. "You're incredibly wrong on that point, Harry. If you have to take a couple of days off as paternal maternity leave, that's okay. But you're not quitting that job."

"I just did," I said, determined.

Brickman said, "Mr. Barrone, perhaps you should explain to your client what might happen in the event we are unable to obtain his cooperation."

I turned to the older man. "Just what the hell is that supposed to mean?"

Barrone reached out and laid his hand on my forearm. "Let me handle this," he whispered.

Anderson leaned forward. "Right now, Mr. Barrone, your client is under suspicion of having murdered one Annie Rogers, an adult, legal resident of Storey County, Nevada. He has also admitted to working as a private investigator in the state of Nevada without a license, which is a misdemeanor."

"This is bullshit," I spat. Barrone squeezed my arm tighter.

"We can take him into custody right now and hold him as a suspect for seventy-two hours, during which time we can proceed with misdemeanor charges. Ordinarily a

judge would not hold someone charged with a misdemeanor, but with everything else, we can tie you up
in paper for days, maybe even weeks. When the bond
hearing comes up, we will, of course, ask for a high dollar
amount as Mr. Denton is a clear flight risk."

"The Storey County jail is overcrowded by at least a
couple hundred inmates," Bouvier said. "Guy like you'd
be real uncomfortable in there."

"And who knows what the forensics lab will turn up,"
Anderson continued. "I mean, we've told you we don't
think there's enough to charge you with murder right
now . . ."

Anderson paused. Brickman finished the sentence for
him. "But that could change."

"And then, of course, you'd completely miss the birth
of your child," Anderson said, finishing me off.

I turned to Barrone. "This sucks, Jacques," I said. "I
didn't sign on for this horseshit."

Barrone turned to me, leaned in close. "I know you're
upset, Harry," he whispered, "but I'm seeing a limited
range of options here."

"You want me to do what these jokers want?" I demanded, my voice louder than it should have been.

He pulled on my arm. I turned around in my chair.
"Harry, look—"

"No, you look," I hissed. "First of all, if they killed
Annie, that means they won't mind doing the same to me
or anybody else who gets in their way. I'm not getting
paid to take those kinds of risks. Second, how do we
know that when they killed Annie they didn't find the
disk she was hiding? Maybe there isn't a disk. Maybe I
can't find it. These jerks here could keep me working at
the Mustang for weeks, months. Hell, the rest of my
life."

"We can negotiate the terms of the deal," Barrone

said, his voice above a whisper, but still low. "But the deal is going to happen."

I decided that it was time for me to get in touch with my inner wounded bitch. "You know, I'm really getting to dislike you people."

Barrone held my gaze for a moment. "I'm sorry for that, Harry," he said, "but we'll get over it. So will you."

"Fuck you," I said, turning back to the table. "Let's hope so."

A Reno P.D. patrol officer drove me back across the county line to the Mustang exit off I-80, then dropped me in the gravel parking lot of a run-down saloon on the other side of the freeway. I walked into the place, ordered a Coke, got a weird look from the cranky old guy smoking a green cigar behind the bar, and sat down near one of the pool tables in the center of the room. About ten minutes later a Storey County Sheriff's Department cruiser pulled up outside and a deputy drove me back to the Mustang.

The deputy left me off at the gate, then pulled away without saying a word. There were four other cars in the lot, and across from me the blond in the souvenir van peeked over the top of her *National Enquirer*. I rang the bell using the employee's code and, a few steps later, opened the front door and confronted Mabel Weyrich.

"Didn't expect to see you back here," she said. "Figured you'd be in lockup by now."

I was in no mood to take crap off this lady. "They cleared me," I said. "I'm off the hook for Raven. I decided to come back to work, that is if I've still got the job. You want to fire me, do it. But don't give me any shit. I've had a bad day."

It was the first time I'd ever talked back to Mabel and I

was more than halfway hoping that she'd can me on the spot. Instead she stared at me as if this were the first time she'd ever seen me.

"So what's it going to be?" I asked. "Do I clock in or go home?"

"Clock in," she said. "Then get back to the kitchen. Miss Mary says one of the seals on the freezer is peeling off."

"Right," I said, walking past her and into the tiny computer room.

"Damn," I whispered under my breath as I typed in my user name and password. I hated this place, hated this job, hated this gig, hated the cops, hated Barrone. Suddenly, everything felt like it was closing in on me. Or I was going to explode. Or both.

The door to the computer room opened and Aphrodite, the black hooker who could've played linebacker for the Rams, stepped in.

"Yo," she said, "what da fug you doin' back here? Thought they took yo skinny white ass off to jail."

I turned to her as she sat down at the workstation next to me. "Nice to see you, too," I said.

Out of the corner of my eye, I saw her punch in a user name and password, although I couldn't tell what they were, and then a different screen from the one I used came up. This was the screen in which the girls entered the service they performed, the time of day, the billing code, and the amount plus tip. This would have been the screen that Annie had access to as she filed the services she performed as Raven.

"Too bad about her, huh?" Aphrodite said.

I turned to her. "What do you mean?"

Aphrodite swiveled the chair toward me. "I mean about Raven, man. It's too bad about her."

I finished clocking in and then clicked the mouse to exit.

"Aphrodite, what do you think happened?" I asked.

"What the fug you care for?"

"Raven was cool," I said. "I liked her. She was good people. Kind of hard for me to imagine someone would want to kill her."

She turned to me, a wide smirk on her face. "Then you ain't imaginin' hard enough."

"What's that supposed to mean?"

She swiveled on the chair and faced me. "Raven had a attitude, man. Look, you want to get along here, you gots to go along. And Raven wouldn't go along."

"Aphrodite," I said, lowering my voice, "what's that mean? What do you have to do here to get along?"

"You start by doing what you're told, whether you like it or not. Boss wants a cup of coffee, you get it for him. Boss wants anything else, you give him that, too. Same's it's always been, Harry. Meet da new boss, same's da old boss."

"And Raven thought she didn't have to play by those rules, right?"

"I got to go back to work, keep my damn mouth shut."

"You think it had anything to do with the kinds of services she provided?"

Aphrodite studied me for a couple of seconds, then shrugged. "Beats me," she said. "I know Raven was into some kinky shit, but that ain't no big deal here. Nothing to get killed over."

"You think a customer might have—"

"Hell, no," Aphrodite said. "Ain't no way a customer could have done this, then got away with it. I mean, we got too much security and shit here."

"Security," I said. "What security? Smiley?"

She flashed me a wide, toothy grin of large even white teeth punctuated by a gold star embedded in the center upper tooth. "Shit, Harry, you just get in off the bus?"

Then she broke into a muted song: "Smile, you're on *Candid Cah-mer-ah*!"

Apparently, my face registered shock without my even being aware of it. "What's the matter, big boy? You too shy to do it for the cameras?"

My eyes widened. "You're shittin' me," I said. "Cameras? Is everything taped?"

"I doubt it," Aphrodite said. "Where would you keep that much tape? Naw, it's just video monitors. They got a set in Mabel's office and I heard Goumba Joey's got monitors in his office as well. Who knows, maybe he gets off on it."

I looked around, suddenly paranoid. "Is this room monitored?" I whispered.

She laughed. "I have no idea, Harry. But there ain't no need to worry about it. Just don't do nothing you don't mind anybody else seeing."

The door opened and Mabel stuck her head in, scowling. "Let's go, girls," she snapped. "How long does it take to fill out a time sheet?"

I looked back at her and somehow managed to hold my tongue. Aphrodite laughed and stood, then squeezed my shoulder as she walked past me out of the narrow room. I stood and followed her.

As I walked through the main-entrance foyer, down the hall past the bar, the hot tub room, and the room once occupied by Raven, I thought about the video-monitoring system at the Mustang. I wondered if the customers knew they were being watched as they engaged in whatever pleasures they'd come to the Mustang in search of. I wondered who had been watching as

Raven and I sat in her room talking the night she rescued me from my dripping-wet clothes.

But mostly I wondered who had been watching the video monitors when somebody at the Mustang Ranch murdered Annie Rogers.

Chapter 21 _____

The knowledge that practically every room in the Mustang Ranch was under the close eye of a video monitoring system drove me to new, undiscovered heights of paranoia.

Or was it depths? Hell, at this point, I didn't know and it didn't really matter.

This opened up a new way to look at things, an entirely new approach to the whole series of events. For one thing, I'd gotten no indication from the police that they were aware of a monitoring system. Maybe they knew and hadn't told me about it, which was possible. Sometimes I think the only difference between the good guys and the bad guys is that the good guys get to carry badges and they generally smell better.

On the other hand, if the police knew of the video system, then why hadn't they torn the damn place down to find it? Aphrodite'd said there weren't tapes, but she could be wrong.

Or she could be lying. But why would she lie to me?

Unless somebody had put her up to it . . .

But who?

Damn, I was getting paranoid.

Hold on, back up, I thought. Let's just assume that the police didn't know about the video-monitoring system. They'd searched the actual crime scene at the Mustang and they'd gone through Raven's room. But they hadn't torn the place apart, and if Mabel and Goumba Joey didn't volunteer that the joint was just jumping with video cameras, then there was no reason to assume the cops knew.

Goumba Joey and Mabel, on the other hand, had every reason in the world not to say anything about the cameras. Can you imagine the headlines in *USA Today*? Can you imagine what Jerry Springer and Sally Jessy and Oprah and Roseanne would have to say about this? Imagine what this would do to Jay Leno's monologues. And the lawyers; good God, let's not forget the lawyers. The potential for invasion of privacy lawsuits on behalf of the Mustang's client list would be a legal Blue Light Special.

The only downside, I thought, would be getting the Mustang to actually pay the judgments.

"What you laughing at?"

I looked up from where I was kneeling on the floor in front of the freezer. Miss Mary stood a couple of feet away from me, staring down with her hands on her hips.

"Pardon?" I said.

"You chuckling like you the cat that done swallowed the mouse and don't nobody know it yet."

I looked back down. "Sorry," I said. "I was just thinking about something and it made me laugh."

"Well, you better fix that seal 'cause if any of this food spoils, Mr. Joey ain't going to be laughing. And won't none of us like that."

"Got you, Miss Mary," I said, pulling out a pair of needle-nose pliers. I'd taken my time getting back to work. There was some cleanup to be done in the toolshed and then a work order to be filled out for the kitchen. I was tired, preoccupied, still trying to figure this mess out. I managed to goof off for about an hour and a half before actually starting to fix Miss Mary's freezer.

As it turned out, it was a pretty easy fix. The metal clips that held the seal in place had been pulled apart over time and come loose. All I had to do was pry them back into their original shape, then pop the seal back on the door and we'd be cool for another six months.

I washed down the seal with some disinfectant and was gathering my tools up when my pager went off. I fumbled to get my tool belt moved out of the way so that I could see the number, thinking all the while that here we go, it's off to the hospital and maternityland. Only it wasn't Marsha's number at Aunt Marty's house. I looked down, didn't recognize the number at first, then it came to me.

It was Kelly.

"Okay," I whispered. "So the day ain't a total loss."

I gathered up the last of my tools and headed out to the toolshed in back. I pulled off my tool belt and hung it on a large nail over the workbench, then sat down and filled out the rest of the work order and filed it away. I picked up the phone and dialed 9 to get an outside line, then punched in the access number for my long-distance carrier, followed by my account number, my PIN, and then Kelly's number off the pager.

She answered on the third ring. "Hello."

"It's me," I said, smiling. "I got your page. It made my day."

"Harry, where are you?" she asked quickly.

"I'm still in Reno. Where'd you think I'd be?"

"You're not in jail?"

The smile went away and I felt my gut spasm, like the time I got ahold of bad Thai spring rolls back home. "What? Why would I be in jail?"

"Why didn't you tell me you were working at the

Mustang Ranch?" she demanded, concern segueing into anger.

"Kelly, what are you talking about?"

"It's on the local news," she said.

"Great," I snapped. "This is perfect. Just perfect."

"You didn't answer my question."

"It's not what you think," I said, tense and angry myself now. "What did they say on the news?"

She hesitated. "Listen, I'm sorry I called."

"Kelly, don't do this to me. Don't hang up. You've got to tell me what they're saying. It's important."

"They showed you being led away in handcuffs, Harry. They interviewed some guy at the Mustang Ranch who said you were on parole from Tennessee, that you were an ex-con, that you were the prime suspect in the murder of a . . . a—"

I heard a snuffling noise over the line, like she was trying to choke back a sob.

"—a, Jesus, Harry, a *prostitute*!"

"Great," I whispered, repeating myself. "Just great."

This sucked on several different levels. First of all, if some bottom-feeding, scum-sucking newshound went back and did some checking and found out that the Tennessee Department of Corrections didn't have a file on me, then my cover's blown and I was screwed. Second, if this went out any farther than locally, then God knew how many of my friends and family were going to see it. I was a little marginal in some of their eyes these days anyway. And let's not even mention the reception that's waiting for me back at Aunt Marty's. Marsha may have been pregnant and bedridden, but she was not any less dangerous as a result.

But the worst right now was what Kelly must be thinking about me. I meet somebody I really like, who seems to like me, and the next thing you know she thinks I work in a whorehouse and kill hookers.

"Listen, Kelly, I know this looks bad. It looks real bad, but please just listen. This is not what it appears. There's a lot more to this than what you're hearing on the news. If you can figure out some way to trust me on this—"

"Then what is going on, Harry? Just tell me. I'll understand and I'll trust you."

I'd already said too much and I knew it. If Goumba Joey had the place wired for video, he wouldn't think twice about tapping a phone line. For all I knew, he was listening to every word.

"I can't talk right now, Kelly." I looked at my watch. It was a few minutes after five. The news story Kelly'd seen must have been the lead item.

"Why? Why can't you?"

"I just can't," I snapped. "Look, I'll call you in a half hour, okay? Just let me get to a pay phone. Will you do that? Will you wait for me to call you?"

There was a long silence from the other end of the line. "I've got to drive to Ely. I'm working the night shift on the flight line. I'll be here about another hour. You can call if you want to."

"Yes," I said. "Yes, of course I want to. Just sit tight and give me a little time, okay?"

More silence.

"Okay, Kelly? Please?"

"All right, Harry. You got one chance to talk your way out of this one."

"If that's the best I can do with you," I said, "I'll take it."

I hung up the phone. One chance to talk my way out of this one.

Wondered what the hell I was going to say to her.

*   *   *

"For Chrissakes, kid," Jake said, opening the door and letting me into his basement apartment. "I watched it on the news tonight. You ain't even going to be able to go into a grocery store."

"You should've been there in person," I said. "It was just a little jaunt to Disneyland."

It was the first time I'd seen Jake in days, what with my putting in all that overtime at the Mustang. I crossed the apartment, sat down in his chair, and grabbed the phone.

"What've the cops got on you?" he demanded, parking himself on the edge of the bed.

"Nothing," I said, dialing the series of numbers to get Kelly back on the phone. "Not a damn thing. But they've got me roped into working for them now."

"What?" Jake yelped.

"It's a long story," I said with the phone to my ear. "I'll go into it later. Just let me make a call real quick."

"Whatever, kid," he said. "Listen, it's cocktail hour. Want me to roll you a drink?"

"I'll pass. You got a cold beer, though, I'll go for that," I said as Kelly picked up the phone.

"Hey," I said before she could say anything. "Look, I couldn't talk earlier. I'm sorry."

"Just tell me what's going on, Harry."

I took a deep breath and held it for a second. I'd thought about what to tell her all the way to Jake's, and I thought I could give her the quick, down-and-dirty version and hope she was willing to live with that until I could explain it in person.

"This is the deal, Kelly. A friend of Marsha's aunt is a lawyer who's been appointed to oversee the Mustang Ranch since it was seized by the feds, only the people who work at the ranch are involved in some very shady financial doings, and the lawyer asked me as a personal favor to sort of go undercover and check some things out for him. And now it's kind of gotten out of hand. But please, Kel, believe me. I didn't kill anybody, I'm not an ex-con, and I wouldn't be caught dead in a brothel if it wasn't part of my work as a private detective. Honest."

There, got it all out in one breath. Okay, I thought, that's it. The next sentence out of her mouth will tell me which way the wind's going to blow.

"Oh, Harry." She sighed, her own breath escaping in relief. "What are we going to do with you?"

I raised my fists to the ceiling, looked up, grinned, and mouthed the word *Yes!* Over by the dorm-size refrigerator, Shaky Jake mimed tipping his hat to me with a skinny joint in one hand and a cold beer bottle in the other.

"You believe me!"

"Yes, I believe you," she said. "Nobody could make up a story like that. It's too insane."

"You should see it from my side of the fence," I said. "It's been crazy. But look, Kelly, as long as you believe I'm telling the truth, it doesn't matter what anybody else thinks."

"Why, Harry?" she asked. "Why does it matter to you that I think you're a good guy?"

"It just does," I said, "and that's the best answer I can come up with right now. But we'll talk about it soon, all right?"

"Yes," she said. "I'd like to see you again, you wild man, you."

I laughed. "I'd like that, too. Soon."

"When?" she asked.

"The baby's due any day," I answered. "And I'm going to get out of this gig as soon as I can. I just want all this behind me. Maybe I'll pick up a car here in Reno and drive it home. I could stop off in Eureka."

"This time," she said. "In the car?"

"Yeah?"

"Water and blankets," we said in unison.

"So did you know her?" I asked Jake as I settled into the chair with the beer he'd handed me.

"Naw," Jake said, relighting his evening doobie and taking a long hit off it. He held the smoke in his lungs, then talked as he exhaled through his mouth, his words causing the smoke to erupt in short, sharp puffs. "Naw, I just used to see her around, you know. I ain't into that stuff she sold. Ya ask me, pain's over here"—he pointed one way with his right hand—"and pleasure's way over there." He pointed to the far left wall. "And the two don't come anywhere near meeting in the middle. I don't have no trouble telling one from the other."

"Me either," I said, swallowing a sip of cold beer. "It ain't my cup of tea, but you know what they say. Different strokes . . ."

I'd spent the previous fifteen minutes after getting off the phone with Kelly bringing Jake up to speed on my day at the Reno P.D. He hadn't talked to Barrone, didn't know what was going on. He was shocked to discover that Raven had been undercover for the Reno P.D. and she was supposed to have hacked into the computer system for them.

"This was one multitalented lady," he said. "She could probably spank your bare bottom and debug your Windows 98 at the same time."

I laughed. "Can you imagine what her fee structure must have been like?"

"Not to mention her bone structure," Jake said.

I didn't know what the hell that meant, but I was in too good a mood to worry about it.

"And you know," he said, "now that I know about all those video monitors, I don't think I'm ever going to feel the same way about being a customer at the Mustang Ranch."

I took another sip off the beer and stared at Jake for a few moments. "So," I said. "What's it like?"

"What's what like?"

"Paying for it," I said. "Paying for sex. I've never done it. Don't think I'd ever want to. Just curious, though. What's it like?"

Shaky Jake let out another continuous column of smoke, emptying his lungs with a satisfied smile. "You poor dumb fool," he said, chuckling.

"What?" I felt my forehead tighten up.

"Never paid for sex." He pointed a finger at me. "Son, let me tell you, you've paid for every piece of ass you've ever had in your life. Paid through the nose for it. You should be so lucky as to have only had to pay cash."

"That's a lousy attitude," I said.

"Well," he answered, leaning over and flicking his ashes into the sink, "it's the only one I've got. After all these years, guess I'm stuck with it."

Chapter 22

I had one more beer with Jake, then turned down his dinner invitation. He had a couple of coupons that would've gotten us the dinner buffet at Fitzgerald's for $6.95, but I just wasn't in the mood for bright lights and noise and clanging bells and people having fun. The last couple of days, my own personal Ronco Stress-O-Matic had been running constantly and it was time to let it cool off before it overheated big time. I was headed up the mountain to face whatever music had to be faced with Marsha, then dinner, a little television, and bed. I was exhausted and had to be back at the Mustang first thing in the morning.

Estella's eyes widened as I walked in the back door. "Señor Harry," she said, "you on TV."

"I know," I said wearily. "It's been a long day. Does Marsha know?"

"*Sí,*" she said quietly.

"How is she today?"

Estella shook her head back and forth. "Dr. Marsha very tired. She maybe sleep."

I nodded. "I'll look in on her," I said. "Then I'll get a shower. Any chance of a sandwich or something?"

Estella's face softened. "I fix you something. You get cleaned up."

I walked upstairs quietly, trying not to make any noise.

I paused at Marsha's door, started to knock, then decided to peek in. The door swung open a crack when I turned the doorknob. The lights were down low, the television on but muted. Marsha was lying there like a series of hills on the horizon, the blue comforter thrown over her pulled into valleys and ridges, peaks and rounds, with alternating lights and shadows. Her chest rose and fell softly, easily, as she breathed.

I turned, my hand still on the doorknob. "So," she said. I stopped and looked back at her.

"You're in it again, aren't you?" she whispered.

I opened the door all the way and stepped over to the bed. "Hi," I said.

A weak smile crossed her face. "How bad is it this time?"

"Not very," I said. "Somebody was killed at the Mustang last night after I left. The cops questioned me—"

"I saw the news," she said firmly, her voice stronger and louder.

"And now I'm back here with you," I said. "They released me. No evidence. I'm innocent. It's over."

"It's never going to be over with you, Harry. After this one there'll be another one and another one and another until one day you get in it so deep, you won't be able to get out."

I stood for a few moments, looking down at her, not knowing what to say.

"Why don't we quit talking about me," I said. "How're you? How's that baby?"

"Quiet now," Marsha said, as if it were the first time all day. "She's very active. Wants to come into the world."

"She will soon," I offered. "It won't be long."

"Are you going to be there?"

"Wouldn't miss it."

"It's going to be pretty messy," she said. "You got a weak stomach?"

"Most men have weak stomachs," I said, smiling. "But when it's important, we manage."

Marsha looked away, out the window into the deepening blackness outside. "Wish that were true," she said.

"Marsh, we've got to reach some kind of peace together. I don't want our daughter to think we hate each other. Because that's not true, at least not from my side."

"I don't hate you either, Harry. Sometimes things work out. Sometimes they don't."

"I want to be here for you, for the baby. Just let me do that, then I'll go back home and be out of your way. Okay?"

She rolled her head over on the pillow and gazed at me with eyes that seemed darker and set deep in her head above dark purple smudges. I saw in those eyes a loss that I didn't know how to fix, didn't know how to make better.

"If it weren't okay, I wouldn't have asked you here."

I knelt down on the bed next to her and took her left hand in mine. I turned her hand over and unfolded it, then gently rubbed the palm of her hand with my two thumbs.

"Would it help anything if I quit?" I asked. "If I just gave the whole thing up and never did that kind of work again?"

Her hand stiffened and she pulled it away from me. "You'd still be you, Harry. You'd still be trying to fill that empty place inside you, and sooner or later you'd explode. You're no house hubby, babe. Forget it."

"I can find something else to do," I said.

"What, sell insurance? Real estate? Become an accountant, a P.R. flack? Is that what you want?"

"I don't know what you want from me," I said.

"It's not a question of what I want from you," she said. "It's a question of what you want. And what worries me the most is that you get what you want. You always get what you want, Harry. And what you want is to live on the edge. That's really it, isn't it?"

"Just because I'm not suited for coat-and-tie work anymore doesn't mean I can't find something else to do if it meant we could bring our daughter up in a real . . ." I stopped.

After a few moments, she said: "A real what?"

"A real home," I answered.

Her jaw tensed. "I *am* going to bring up our daughter in a real home."

"I didn't mean it like that," I said. "I'd just be willing to give up my work if that meant we could give her something together."

Her head settled onto the pillow, the flesh of her face going limp, almost melting around her bones. "She'll be fine, Harry. And so will we."

"Will we?" I asked.

"I'm tired now," Marsha answered. "Think I'll sleep for a while."

The next morning Marsha was well enough to sit up in bed and eat a little breakfast. I made her and Estella both promise to page me if it even looked like she was about to go into labor. We set up a code: If it was labor and they were on their way to the hospital, they'd punch in a series of nines. If there was time for me to come home first, there'd be a series of threes. If it was anything else, they'd just punch in the number and I'd call when I got a chance.

But Marsha said she didn't feel like it was going to happen today, and the doctor had said they were going to give her through Sunday before inducing labor. I didn't understand much of this but figured that since Marsha was both a doctor and a woman, she could probably make up for my ignorance.

I'd slept fitfully that night, partly as a result of Estella's black bean casserole and a couple of glasses of wine and partly because I couldn't turn my brain off. I kept thinking of Raven and my last conversation with her and trying to imagine what it must have been like for her as she lay in bed after I left, thinking that the evening was over for her and she could fade into sleep, and then the door opening, surprising her, and then a little more time passing until her sudden realization that what was happening was not good. And there would have been that initial shock of fear and denial, that moment when the loud inner voice thinks, *This can't be happening!* and then the panic and fear as her murderer grabs her around the throat and the struggles begin and then the moment when she first sees that her killer has her outstrengthed, outmaneuvered, and the futile grappling, the desperate, horrible panicked exertion and gasping for air, followed by the tingling in her limbs and her throat, the gradual loss of feeling and sight as the optic nerve and brain are starved for oxygen.

Then the plunge into black . . .

I wondered what she'd seen. Had the final image imprinted on her brain been the eyes of her murderer—the look of glee or anger or revenge or the coldness of someone simply doing a job—or was there something else? A blinding white light at the end of the well, the tunnel, that gave way to the opening arms of a long-lost loved one. Perhaps a grandparent, someone who had loved her as a child, one of the few who had treated her with kindness and gentleness before the evil of the world had turned her into the kind of person who would sell her body and soul for drugs and cash to the highest bidder.

I pulled to a stop sign at the Mount Rose highway and took a long sip off the travel mug of hot coffee Estella had fixed and handed to me as I walked out the door. Her concern and kindness was a contrast to the way I felt about the world today.

Damn, humans are savage.

Saturday morning at the Mustang Ranch was traditionally a busier time than one would think. Maybe it was the large number of customers who had commitments elsewhere on Friday night—husbands dining with wives at the country club or favorite restaurants or cowboys taking their girlfriends line dancing. And the next morning: "Dear, I'm going to run a few errands downtown," or "Honey, I'm going into the office for a few hours, but the switchboard's closed so you can't call me."

I came into work Saturday morning and had trouble finding a parking space. I had to park on the other side of the souvenir van. Mabel was waiting at the front door when I pushed it open.

"You're late," she said.

"Dock me," I shot back at her.

"Don't worry, I will." She followed me into the computer room, where I typed my name and password and clocked in.

"You're going to get some overtime today," Mabel announced. "I want you to clean out Raven's room. I want her stuff out of there and carried over to one of the trailers and stored. Then get back here and paint her room. We've got another girl coming in tonight. I want the room ready by eight. There's a big convention in town and we're expecting a crowd. Got it?"

I turned to her and scowled. "Damn it, Mabel, can't you get somebody in here to help me?"

"Deal with it, Harry," she instructed. "It's your reality du jour."

"What about Gary?"

"Gary doesn't do maintenance," Mabel said. "He's a manager."

"From what I can tell," I said, standing and pushing past her, "Gary doesn't do much of anything."

"Hey," she barked to the back of my head. "That's my boy you're talking about."

Something in the tone of her voice let me know that I was borderline copping too much of an attitude with her. You could push Mabel only so far before she got seriously ugly on you. And I didn't want that right now. As much as I resented having to be here, her orders gave me the perfect excuse to search Raven's room.

"Okay," I said, without turning around. "Fine. All right. I'm going to the supply room and dig up some boxes to load Raven's stuff in."

I could hear her breathing in short rasps behind me. I turned, looked at her. She was old and mean and gristly, and I'd had enough of tangling with her.

"That okay?" I asked in as supplicating a fashion as I could muster.

"Go," she ordered. "And stay out of my way today. I've had about as much of your mouth as I'm going to put up with."

"Yes, ma'am," I said, walking off.

The supply room was in a little alcove off to the right of the kitchen, just to one side of the small porch that served as a freight dock for the Mustang. The restaurant supplies, linens, and other laundry, as well as the cleaning supplies and maintenance items, were all delivered through the back porch.

Miss Mary was at the stove stirring a big pot of something that smelled delicious as I passed through.

"You hungry, Harry?" she called as I went by. The kitchen and lounge were empty except for the two of us; guess all the girls were otherwise engaged.

"I wasn't till I walked in here," I said, stopping and looking over her shoulder. "Damn, what is that?"

She turned and bumped me with her shoulder. "Watch your mouth, boy, 'fore I have to whup you."

I laughed.

"What you laughing at?" she demanded in mock anger.

"Just the thought of being told to watch your mouth in a whorehouse," I said.

Miss Mary shrieked. "Oh, you are so bad, bad! You so bad!"

"What is that, stew or something?" I leaned over, trying to see into the pot.

"Listen to you," she said. "Stew, my eye. This is my famous Delta chili."

I patted Miss Mary on the shoulder. She was one of the few people around here I was going to miss. "If it's as good as it smells," I said, "then, yes, I want it. All of it. I don't know what everybody else is going to eat."

She giggled, embarrassed. "Boy, you'd talk a nun out of her drawers."

"That's me," I said, walking away. "Mr. Charm."

I pulled my key ring out of my pocket and found the key to the storage room. I'd been issued keys to the storeroom and the workshed, the laundry room and the electrical room, but none to any of the other rooms, including Joey's and Mabel's offices. That was a problem I was eventually going to have to work my way around.

Inside the storage room, I found a stack of broken-down boxes that hadn't been recycled yet. I pulled out a half-dozen of the ones in the best shape and carried them down to Raven's room. The yellow crime-scene tape had been removed and the door left unlocked. I touched the doorknob and felt something gritty. I held my hand up; residue from the fingerprint powder left a black smudge. I wiped it quickly on the leg of my jeans.

I opened the door, reached in, and switched on the overhead light. It was an understatement to say that it felt a bit weird being back in Raven's room, but I tried to put it out of my mind. I looked around: the room was pretty much a mess. The sheets and pillowcases had been stripped off her bed, along with the plastic cover that protected the mattress from bodily fluids and God knew what else. I guess the crime-lab techs had bagged those up yesterday, which seemed so long ago now.

There was black fingerprint-powder residue on the windowsill, the interior doorknob, and on the posts of her bed. I set the boxes down on the bare mattress, then gave a cursory examination to the rest of the room. I could tell the walk-in closet had been searched, but Raven's belongings were not in as much disarray as I would have expected. Other than powder residue on the sink faucets and the toilet handle, the bathroom was largely undisturbed.

The room was deathly quiet and still, with dust already beginning to settle on the unused furniture. A chill tickled the nape of my neck and I squirmed around a bit, trying to shake the tension out of my neck and shoulders.

I thought for a few moments. There were two ways to approach this: search everything as I packed it or box it all up, get it over to the storage trailer, then search it off premises. The advantage of doing it offsite was that I'd be out from under the Mustang's video surveillance system. But if I waited until I got to the trailer, that might take too long. If I was gone too long, at the very least I'd raise some suspicions; at the very worst, I'd get another tongue-lashing from Mabel.

I looked around the room again. If I just knew where the camera was, I could at least try to stay out of its way. My eyes scanned the ceiling, the molding. Surely the center of the camera's view would be the bed. I walked over by the head of the bed, turned, and faced the opposite wall. There were no paintings or pieces of art or anything else to camouflage a hole in the wall that would accommodate a camera lens. Just below the ceiling molding was a thin, perhaps three-inch strip of decorative wallpaper border that ran all the way around the room. Raven's room was painted a dark lilac and the wallpaper border consisted of a Victorian pattern of flowers and vines interwoven in a complex design. I studied the border as if trying to figure out how I was going to paint around it. My eyes went back and forth, struggling in ways they hadn't had to even five years ago. The price of surviving into middle age . . .

And then I saw it.

I looked away quickly, not wanting to stare directly into the lens. I busied myself moving a couple of furniture pieces away from the wall, glancing back over my shoulder at the area in the wallpaper where I'd seen the tiny black hole that was almost completely hidden by the painted shadow of a vine on the dark paper.

That was it, though. I checked it several times, from several different angles, and I could see that what they had done was go into the attic and bore a hole at an angle down into the wall just below the molding, then mounted the camera in the attic and papered over the hole to disguise it.

I walked out of the room and down the hall toward the back door. "Damn clever," I whispered.

I picked up my tool belt, a two-inch roll of strapping tape, and a box opener, then came back in, walked past the bar and the entrance area and down the hall to Mabel's office. I knocked twice on the closed door.

"Yeah?" she grumbled.

"Harry here, Mabel. What color you want Raven's room painted?"

"There's five gallons of Etruscan Red in the store-room," she called through the door. "Use that."

"Okay, but I'll have to tear down that border at the ceiling."

Suddenly, there was a scramble from inside her office, the sound of a cabinet being shut and a chair being jerked out from under a desk, then footsteps.

"No," she snapped, opening the door. "Leave the border alone. We don't have anything to replace it with."

"Yeah," I said amiably, adding just a lilt of Tennessee drawl to my voice, "but it ain't going to match."

"What are you, an interior decorator?" she demanded.

"No, it's just—"

"Just do what I tell you. You got that?"

I shrugged. "I could paint over it if you want."

Her voice went down about half an octave. "Leave the border alone, damn it. Mask it off and paint below it. Just like I told you. Understand?"

I nodded and smiled. "Yes, ma'am," I said. "Got you."

She slammed the door in my face. I grinned, turned around, and headed back to Raven's room. I'd been right about the camera.

I liked being right for once.

Chapter 23

I started with Raven's closet, since that and the bathroom were the only two places in the room where I could be reasonably sure I was not under video surveillance. Okay, if somebody was really twisted, he or she could monitor the bathroom. But a walk-in closet? What's the point?

A bare bulb hung down from the center of the ceiling. I pulled the string and the harsh light flashed on. I turned away, squinting, and studied the closet. Raven had been into the leather/dominatrix scene and she'd certainly liked to dress the part. Several leather catsuits in different colors—red, black, purple—hung from padded-satin coat hangers. There were also leather coats, leather pants, and a cherry-red leather vest with gold snaps. Also bustiers and capes and sheer robes. There were also some civilian clothes: blouses and slacks, pairs of faded jeans, several flannel shirts, a velour bathrobe.

Anderson had told me that I should probably look for a 3.5-inch floppy, the kind now available in grocery stores or drugstores everywhere. Something that small could be hidden in a hundred places, with no guarantee that Raven hadn't stashed it away somewhere else at the Mustang. But it made sense that she would keep it near her, to cut down on the risk of someone else accidentally coming across it, and hide it as well as she could. I'd have to search carefully.

In a weird sort of way, which I can't quite explain, I also felt that I owed it to Annie/Raven to treat her belongings with at least a bit of respect, which God knows she got little enough of in life. I don't know why it meant something to me to carefully examine each article as it came off the hanger, then fold it neatly and place it in the box. Maybe she had family somewhere and maybe somebody at the Mustang would take the time to track them down. Perhaps someday they'd come for the stuff she'd left behind. If so, the least I could do for her was have all her things in some kind of order.

I went through the leather suits and clothes, working quickly but thoroughly, and found nothing. I'd filled up five medium-size boxes of clothes without finding anything. Annie was obsessively neat, I discovered. There wasn't a single business card or a crumpled tissue or even a matchbook in her clothes. The pockets were all empty, the hems intact; no secret compartments or pockets or chambers to be found anywhere.

I taped together several more boxes and went back into the closet. I finished the last of her clothes, then started boxing up the thirty or so pairs of shoes. Annie had small feet; there was no way something as wide as a floppy could be hidden inside a shoe. But I checked them all anyway.

There were maybe a dozen small white boxes on the shelves, the kind used as gift boxes for shirts or blouses. I went through each one, unfolding the article of clothing, feeling for something, then examining each visually. Finally, I refolded it neatly into its box, then stacked the boxes together.

The last things to get boxed up hung from racks mounted on the narrow right-side wall of the closet.

They were the tools of her trade, I guess you'd call them: whips, handcuffs, blindfolds, a short chrome chain with an alligator clip on each end, a spiked dog collar lined with fur. Just the usual stuff available in most suburban households in the Nineties . . .

Then I examined the interior of the closet, searching for a hidden compartment in the drywall, something taped to the underside of a shelf, or a piece of flooring that had been pried loose and then replaced.

Nothing.

I spent nearly an hour inside the closet with no success. I'm sure that when Mabel told me to clean out the room, she meant for me to get rid of everything in the fastest, most efficient way possible. I didn't have all the time in the world.

Next, I stepped into the bathroom. Each room had a private bathroom that became a kind of sanctuary for the woman. Customers weren't allowed in there and I imagined most of the girls stuck to that rule. When you're in the business they're in, there's got to be a certain amount of hygienic housekeeping that has to be done on a regular basis. Well-kept bodies in this business tend to be high maintenance.

Annie was no exception. I packed one medium-size box with nothing but makeup, most of it leaning toward the theatrical. Then I filled two boxes with over-the-counter feminine products, grooming aids, medicines to combat a variety of routine human ailments that could seriously cut into a girl's income if not controlled.

I learned even more about Annie from the contents of her medicine cabinet. Besides the other medications, there were several brown pill bottles containing prescription tranquilizers, antianxiety agents, stomach medications, and two different types of antidepressants. Somehow these pills made her more Annie and less Raven to me. The domineering woman dressed in black leather and wearing the scowl with the abusive angry act was, in fact, anxious, insecure, depressed, and plagued by a bad gut.

I tried not to think about that, to keep working as quickly and efficiently as I could. I took the lid off the toilet tank and examined it, looking for a floppy in a Ziploc bag hidden next to the flapper. I got down on the floor to examine the cabinet under the sink and felt all over the pipes and the underside of the sink.

Nothing.

If Annie had hidden the floppy anywhere in this room, she'd done it well.

I examined the empty medicine cabinet, yanking on it to see how securely it was anchored to the wall. It wouldn't budge, which I took as a safe assumption that Annie wouldn't have done any major construction or demolition to hide the floppy because it would have drawn attention to her. Mabel or Gary would surely have wanted to know why hammering and banging was coming from her room, since that kind of activity was beyond even Annie's repertoire.

After about thirty minutes, I determined that the bathroom was clean. I had no choice now but to start on the bedroom, but once in there I'd be under the watchful eye of Mabel and perhaps even Goumba Joey as I worked. I'd have to be extra careful.

I stacked the packed boxes, which now numbered a dozen, out in the hallway. Then I turned back to her room. One of the things I wanted to do was examine each drawer in her bureau. A floppy could easily be taped to the back or underside of a drawer. But how to do it without being obvious about it?

I thought for a moment, then it hit me. I went into actor mode and began huffing and puffing and stomping around the room like I was really pissed off at having to do this chore. I yanked each drawer out of the bureau and turned its contents upside down on the bed. While doing so, I checked each side of each drawer.

The first one was full of underwear, of course. Annie's taste in lingerie was about what you'd expect from someone in her line of business. Not a lot of cotton granny panties . . . Some interesting stuff, and a couple of items I didn't even recognize. I wasn't into taking notes right now, though. I was looking for something.

And it wasn't here. I was careful to check inside the frame of the bureau, which I also pulled away from the wall. I checked the back and under it, all the while trying to look busy for the camera.

I looked around the room one more time, frustrated. Then I went over to the large, three-drawer nightstand next to the bed and started the drill on it. The first drawer contained a variety of condoms, lubricated and unlubricated, shaped, formed, textured, and tasty. There were massage oils, lubricants, smelling salts, and some liquid in a little brown bottle labeled LOCKER ROOM.

Call me naïve. Okay, call me *stupid*, but there was so much of this kind of stuff that I couldn't imagine anyone actually using all of this junk. I gathered up the bottles, tubes, and foil-wrapped packages and dumped them into a box. Then I pulled the drawer out and looked it over quickly.

The second drawer contained . . . well, I guess you'd call them more tools of the trade. Vibrators and other mechanical devices. I didn't even want to touch these guys, so I dumped the contents into a box in one swift motion. There was a limit to how much respect even I was willing to show to this debris.

The third drawer was full of CDs. *Okay,* I thought, *now we're on to something.* But how could I examine them all without looking suspicious? My brain in high gear, I dumped the CDs out on the bed and packed them quickly, opening each and examining it in a show of making sure the CD was in its right case and in order.

Nothing.

I picked up the empty drawer and rotated it quickly on all sides, looking for the floppy.

Again nothing.

I slid the drawer back in, then reached down and picked up Annie's boom box and put it on the bed next to the CD box. I stood there a moment, thinking as fast and hard as I could. I'd searched everything, torn the place apart and put it back together again as neatly as I could. All of Annie's belongings were in taped boxes on the bed, the bedroom floor, and the hallway. Not much to show for a lifetime, but then again Annie hadn't exactly had a very long life. Not quite a quarter of a century.

The one thing I knew for sure was that I couldn't stand around here staring for very much longer with Mabel watching me on the video monitor. I left the room and walked out the front door, then pulled the truck around to the back entrance and parked. The temperature had dropped and the wind had picked up to the point where I could hear it whistling past my ears. I quickly went in through the back door, put on my jacket, and started carrying the boxes out to the truck. None of them were heavy, but they were bulky and I could only carry a couple, maybe three, at a time. I put all the boxes in the truck bed except for the CDs and the boom box, which went in the truck cab. I figured I'd at least get to listen to a few tunes. Maybe I'd even bring the boom box back in and set it up so that I could listen while I painted for the rest of the day, which was something I was definitely not looking forward to.

I walked back through the hallway out to the lobby,

then down the adjacent hallway to Mabel's office. I
stopped, straightened my shirttail, then knocked softly.

"What?" that gravelly voice called. *God,* I thought,
how many years has she been smoking, anyway?

"I've got all of Raven's stuff boxed up," I said to the
closed door. "Where do you want me to take it?"

I heard the squeal of the wheels on her chair as she
backed away from her desk. A moment later she opened
the door a crack and held out a key.

"Took you long enough," she grumbled. "You know
where the trailer park is?"

"I think so," I said. "You go back to the access road,
turn right. Couple miles down."

"Yeah, that's it. Here's the key to sixteen." She handed
me the small key. "We use that one for storage. Dump
that junk off and get back here as quick as you can.
Don't dawdle, and don't stop off at any of the other
trailers."

"What?" I asked, confused.

She glowered at me. "Girls, you idiot. The trailers are
rented to the girls."

"Okay," I said, wanting to slam her against the wall
and ask her what made her think I'd stop off there in the
first place. "I'll be back as quick as I can."

"See that you do," she ordered. Then she shut the door
and locked it.

"Bitch," I muttered under my breath as I walked away.

Outside, the wind was howling now, picking up dust
in a bitter freezing mix that made it hard to breathe and
see very far. It was like one of those scenes in a movie
where the grizzled old prospector was trying to make it
back to civilization while battling the elements, ban-
ditos, thirst, and cranky mules.

My cranky mule was the ragged pickup, which suddenly didn't want to start. The engine bucked and ground

away until it caught with a backfire that sounded like a gunshot. I looked out over the windshield and could barely see fifty feet ahead. It was turning into a rotten day, and what's worse was that there was so much left of it.

I kicked the truck into gear with a loud *thunk* and pulled away from the Mustang, through the parking lot, and under the railroad trestle. I stopped on the other side of the bridge and pulled over. I'd never been able to get the radio on the truck to work, and as long as I had this box of CDs, I might as well enjoy them. I dug through the box and came up with a Chris Isaak CD, *Forever Blue*. I hadn't heard that one in a while, so I hit the button to raise the lid on the CD player. I slid the disk in, pressed the lid shut, then hit the PLAY button.

Nothing.

"Damn it," I muttered. "Typical."

I picked up the boom box and rotated it so that I could see the controls. I turned the knob labeled VOLUME and clicked it on, turning it all the way clockwise.

Still nothing.

"Crap," I said out loud. I wanted to hear some music and I wanted to hear it now. The way my life was running, *Forever Blue* was perfect and, by God, I was going to hear it even if—as Slim Pickens said in *Dr. Strangelove*—it harelips everybody on Bear Creek.

Apparently, the boom box felt otherwise.

"I'll beat you yet, you S.O.B.," I said, realizing that once again I'd come to a place in my life where I was talking to myself and inanimate objects. I turned the boom box over, looking for the battery compartment, hoping that there was a power cord in there that would work with a car's cigarette lighter.

I found the plastic panel and pushed it until it clicked, then took it off.

No batteries. Of course.

I dug around for the power cord with my left index finger. It was tangled up inside the back part of the battery compartment, tucked out of the way to make room for the batteries. I hooked it with my finger, then yanked it out.

"Great," I grumbled. The cord was for a 120-volt line only. No tunes in the car today, I thought.

I slid the boom box on the seat next to me and put the truck back in gear, then pulled out onto the gravel road. At least, I thought, I could plug it in at the trailer and have some music out there. Then maybe I'd borrow it and take it back to the Mustang with me. Then I could plug it into the wall outlet in Annie's—

Wait a minute.

The wall socket! In Annie's room! There were no batteries in the boom box, and yet when I found it in Annie's room, it hadn't been plugged into the wall. Why wouldn't it have been plugged in if there had been no batteries?

"Jesus H.," I mumbled. "I mean, maybe there's a . . ."

I pulled over on the side of the road again. The dust was so thick, I couldn't see a quarter mile in front of me. It was like a brown fog now. If Mabel or Gary or Joey or anybody came by and wanted to know why I was pulled off the road, at least I had an excuse.

I picked up the boom box and held it in front of me on the dashboard over the steering wheel. Where could it be?

I turned it over, yanked the plastic plate off the battery compartment again, and stuck my finger in as far as it would reach. I couldn't feel anything except the power cord and I could reach all the way back to the end of the compartment. I took out the Chris Isaak CD, held up the boom box, and shook it. Nothing was loose inside. Other than the lid to the CD drive and the battery compartment, there were no other pieces of plastic on the thing that came apart.

"There's got to be," I said. "C'mon, think!"

I turned the boom box back over and stared at the bottom of the battery compartment. Four brass screws in each corner of the square compartment held everything in place. I reached in, stuck my fingernail in the slot of one of the screws.

It turned easily.

"Hot damn!" I yelped. I pulled out my pocketknife and unfolded it, then quickly removed the four bright screws. I set them on the seat beside me and used the knife blade to pry loose the piece of black plastic held in place by the screws. It popped up. I strained in the dim light to see inside.

Wedged against one of the circuit boards was a black plastic 3.5-inch floppy disk.

My jaw dropped. "Dumb luck," I muttered. "Dumb fuckin' luck." If Chris Isaak hadn't done *Forever Blue* and I hadn't had a hankering to listen to it, none of this would've happened. I'd never have found it. Now I had it. Annie Rogers's secret, her treasure, the thing that she'd risked so much for and died for, the data that would expose and blow the lid off a multimillion-dollar money-laundering operation was sitting in my lap, tucked up inside a cheap boom box that was missing three bucks' worth of D cells. And it was all thanks to Chris Isaak.

"Chris," I said, setting the boom box beside me and chunking the truck back into gear, "you da man."

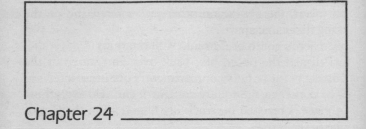

Chapter 24

Elated, I drove through the swirling dust the two miles or so to the trailer park. The road into the park was gravel, and the trailers—nearly all of them small traveling trailers at least twenty years old—were arranged in cluttered rows. At the end of the gravel road a filth-encrusted Dumpster served as the community trash receptacle. I saw no evidence of running water or sewer facilities, just a bunch of old trailers lined up in the desert. I found number sixteen at the end of the second row and, choking all the while on dust, got the door open. Inside the trailer was a single room with a ratty sofa against one wall and a bunch of other junk piled in there, all of it mildewed and musty. I didn't see how anyone could live for very long in one of these things.

It took about five minutes to get all of Annie's boxes unloaded and stowed inside the trailer. Then I sat back in the cab of the pickup truck wondering what to do about the boom box. On one hand, Annie had chosen such a good hiding place for the floppy that it might be a good idea to leave it there. On the other hand—and I don't mean to be tacky here—the lock on the trailer didn't look very secure and leaving a boom box, even a cheap one, in a trailer park full of hookers might not be the best idea either.

I decided to take the floppy with me. I carefully pried it

out from inside the boom box and slipped it into my shirt pocket, then put everything back together. I took the boom box and the carton of CDs into the trailer and locked the door as I left.

I'd be surprised if any of it was there tomorrow.

The wind was still up. My eyes felt as if somebody had held them open and emptied a salt shaker into them. I blinked, trying to stop the burning, and strained to keep the road in focus. A car came out of the dust heading straight for me and I jerked the truck over to avoid a collision, the right front wheel jumping and shaking as it rode the edge of the road and a shallow ditch. I cursed under my breath, fought to get the wheel straight, then made the turn onto the gravel road leading to the Mustang.

As I pulled the truck to a stop in the now thinly populated parking lot, I eased the floppy out of my pocket, leaned down, stuck my hand under the seat, and wedged the black plastic square in between the springs and the cushion. It would be safe there, out of sight, until I could get it to the cops or Barrone.

My first instinct was to drive into town right now, hand the floppy to Sergeant Anderson, politely inform him which part of my anatomy he could kiss, and then walk out. Unfortunately, I'd been around enough cops to know that that wouldn't work. For one thing, I didn't yet know what was on the floppy. In fact, it might be prudent for me to find a computer and check out the contents before I even called Anderson and Barrone. I felt certain that the data they wanted, what they'd pressured Annie to get, was there. But something told me to play my cards close to my chest on this one, and part of that was to continue the charade at the Mustang. If I bolted in the middle of the day, it would only raise suspicion. I'd give the floppy to Anderson later, and if it was what he wanted, then I'd simply turn in my resignation at the Mustang and be done with it.

"Yeah," I whispered to myself as I got out of the truck and headed inside for some of Miss Mary's chili, "that'll work."

I had a plan and the plan was working. Once again, it felt good to be right.

I spent the rest of the day being a good soldier, keeping my mouth shut and going about my work with as little fuss as possible. Miss Mary fed me, the girls ignored me, and I went back to Annie's room. I moved the furniture into the middle of the floor and covered it with some old sheets, then spread tarps around on the rest of the floor. I carefully masked the border at the top of the room and the molding at the bottom. After that, I did the best down-and-dirty estimate I could of how much paint it would take to cover the walls, then mixed it in a large plastic bucket and stirred it for about twenty minutes to get it all blended together. The paint was thick and dark, the color of brick or the red clay of Tennessee I'd grown up around. I took a small brush and did the cut-ins, the close work around the masked areas and the corners. The work wasn't hard, but it was tedious and required a lot of careful attention. My shoulders knotted up from tension and my neck ached.

It was nearly four in the afternoon by the time I finished the prep work and the detail and got down to rolling out the rest of the room. It's curiously satisfying to roll paint over large areas of wall; it's instant gratification. When the rewards for so much effort in life take forever—if they come at all—it's almost a delight to get such quick returns on work. I thought of how rough the last couple of weeks had been, but somehow it felt like my luck was turning. I'd set out to find the truth about a part of the world and I'd found it. The police would have what they needed to crack the money-laundering operation; if they were any good, they'd put the heat on everybody involved until someone cracked and Annie's murderer was discovered. I'd hang around until my daughter was born and I could make some kind of peace with her mother, and then I'd go back to my life.

I felt as calm and grounded as I'd felt in weeks as I rolled out the last of the paint and then began cleaning up the mess. I'd covered everything in the room, but I had rolled the paint on quickly and more sloppily than I intended. My jeans were splashed with streaks of red paint and when I stepped into the bathroom, I saw that paint was in my hair and on my face, under my fingernails and ground into the hair on my forearms. I laughed at my own reflection in the mirror. No matter; the paint was a water-based latex. I'd clean up the mess here, go back to Aunt Marty's, and scrub it all off in the shower.

I finished cleaning the rollers and brushes, then put away the rest of the equipment. As I started to roll up the sheets and paint tarps, I realized how tired I was. Another twenty minutes or so, though, and I'd be out of here and on my way home.

That's when my pager went off. I pulled the bundle of paint-splattered sheets out of the way and looked down at my belt.

On the pager's display: a row of nines.

The next thing I remember was hitting the exit ramp off I-80 about forty miles an hour faster than I should have. Tires squealed, then screamed, as the truck began an outbound slide toward the guardrail. I let up on the accelerator and countersteered enough to transition from an out-of-control slide to a controlled one, then downshifted and braked to a stop at the intersection.

I vaguely remember running past Mabel and Goumba Joey on my way out of the Mustang. They must have seen the look on my face as I went by because they didn't try to stop me.

"What the fuck!" Joey yelled. "Where ya going?"

"Personal emergency!" I yelled back as I went through the front door.

I don't think I even clocked out. To hell with it.

I yanked my wallet out of my pants and extracted the handwritten note from Marty with directions to Washoe Med. Center. It was off Mill Street, near downtown, just around a curve. Marty'd told me to watch for the big blue medivac choppers on the right next to a police substation.

The guy behind me laid on his horn. I looked up; the light had turned. I stomped the gas pedal and shot out into the intersection, leaving a black-and-blue cloud of smoke and burned oil all over the rude bastard behind me. That'll show him, I thought. If I want that kind of treatment from motorists, I'll go back to Nashville.

I went through a bunch of traffic lights and late-Saturday afternoon traffic that all of a sudden seemed to be thick as flies and going about two miles an hour. I weaved in and out, using every one of my advanced skills as a southern driver to maneuver my way through the traffic, all the while glancing first at my note, then the street signs. Finally, I spotted East Second Street up ahead, stomped on the gas to pass some guy in an early Seventies Cadillac with fur around his rearview mirror, then cut across two lanes and made the turn. Horns blared, fingers were raised. I didn't care. A baby was coming; get out of my way.

I made another left, then a right onto Mills. Ahead of me sat a huge blue chopper on a landing pad and I knew I'd found the place. I pulled into the first parking slot I found, ignored the meter, and ran up the sidewalk and into the front door.

"Ohmigod!" the receptionist screamed, jumping up out of her chair. She pointed to her left. "Emergency room's that way!"

I stopped. "What?" I asked, wondering which one of us had lost our mind.

"Down there, quick!" she yelled, eyes bulging, as she backed away from the counter. Her glasses slipped off her nose and dropped down onto her chest, held there by a blue lanyard.

I looked down at myself. "Oh," I said, holding out my palms in supplication. "No, ma'am, you don't understand. It's paint."

Her jaw dropped. "It's what?"

"Paint," I said, laughing. "I was painting when I got paged. My . . . my wife's having a baby. I didn't have time to clean up." I also didn't have time to explain my relationship to Marsha, so *wife* would have to do.

She dropped her arms and glared at me. "You scared me to death," she snapped.

"I'm sorry," I said, trying to control my laughter. "Would you please direct me to the maternity area?"

The lady sighed irritably. "Down that hall to your right," she said. "Through the double doors, then follow the red arrows."

"Thanks," I said over my shoulder as I took off. Guess I'd better be careful charging through a hospital looking like the victim of a drive-by shooting.

I ran down the hall and through the double doors, nearly barreling into a guy pushing a cart loaded with food trays in the process. A series of red arrows on the wall led me through the maze until I got to another set of double doors with a sign that read BIRTHING CENTER.

I pushed through the doors and came to a curved desk

with several nurses behind it, all of whom turned quickly and stared at my appearance.

"It's paint," I blathered. "I was painting when I got the call!"

An older woman in a starched white uniform and a blue sweater who had the look of someone in charge grinned. "Okay. You're okay. Calm down. Who is she?"

"Marsha," I gasped. "Dr. Helms."

The charge nurse looked down at a clipboard. "She's in suite three, but you can't go in there looking like that." She turned. "Bertie, would you help Mr. Helms clean up a little bit? Get him gowned so he doesn't scare the baby."

The other nurses laughed and a younger woman with a kind, round face stood. "This way, Mr. Helms," she said, motioning for me to follow her.

"Actually," I whispered to the back of her head as I followed her down the hall, "it's Denton. Harry Denton. The mother and I, well, we aren't—"

She turned. "Don't worry, you're not the first. And it doesn't affect the process."

"Good," I said. The young nurse stopped in front of a door and opened it. At that moment, across the hall and maybe twenty feet farther along, Marty stepped out of a room wearing green surgical scrubs.

"Marty!" I said loudly. I dashed past the nurse, who shook her head and smiled.

"What in God's name happened to you?" Marty demanded, her patrician Virginia drawl accentuated by the volume.

"I was painting," I explained for the forty-millionth goddamn time. "I was painting when you guys paged me. I'm sorry. This lady's going to clean me up. How is she?"

"Slow down, Harry," Marty said, patting me on the

arm. "You're going to have a heart attack if you're not careful."

"How is she?" I snapped.

"She's fine. She's still in the first stage. You've got time."

"First stage," I said, feeling like a babbling idiot. "What does that mean?"

"She's dilated about seven centimeters," Marty explained. "Three more to go. The contractions are coming faster and faster, but there's still time."

"Good," I said, whipping around to face the nurse. "Let's go."

"Harry," Marty said soothingly, holding on to my arm. "You're going to have to calm down. Marsha's fine. She's a doctor. She knows how this is going to work. She knows what to expect. But if you go in there like a hysterical banshee, then you're going to throw off her rhythm and get her all upset and then this is all going to get very difficult."

I looked into Marty's face for a moment, saw her concern and her warmth and kindness toward me.

"I'm sorry, Marty," I said. "I'm just scared."

"We all are. But it's going to be okay. Go run some cold water on your face, take a few deep breaths, get centered, and then go hold Marsha's hand."

"I don't know what to do," I said. "I didn't prepare for this."

"That's okay," Marty said. "I'll be in there with you. The people here are very nice. They'll tell you exactly what to do."

I turned. The young nurse smiled at me. "She's right," she said. "C'mon."

I looked back at Marty. "I'd hug you, but I'm too dirty."

She laughed. "Later, Harry. We'll do it later."

"All right," I said to the nurse. "Let's go."

"Oh, Harry," Marty said.

"Yes?"

"Congratulations, dear."

I felt a lump rise in my throat. "Thank you, Marty."

Ten minutes later, and after removing the top three layers of epidermis over most of the exposed skin on my body, I walked into the room where Marsha was lying alone in a hospital bed, the back of it raised about forty degrees. On the side of the bed opposite the door, an IV pole stood, with a clear plastic bag hanging below it. It was cool in the room; the lights were turned down low and soft music played from hidden speakers. Marsha's eyes were closed as I walked in. There was a thin sheen of sweat on her skin and she seemed to glisten in the subdued light. She panted softly as I approached the bed and opened her eyes just as I touched the bed rail.

"Hi," I said, trying to keep my voice level and calm. "Where is everybody? They decide to go on a break?"

"Harry?"

"Yeah," I said, leaning down and kissing her softly on her forehead. The nurse had told me that I didn't have to wear gloves or a surgical mask yet, but the attending doctor might ask me to later.

"How are you?" I asked.

"Okay," she said wearily. "Tired."

"I saw Marty outside. She said you're getting close."

"My water broke about three-thirty," Marsha said.

"I appreciate you guys paging me. I got here as fast as I could."

Suddenly, her face screwed into a tortured mask of pain and she reached out and grabbed my hand. She growled and cranked down on my hand like a vise. I squeezed back, my whole body tensing with hers as she practically bounced off the bed. Then she let loose with a howl that made the hair on the back of my neck stand up.

"Hold on, baby," I said, trying not to panic. "Hold on. It'll pass, Marsha. It'll pass."

Her whole body seemed locked in a rigid spasm for maybe thirty seconds, then she began to settle, to relax, back onto the bed.

"That's easy for you to say," she wheezed.

"God," I said. "That's pretty damned impressive."

"You should see it from my side."

"Do I need to call the nurse?" I asked.

"Not yet. But when the next one comes," she said, pointing to the wall across from her, "use that clock to time it. Measure from the beginning of one contraction to the beginning of the next."

"You got it," I said as she began a rhythmic panting. "Can I get you anything?"

"Oh, I don't know," she whispered. "Maybe a Stoli martini, dry, straight up, a pearl onion instead of an olive."

"Would you settle for some ice chips?"

She nodded, exhaustion and weariness etched on her face.

I spooned her some ice chips, then wet a washcloth and wiped her face. I lifted her up in bed a little and positioned myself so that I could massage her neck and shoulders. She said little during all this, only moaning faintly while I rubbed her. Then the next contraction hit, and it was a big one. I glanced up at the clock and made a mental note, then grabbed her and held on as wave after wave coursed through her body as if she were being put through a wringer. I'd never seen anything like it; it scared the hell out of me but also fascinated me and kept me absolutely in awe of what a human body can go through and still survive. My thoughts turned to my mother, now retired with my father in Hawaii, and her tendency to describe to me every little ache and pain in exhaustive detail. I thought, *She went through this for me?*

Then it was over, those forty-five seconds feeling more like a couple of hours, and we went through the same routine until the next one hit and we held on for dear life again. When it was over, Marsha turned to me, her head as limp as a dishrag on the pillow.

"How long?"

"Not quite six minutes," I answered.

She groaned.

"Is that good? Bad? What?"

"It's nothing, Harry," she answered. "It just means we aren't there yet."

Which turned out to be the truth, as we sat there for hour after endless hour. The initial stages of labor had gone so quickly, but now she was stalled. Marty came in and offered to spell me, but except for a bathroom break I decided to stay put. Nurses came in and checked the IV, took Marsha's blood pressure and pulse, and time dragged by, with the contractions seeming to speed up only a bit. The doctor came in once, then again an hour or so later, and then a third time around nine-thirty that night.

"What's going on?" I asked as he leaned down at the foot of the bed, making yet another examination. Then he hooked up his stethoscope and pressed it against Marsha's abdomen, listening intently for a few moments.

He raised his head, a dry professional look on a face that seemed to me terribly young.

"Marsha, you seem to be hung at about nine centimeters," he said. "We just can't quite make the jump to transition and phase three."

Marsha raised her head. "Any sign of fetal distress?"

"Baby's heartbeat is fine, there's no staining in the amniotic fluid. No discharge or blood. We can give it a few more hours or we can go with the oxytocin now. What do you think?"

Marsha laid her head back down on the pillow. "I don't know," she said listlessly.

"Excuse me, guys," I said, standing. "Unlike the two of you, I did not go to med school. Anybody want to tell me what's going on?"

The doctor smiled. "None of this is particularly troubling yet," he said. "First babies just take a long time sometimes. It's totally unpredictable. We can let nature take its course or we can jump in and intervene."

"What's the right thing to do?" I demanded. "You guys are the doctors. I just carry the ice chips."

"The baby's doing fine," he said. "My concern right now is for Marsha. If she gets so worn out that she can't see this through till the end, then we may as well go ahead and speed things up. Get it over with."

I stepped to the head of the bed and leaned down. "How about it, baby? What do you want? Can you hold on?"

She stared at me. "Will you stay with me?"

"They'd have to drag me out of here with a bulldozer," I said.

She smiled. "You always did have a way with words. Let's hang in a little while longer."

"Okay," the doctor said. "I'll be back to check on you in about an hour."

And the waiting began again. The contractions became a little more frequent, but not much, and I could tell Marsha's weakened body was running out of power. She drifted in and out of consciousness, it seemed, and she was sweating like crazy. The nurses came in and we changed her hospital gown and the sheets, and about the time we got her settled again, the mother of all contractions hit. Marsha's skin stretched tight over her face and the vessels in her neck and forehead swelled as if there was something inside her trying to burst out through the top end instead of the bottom.

This one scared me. I turned to the nurse, who read the look on my face.

"Don't worry," she said calmly. "It won't be long now."

"How can the human body go through this?" I hissed.

She grinned. "Happens all the time," she offered. "Just be glad it's women who do it and not men."

"I already am," I said as the wave passed and Marsha's death grip on my hand began to loosen.

The doctor came in a few minutes later, and then it all seemed to hit the fan. He examined Marsha again and whatever he saw down there sent him scurrying away. He disappeared for about five minutes, and then suddenly the room was full of people in a buzz of activity. The bed was yanked away from the wall to the center of the room, the foot piece removed from it, and two stirrups attached to the frame. One nurse pushed me to the head of the bed and told me to stay there. They erected a little curtain across Marsha's abdomen and yanked up her hospital gown. Then the doctor came in, scrubbed, gowned, and gloved, with this goofy paisley cap on.

"Okay, folks," he announced, "it's *showtime*! Let's make a baby!"

One nurse cranked the bed up, forcing Marsha higher in the bed. Instructions seemed to come from every direction. "Breathe this." "Push that." "Turn this way." "Okay, count for me," "Breathe now!" "Push hard!"

I stood on one side of the bed, leaning down, holding Marsha's hand as she pushed and heaved with all her might. Marty stood across from me, her eyes shimmering as she rubbed Marsha's shoulders.

"We've got crowning here, Marsha!" the doctor said calmly. "Relax, relax, there, that's it. Hold on . . . hold on . . . That's it . . . Now push, Marsha, give it all you've got!"

Marsha grunted, took a deep breath, her face literally corkscrewing into a frozen bright red mask. It was hideous and frightening and awe-inspiring and wonderful, all at once. I heard a noise that can only be described as *squishy* and then this awful smell filled the room, but nobody seemed to pay much attention to it. The whole medical team moved like clockwork. My heart pumped like crazy, and I realized I was hyperventilating. I fought to slow down, to relax, and just as I did, Marsha let out with a horrible scream that went on and on and on, then the doctor yelled, "All right!" and suddenly it was like all the air went out of her and every muscle in her body went limp and she collapsed. I stepped closer to the middle of the bed, straining to see over the curtain, then I saw this tiny lump of wet, red baby barely bigger than the doctor's two hands covered in goop and white slime. My eyes widened.

"How is she?" Marsha gasped, unable to raise her head. I tried to say something, but the only thing that came out was a strained squeak, which caused a couple of the nurses to burst out laughing.

The doctor was smiling so broadly that I could see it beneath his surgical mask. "She's fine, Marsha, she's just fine." Three nurses huddled around the doctor and the foot of the bed, their arms like buzz saws around the baby. "We're just going to clean her up a little bit." The doctor looked up, saw my face. "Would you like me to take care of the cord for you?"

I nodded.

A minute or so later the doctor stood and held the baby, wrapped now in a small hospital blanket, over the curtain and set her down on Marsha's stomach.

"Marsha, Harry," he said. "Meet your daughter."

I stared at her for a second, her eyes closed, her skin pink and wet and shiny and all shriveled up, and suddenly my eyes were wet. I looked at Marsha; her mouth was open as she slid her hands up from the sides of the bed and gently cradled the baby for the first time. She pulled the baby to her, then looked over at me. I held out my hand and saw that it was trembling, as if it were detached from me, separate with a mind of its own, and then I reached over and gingerly, carefully touched the top of my daughter's head.

And then I wept.

Chapter 25

And so it came to be that at 10:47 P.M. on a chilly Saturday night in Reno, Nevada, I became a father. Alexis Martha Helms came into the world weighing six pounds, ten ounces. Her first APGAR score was eight; five minutes later she scored a ten. At less than thirty minutes old, my daughter was—like her mother—already an overachiever.

One is apt to get sloppily sentimental at times like this and I fought the impulse as hard as I could, with limited success. *Maudlin* was not the right word, although it was close.

Oh, hell, maybe it was the right word.

There was still much to do even after the birth. I didn't know that there was yet another stage of labor for Marsha, where she had to expel the placenta and the rest of the goo left over from childbirth. I didn't pass out during that one, although a couple of times I did have to turn away and not look.

Marsha seemed exhausted and relieved and over-whelmed all at the same time. Whatever gulf had come to separate us had—for the moment, at least—closed a bit. The nurses took Alexis away briefly to clean her up some more and run the necessary tests. Then they cleaned Marsha up, changed her gown and bedding again, and got her prepared for the baby's return. In a short while, they brought Alexis back and Marsha breast-fed her for the first time. The sight of my daughter at her mother's breast gave me this sense of wonder, of miracles, of the potential of life. Aunt Marty took pictures of the three of us and I was profoundly grateful to her.

A little after midnight they sent me home. Marsha was exhausted, Marty had already made arrangements to spend the night, and after a long day at work and a long, nervous night in the delivery room, I was frankly starting to be a bit gamy. I needed a bath and some dinner and probably, like many a new father, a couple bottles of beer in order to get to sleep. I kissed Marsha and the baby, gave Marty a long overdue embrace, then walked out into the cold Reno night.

Reno, of course, refused to recognize the existence of night and held it off with millions of flashing lights. I walked to the truck, pulled the three parking tickets off the windshield, and threw them in the cab. The truck engine rumbled and groused for a few seconds, then caught with a deep rumble.

All the way back to Marty's, I kept thinking of what I had just witnessed. I'd heard from so many new parents of the miraculous nature of the experience, of how the biggest amazement of childbirth is the realization that you can love something so totally, so unconditionally, with such complete abandon and acceptance. With the arrogance of the uninformed, I'd always taken it as something sweet and nice. It was only tonight that I understood what they were all talking about, what they meant by the notion of watching one's child come into the world as the most profound of all human experiences.

I started up the mountain in the pitch-black night with the glimmer of Reno in the rearview mirror. In the midst of this miracle, I wondered if there wasn't another chance for Marsha and me. Was it possible for a child to bring two people together who otherwise might have given up?

I knew in the rational part of my brain that parenthood was the lousiest excuse for two people to stay together, for the child and the parents. Still, there was that little spark of hope.

Ahead of me a doe leaped across the Mount Rose highway, a flash of white and brown reflected in the headlights. I slowed in case there were others behind her, then made the turn on to Marty's street. A couple of minutes later I parked the truck and unlocked the back door.

Estella was in bed, long asleep, but there was a note on the kitchen counter that said there was a casserole in the oven still warm for me. Whatever it was, it smelled wonderful. I opened a bottle of beer, turned up the oven to get the food a little hotter, then ran upstairs for a quick shower. I stripped, stood rock-still in the shower, and let the hot water run over me. I didn't realize how tight I was until my shoulders and neck began to loosen up and the pain began. I was going to be sore as hell tomorrow.

I went downstairs in my bathrobe and loaded some black bean casserole onto a plate, opened a bottle of beer, and took them into the living room. I turned on the television, the volume down low, and channel-surfed until I found an old movie, then settled back on the sofa.

It was hard to concentrate on the film, though. This day had just been too much. My thoughts turned again to the baby and in a roundabout, chaotic pattern, I jumped from one thing to another in my head. I thought of Annie again and wondered whether on some Saturday night a long time ago, her father had looked down at her nursing for the first time and felt such hope, such potential, such love. And what had gone wrong? I wondered. What had gone so terribly wrong, that the beautiful, precious treasure that Annie Rogers had been as a

baby turned into a hooker/dominatrix called Raven who
would be murdered so horribly?

The more I thought about Annie Rogers, the worse I
began to feel. She had been caught in a horrible dilemma,
either to work undercover for the police at a terrible risk
to herself or to refuse their demands and go back to jail.
She had made the wrong choice and paid the ultimate
price for it.

I had to give her this much: Annie Rogers had had
balls, metaphorically speaking. Someone had discovered her treachery, her infiltration of the computer system, and he or she had no doubt demanded that she
turn over what she had. Maybe all she had had to do
was give up the floppy disk and he or she would have let
her live. But she'd refused and the killer had beaten the
crap out of her and then murdered her. And she hadn't
given in. If she had, I never would have found that hidden floppy disk.

I wondered if I would have had that kind of guts. If
someone held a gun to my head or started beating the
hell out of me, I'd probably trip over myself pulling that
damn floppy out. In a way, it didn't make any sense to die
for something like that. But Annie had done it. Whoever
had killed her, they'd done it without getting what they
wanted out of her.

Maybe it hadn't been guts; maybe Annie had known
that even if she gave up the floppy, she'd be killed anyway. But that went against all human instincts. Unless
we're suicidal—and there's no indication that Annie
Rogers, as troubled as she'd been, had had those kinds of
problems—we hang on to life with every thread of our
being. If there were even the slightest hope of life, she'd
have done anything to keep breathing.

I don't mean to cast aspersions on the profession, but
the truth is that you don't often hear hookers described

as noble and courageous. In the movies, maybe, but in real life hookers have already sold body and soul, so what's the point in being noble?

I put the beer bottle down on the coffee table and stared into the empty fireplace.

Something stinks.

I thought I had this figured out. I thought I knew how this all had gone down. Now I wasn't so sure.

Why would Annie have died for a stupid floppy disk? It didn't make any sense. And if it didn't make any sense, then something else must have happened.

In its own twisted way, murder always makes sense.

Except in the cases of psychos in bell towers blowing away people indiscriminately, there's always a logic and consistency to murder. There's always a reason, a motive, and suddenly this one didn't fit.

Okay, if this one didn't fit, I should go back to the beginning. There were only a very few reasons to commit murder. Greed, for instance, for either money or power or drugs or control. And then there's passion in some form or other, whether it be hatred or revenge or the warm, fuzzy feeling that comes to some people from the exercise of pure malevolent evil.

Greed and passion. If Annie hadn't died for greed, for the return of the data that would protect a fortune in illegal profits, then she'd died for passion.

A hooker dying for passion: What a concept.

Passion.

I stared into the fireplace.

Lust.

The bricks began to vibrate, to shimmer in and out of focus.

Revenge.

My heart caught in my chest.

I knew.

I'd been wrong all along. I'd assumed one thing that led me on a trail that fooled me into thinking I was getting what I wanted. I got what I wanted and what the cops wanted and what Barrone wanted, but I didn't get the truth.

Now I knew.

I went into the kitchen and grabbed the phone and the phone book. I dialed a number; it rang maybe twenty-five times before somebody answered.

"Reno police," a sleepy voice answered. "Officer Zoeller."

"Good evening, Officer Zoeller. I need to speak to Mike Anderson, Sergeant Mike Anderson."

"He ain't here," Zoeller said. "You got any idea what time it is?"

"I have to speak to him now," I said. "It's an emergency. It can't wait until morning."

"Listen, bud—"

"No," I said. "You listen. I'm going to find Anderson one way or another, and when he finds out that Officer Zoeller refused to pass along my message in a murder case, I suspect that this isn't the only Saturday night you'll be manning that desk."

"Hey, easy," he said. "Jeez, I can't give you his number, but I'll take a message and pass it along."

"Good, I need to hear from him in the next ten minutes. Tell him it's Harry Denton calling."

I gave Zoeller the number, then apologized for being such a smartass and thanked him. Then I went upstairs and changed back into street clothes. By the time I got dressed, the cordless phone on the bed chirped loudly.

"Mike?" I said, pushing the button to talk.

"You got any idea what time it is?" Anderson asked. His voice was thick, almost slurred, with sleep.

"Yeah, half-past late," I said.

"This better be good," he said, sighing.

"I found your floppy disk," I said. "I've got it."

Anderson was suddenly much more awake. "Where?"

"Annie hid it. I found it. I've got it with me."

"Great, Denton," he said. "Great. But couldn't it wait till the morning?"

"The disk can wait. This can't."

"What?"

"You want Annie Rogers's killer?" I asked.

There was a long pause. "You serious?"

"What was it you said to me? 'As a heart attack,' " I answered.

"What are you up to, Denton?"

"Look, *Anderson,*" I said, "you want Annie Rogers's killer, grab a couple guys and meet me at the Mustang in an hour."

"Wait," he snapped. "What are—"

I hung up the phone and reached for my jacket.

As I pushed the pickup as hard as it would go east on I-80, a huge golden moon rose over the mountains. It seemed to rise so quickly that I could see an advancing line of illuminated landscape coming toward me. By the time I pulled into the parking lot of the Mustang Ranch, the gravel was sparkling in an eerie yellow glow.

I checked my watch. It was nearly two in the morning, with only a few cars and a couple of pickups in the parking lot. I walked up to the gate and paused. Maybe it was better if I didn't use the employee code this time. I pressed the buzzer one long time. The metal gate clicked and buzzed. I pushed it open.

By the time I got to the front door, Aphrodite had opened it for me. She stood there, a full two inches taller and fifty pounds heavier than me, wrapped in a sheer bright red robe and wearing a one-piece bathing suit beneath that. Her skin glowed darkly in the subdued light. Two other girls—Serena, the slight blond, and Julie, the Cher look-alike—emerged from the hallway behind us in the traditional lineup of all available talent.

"Harry," she complained. "What tha' fug you doin' here and why didn't you use the staff code?"

"Maybe he ain't working," Serena said. "Maybe he's here as a customer."

Aphrodite turned to me. "That it, Harry? You looking for your employee discount?"

"No, I'm here on business," I said. "You other girls go on back to wherever you came from. Aphrodite, I need to talk to you."

Serena shrugged her bony shoulders and Julie gave me a dirty look. But they turned and walked off without another word. Guess they were used to being told what to do.

I reached out, touched Aphrodite's arm. "I got to talk to you," I said.

"Whussup, Harry?" she asked as I led her down the hall toward Goumba Joey's office. I raised my finger to my lips as we passed Mabel's office. There was light coming from under the door, but I couldn't hear anybody in there. The lights were down low at the end of the hall, Joey's door in shadow. I pulled her to the side and lowered my voice.

"Who's working security tonight?" I asked.

"Just Smiley," she said. "Smiley Gilstrap."

"Thought there was a second guy on Saturday night."

She leaned in close, towering over me, covering me with her own shadow. "Things are slow," she said, her voice deep and low. "Smiley sent him home. What tha' fugs going on, Harry?"

"Where's Gary?"

"Gary?" she said, almost surprised. "What you want with that l'il weasel?"

"Just where is he?" I asked.

"I don't know. I ain't seen him around here in hours."

"Who's been greeting the guests?"

"I have most of the night," she admitted. "Things been kind of slow for me, given that I'm sort of a specialty act."

"What you talking about, girl?" I said. "You be gorgeous."

I paused, my head spinning, as I tried to figure out how to pull this off. I hadn't exactly planned much further than this moment. And if I didn't do it just right, then Anderson was going to be here and it'd be too late.

"Aphrodite, I got to know where Gary is."

"Why?"

"Never mind that. Is the new girl here yet? The one who was taking Raven's room?"

Aphrodite snickered. "Yeah, but Smiley and Gary had to finish putting the place back together after you ran out of here so quick. You in deep shit with Gary."

"Doesn't matter," I said, distracted. Then it hit me. The new girl.

"You seen the new girl lately?" I asked.

"Not in a while. She was back in the kitchen grabbing a bite earlier."

"And you ain't seen Gary?"

She shook her head. "Wait a minute," she said. "You don't think . . ."

"Five'll get you ten he's breaking her in," I said. "Has he ever let a new one in without taking first crack at her?"

Aphrodite's brilliant white teeth glowed as she smiled. "Yeah, that's where he is, all right. But what's going on, Harry? What you care where Gary is?"

"Aphrodite, I think he killed Raven. And I think he killed her because she wouldn't give him freebies."

"You crazy," she said.

"Think about it," I said. "You said it yourself. Raven had an attitude. She wouldn't go along to get along. Right? What other reason could there be?"

"Maybe he just didn't like her."

"Yeah, maybe. So why didn't he go to Goumba Joey and Mabel and get her kicked out of here?"

"I don't know," she said.

"I do. Because Joey and Mabel don't know he's, uh . . . dipping his pen in the company ink, so to speak."

"I do know Gary ain't used to having anybody say no to him," Aphrodite said.

"I've noticed that, too," I said. "I think he kept trying and trying, and Raven, her specialty being the one in charge, kept going into her act, and it was driving him nuts. Finally, he went off the deep end."

"That muh-fuggah," she said. "That piece o' shit."

"Yeah, yeah, all that," I said. "But we got to nail him. We got to get him to admit it."

"How we going to do that?" Aphrodite asked.

"First thing we got to do is get me alone with him," I said. "I seem to be able to piss him off fairly easily. Maybe I can get him to blow up."

"Harry, if he killed Raven, he ain't going to worry about yo' little skinny white ass. You don't wanna wind up like her."

"That ain't going to happen," I said, looking at my watch. If Anderson was on time, I had about ten minutes. If he wasn't, nobody knew how long I had.

Then it hit me. The hallway in front of us was still empty. Smiley was down in the lounge, probably napping on the couch or watching a movie on the big screen. It might work.

"You in this with me?" I asked.

"Will it put his ass away?"

I nodded. "For a long time."

"I'm with you, baby. Le's do it."

I led her back down the hall to Mabel's door. I turned the handle; it was locked. But the door wasn't made for real security, just convenience. I twisted the doorknob, tried to push the door far enough away from the jamb to slip the latch out.

I grunted and heaved again. Aphrodite grabbed my shoulder. "Here, get out of the way."

She pushed me aside, turned sideways, put her right hip against the door. Then she set her feet and with one smooth motion brought her torso out to her left, her massive hips swaying, her arms out like she was doing the hula, and snapped hard to the right, her hipbone hitting the door just above the lock.

The jamb splintered with a loud crack and the door flew open.

"Jeez," I whispered.

"I'm yo butt-Mama-monkey-love," she chimed. I followed her into the office and closed the door behind us. The office was tiny, maybe eight by ten. But on the wall opposite Mabel's desk, adjacent to the door, was the recessed cabinet with the two wooden doors I'd seen my first day here. I grabbed the knobs and pulled them open.

"Well, how about that?" Aphrodite said. "We was right."

I turned to her. "I knew you were. I found the camera in Raven's room."

Twenty eight-inch security monitors were arrayed on the wall in neat rows of five. The Mustang's sixteen rooms were on camera, along with the two hot-tub rooms, the lounge, the party room, and the foyer. I scanned the monitors, trying not to look too hard. I didn't want to know what was going on behind those closed doors; I could live without that.

Most of the rooms were empty, including the party room. Two were dark; presumably the girls were off-duty and asleep. Smiley Gilstrap sat staring at the big-screen TV in the lounge, vigorously scratching himself in a manner he probably wouldn't have been doing if he'd known we were watching.

The two hot-tub rooms were occupied by foursomes: two guys and two girls in each, who, at the moment, were simply enjoying the water.

"There he is," I said, pointing to one of the monitors. And sure enough Gary Weyrich was lying back on the bed, naked except for a pair of cowboy boots, smiling beatifically at the camera in Annie's old room, his hands clasped behind his head. On the bed next to him was a brunette whose face I couldn't see because she was kneeling over him performing an act that was still illegal in a couple of states and that had nearly cost a sitting president of the United States his job. Her head bobbed up and down so fast, her hair bounced over his torso and legs.

"I could've gone a long time without seeing that," I said.

"Don't be such a choirboy," Aphrodite said. "Hey, we got sound here?"

"I don't know." I reached over and twisted a knob, which produced a loud crackling over a tinny speaker. Nobody was talking, but there was considerable moaning going on.

"So what you going to do?" she asked.

"I don't know," I said, "but I got to do it now."

On the wall opposite the monitors, behind the desk, was a corkboard with a bunch of keys hanging, little white disks attached to each. Annie's room, I knew, was number fourteen. I stepped over, grabbed that key off the rack.

"Okay, I'll wing it," I said. "You stay here, listen carefully. You're my witness."

"Witness to what?" Aphrodite demanded. "What tha' fugs going on, man?"

I stepped over to her. "Listen, sweetie, the shit's about to hit the fan around here. I can't tell you anything more than that, but when it does, I can help you. All right? I know it's tough, but you've got to trust me on this one."

Aphrodite stared at me for a couple of moments. "Okay, Harry," she said, "you go do what you gotta do."

Chapter 26

It occurred to me as I walked down the dark hallway toward Annie's room that I was about to interrupt a murderer in the middle of a sex act and all I had as backup was a hooker with an attitude and a little bit of hope that the cops were on their way.

"Oh, well," I whispered. "I can't worry about that now."

Yeah, right, I thought. *You and Scarlett O'Hara.*

The bar was empty of customers. The bartender slowly wiped glasses as I walked by, pausing only to glance up at me. I crossed the bar to the right hallway and walked quickly to number fourteen. I reached down, twisted the knob gently, quietly. It was locked. Through the door, I could hear muffled moans and voices.

I leaned over, slipped the key in, then held the doorknob and turned the cylinder. The door opened easily. I set my weight, twisted the doorknob, then stepped in quickly and slammed the door behind me.

The girl looked up, surprised, but not the least bit embarrassed. As for Gary Weyrich, despite his Neanderthal level of intelligence, he was definitely *homo erectus* at the moment.

"What the fuck!" he snapped.

"I don't mean to be rude," I said to the girl. "I know

290

we haven't been properly introduced. I'm Harry, the maintenance man, and I need to talk to Gary."

"*Were* the maintenance man, you turd!" he said, grabbing the blankets to cover himself. The girl, an attractive brunette in her early twenties with a slightly skewed nose, got up on all fours and looked at me. She was completely naked, the entire lower half of her face wet and shiny in the light.

I turned away, repulsed. *Jeez, there are limits, you know.*

"What the hell do you want?" Gary yelled.

"I told you," I said. "We need to talk."

"Later," he growled. "I'm busy right now."

"It can't wait," I countered. A red satin robe was thrown haphazardly across the top of the bureau. I stepped over to it, picked the robe up, held it out, and straightened it.

"Sweetheart, would you mind stepping down to the lounge for a few minutes? Maybe get a Coke, something to take the bad taste out of your mouth."

Weyrich's face reddened. "You're asking for it, Denton," he warned.

I looked the girl in the eye and suddenly remembered a line from a movie that was so apropos I couldn't resist. "Get up, sweetheart," I said. "You look like a Pekingese."

The girl sat up on her knees, like a Vargas painting or a Betty Page photo, then turned and looked at Gary.

"We'll finish this later," he said under his breath. "Go on, get out of here."

The girl faced me, rolled her lower lip out in a pout, then climbed off the bed and took the robe from me. I helped her into it. Under ordinary circumstances and given how long it had been since I had—what's the euphemism?—*been with* anyone, I would have be panting right about now. Fortunately, I really did h other things on my mind.

The young lady tied the robe around her tiny waist, then smiled at me. "Later," she said, her voice high and sweet.

"Sure," I said. "Later."

She closed the door behind her and I locked it. "How'd you get in here?" Weyrich demanded. He'd pulled the covers over him but was now looking around the room, searching for his pants.

"Magic," I said. "I'm a wizard with locks. But I didn't come here to impress you with that. I came to offer you a business proposition."

"The only business proposition I'm interested in right now is how much I can get on the transplant market for all your fuckin' organs." He fidgeted, running his hands under the blankets. Then he found what he was looking for and scrambled around under the covers. When he finished, he threw back the covers and sat up wearing a pair of boxer shorts.

"Oh, you don't mean that," I said. "Gary, you and I are going to be great buddies."

"Yeah, I'll put flowers on your grave every Memorial Day." He got up, reached over and grabbed his pants off the back of a chair, and started climbing into them. They were baggy and slipped easily over the boots.

"That won't be necessary," I said, hoping I was right. "You see, I know what's going on here at the Mustang. And I know what happened to Raven."

He stopped, turned, and stared at me with the stone-cold darkest eyes I'd ever seen.

"What are you talking about?" he asked, his voice calmer.

"I just want in," I said. "All I want is to be your buddy. now you killed Raven because she wouldn't put out you. What the hell, why should I care? She was a er, a paid piece of ass. No more value than any other feedlot animal. You're hungry, you slaughter some fresh meat on the hoof. You need sex, you get it. And if anybody gives you any shit, you get rid of them, right?"

Gary looked around the room, as if checking to see if anyone else was around and he could really believe his ears. It was the middle of the night; everything was a little surreal, a little weird. Was this really happening to him?

"And I know all about the money laundering," I said. "I know the Mustang don't do the kind of business you guys report. So you run eight or ten million a year through here to clean it. I think it's smart of you, really. I just want to help out. I'll smurf for you, I'll count it, I'll weigh it, I'll bag it. Whatever."

His face relaxed. "So how'd you figure all this shit out?"

"Actually, it was me and Raven together. She and I got to be friends. One slow night she tells me she's cracked into the computer, found the duplicate books. I don't believe her, so over the next couple of weeks I count cars. Count the customers. And you know something, Gary?"

"What?" he snarls.

"The whorehouse biz just ain't what it used to be. I don't blame you guys for making up the shortfall some other way. It's just good business. So am I right, Gary? At least give me the satisfaction of knowing."

He pulled on his shirt and started buttoning it. "Okay, smartass, you're right. Ma was really pissed at me when I told her I took the bitch out. She thought she'd set you up pretty good to take it for me. Guess you're a lot smarter than we thought."

"But look at the upside, Gary," I said. "When Mabel finds out you killed the woman who was hacking into the computer and setting you guys up, think how happ she'll be."

I gave him the biggest, broadest smile I could, all the while wanting to strangle him as hard as he'd strangled Annie. He smiled back at me.

"You got a point, Harry," he said. Then he reached under the pillow and came up with a shiny chrome pistol and pointed it right at me. It looked tiny at first, but it seemed to grow larger with each second until finally it felt like I was standing in front of a cannon.

My mind seemed to empty itself of all thoughts and all images save one: me touching my daughter for the first time.

"You don't gotta do this, Gary," I said, my voice trembling in real fear now. The act was over. "If I wasn't being straight with you, I would've just gone to the cops. I only came to you like this 'cause I want to work for you. Let me prove it. Let me show you how good I can be."

He held the gun on me with one hand while tucking in his shirt with the other.

"Sorry, Harry," he said. "There's a hiring freeze on. In fact, we gotta lay you off."

"You kill me, Gary, you're just going to draw more attention to the situation. Mabel—Ma—won't like that."

"Ma won't give a shit one way or the other," Gary said. "As long as it don't come back here."

"How you going to stop that, Gary? You can't kill me here."

"Who said anything about here?" he demanded. "We're going to take a little drive. A few miles out I-80 into the desert. We take a ten-minute walk off the highway and nobody'll ever find you, at least not until the bones are picked clean."

He waved the pistol. "C'mon, move. Out the front door."

Gary pulled on a jacket, deftly switching the pistol

from one hand to the other as he slid his arms into the sleeves. Then he tucked the pistol into the right pocket and kept his hand firmly on it.

"Let's go."

"Gary," I said, my voice breaking for real. "Look, just let me go. I'll jump in my truck, head back to Tennessee. You'll never hear from me again."

"I'd like to be able to trust you, Harry." He grinned meanly. "Unfortunately, I can't."

He waved the gun in his pocket. I raised my hands.

Gary scowled at me. "Don't be stupid," he said. "This ain't a fuckin' movie. Put your hands down. Just stay in front of me and don't try no funny shit, 'cause I'll put one in your back if you do."

I turned. "Open the door," he ordered.

We walked out into the hallway. "Look, Gary, there's one other thing you need to know."

"Yeah? What's that?"

I turned, looked over my shoulder at him. "I'm a cop, Gary. Reno P.D. Financial Crimes Unit. My supervisor is Detective Sergeant Mike Anderson. You know him?"

"Nice try, Harry. Keep walking."

"Seriously, man," I said. "How come you think they cut me loose when you and Mabel had set me up so well? I'm one of them. You don't want to kill a cop in the line of duty, do you? You get the bitch for that one, Gary. You take the long walk for that one. Z'at what you want?"

He stepped forward, slammed the pistol into my kidney, pushed me hard down the hall. I grunted—it hurt like hell—but beneath the pain I knew that if I walked outside this building, that was it. He had me. Whatever I did, I couldn't go through that door. Maybe he'd kill me right here. It wouldn't be his first time. But at least I had a chance here.

We passed the bar. The bartender wasn't there; th

room was empty. We entered the foyer. The front door was ahead of us. I knew if I went through that door, I'd never see Alexis or Marsha again, and suddenly that made everything different.

I had to take my chance now.

I stopped, set my feet, started my turn to grab him.

I never got the chance.

There was huffing and the floor shook beneath us. I turned, and without warning all the light was gone, completely blocked out, and something slammed into me harder than I'd ever been hit before. My breath was gone before I even hit the floor, and when I did hit, everything sparkled and glittered red and green and gold, and something popped in my shoulder.

I heard this horrendous yell from Gary. "Wha—" And then a long, extended *Aaiiiiii!!*

I rolled to my left and found myself against the wall, stunned. There was screaming and yelling all around me. I forced myself to roll over and focus.

Aphrodite sat across Gary's chest, her knees on the floor, straddling him, pinning him down. He was screaming and jerking, but helpless, and she was raising her right arm, doubling up her fist, the size of a small ham, and then slamming it down on his head.

He screamed with each blow, in agony and panic. Aphrodite raised her left hand, cocked it, and brought it down hard on the other side of his face. I heard a sharp crack followed by a sickening thud. Behind us, the gate buzzer rattled loudly. Boy, I thought, was this customer in for a surprise. One of the girls walked over, zombie-like, and hit the button to open the gate.

I looked back down just as Aphrodite grabbed Gary's hair right at his forehead, raised his head up, and slammed it into the floor.

Gary howled. *"Mothafuggah!"* Aphrodite bellowed

over and over. She slammed his head into the floor again in time to her curses.

"Get . . . her . . . offa . . . me," Gary whimpered between snaps.

Behind us, the bartender, a couple of the girls, and three or four customers stood staring. Then I heard Smiley Gilstrap's voice as he ran up to the scene.

"What the hell's going on here?" he yelled, stopping a couple of feet away from them, not wanting to get caught in the middle of all this. "Aphrodite, get the fuck off him!"

I raised myself up on one elbow and held out my hand. "Wait," I said, but my voice was weak.

Through the gap between Aphrodite's massive form and Gary's almost unconscious one, I saw Smiley reach into his belt, pull out a revolver, and point it at the three of us.

"I swear, Aphrodite, if you don't get off him, I'm going to blow your shit away!"

Then the front door flew open and Mike Anderson, followed by about a half-dozen uniforms, burst into the foyer, guns drawn.

"I don't think so, mister!" Anderson barked. "Put it down. Now!"

All the breath went out of my body and I lay down on the floor.

"I don't think it's dislocated," the EMT said to me. "You might want to get it X-rayed, though."

"If it still hurts in a couple of days," I said. "I've had enough of hospitals for tonight."

The tech packed up his bag and left. I was in Goumba Joey's office, sitting on the leather couch beneath the open cabinet of video monitors.

"So they watched everything," Anderson said.

I nodded. "Kinky, huh?"

"Go figure."

I looked up. "So what's next?"

He sat down in Goumba Joey's chair and put his feet up on the desk. "We woke up the D.A. He'll seek a court order to shut this place down. In the meantime, we've impounded the computers and we'll close the place down as a crime scene. Gary's on his way to the hospital, but the doc says he'll live. God, that fat black bitch beat the stew out of him."

I looked up. "Her name is Aphrodite Jones," I said. "And she saved my life. You treat her right if you want my cooperation in this."

"Chill, Harry," he said. "We want her as a witness, too. She'll be treated well. Besides, given the circumstances, we couldn't even hold her on simple assault."

"Good," I said, rubbing my shoulder. "Don't even try."

"Say," Anderson said brightly. "Did you really tell that pig you're a cop?"

"The Supreme Court has ruled that subterfuge can be used in obtaining a confession from a suspected perpetrator."

"Yeah," he said, grinning. "The cops can do that. But you were impersonating a law-enforcement officer. That's a felony in this state."

"Yeah," I said, raising my head and glaring at him. "So sue me."

Anderson got up. "Look, why don't you go on home. You look beat. Come down tomorrow, get the paperwork out of the way. Okay?"

"Thanks, Mike," I said. "I am tired."

He walked out from Joey's desk. "Hey," he said. "How's that girlfriend? You guys had the baby yet?"

I looked up from the couch, smiled at him. "About six

hours ago," I said. "A girl. Six pounds, ten ounces. Completely, absolutely perfect in every way."

"Congratulations!" he said. "What'd you name her?"

"Alexis Martha," I said. "And she's incredibly beautiful."

"Mazel tov, my friend," he said, throwing an arm around my sore shoulder as we walked out of Goumba Joey's office for what I hoped would be the last time.

"I got two daughters myself," he continued with a wide grin on his face. "Ah, kids. You gotta love 'em."

Epilogue _____

Thankfully, life calmed down a bit during the next few days. After an awful pregnancy, Marsha's delivery had been so routine that they sent her home late the next day. She was tired and sore, but so glad to be out of the hospital that she was up walking around that night. Alexis made the transition from hospital to home in magnificent style. Nothing I'd ever seen or done in my entire life gave me as much pleasure as simply watching her sleep, which by the way she did a great deal of, and with equally magnificent style.

I went down to Reno P.D. headquarters Monday morning and gave a statement to Mike Anderson that took about two hours and was videotaped in addition to being transcribed. There were two FINCEN field guys there as well, along with Jacques Barrone, the local U.S. attorney, the two local Secret Service investigators, and the Storey County D.A. It was a crowded room and quite an interesting morning.

Goumba Joey, Gary Weyrich, Smiley Gilstrap, and Mabel Weyrich were already in custody, and the cops were looking for a few others as well. Barrone was cleared of any involvement in the money-laundering operation and agreed to cooperate fully with the investigation and the prosecution. The Mustang Ranch was apparently closed for good this time, although the place seemed to me to have more lives than a cat. I wouldn't bet the rent money on it staying closed.

Speaking of money, I decided this time to do something I'd never done before. I figured out how many hours I'd put in working for Jacques Barrone and the cops and decided that it simply wasn't enough compensation for a job well done. They'd pushed me into doing something I didn't want to do in the first place and they nearly got me killed at a time when life suddenly seemed a lot more precious to me than it ever had before. When I saw what they owed me, I decided to triple it and invoiced Barrone for fifteen grand. I think he swallowed hard, but he paid up. I didn't ask where the money came from.

I did a little car shopping in Reno and found a perfectly bland, well-maintained Toyota that was only six years old and a bargain for just under five grand. It was the newest car I'd had in a decade. My friend Lonnie back in Nashville had taken care of the paperwork for my replacement driver's license and mailed it to me, so I was street legal again. I paid cash for the Toyota and drove it off the lot. That afternoon I sat down with Marsha and handed her a cashier's check for the rest.

"Harry, you don't have to do this," she said. "You don't have this kind of money."

"I'm in better shape than I've been in a long time. And things are definitely looking up. Go on, take the check."

"I don't need the money. Alex and I'll be fine."

"Look, she's my daughter, too," I insisted. "And I want to do right by her. If you don't need the money, then take the ten grand and have Marty invest it for her. I'll kick in more whenever I can. By the time she goes to college, it'll be worth something."

She took the check and stared at it. "Okay," she agreed. "I'll do it for Alex."

The baby was asleep, Estella was in the laundry room, and Marty'd gone into Reno for a board meeting of the local Easter Seal Society. It was the first time Marsha and I had been alone in the week that she'd been home.

"So what are you going to do?" I asked. "Where're you going to be?"

She picked up her cup of hot tea and sipped it carefully. "I don't know," she said after a moment. "I'll be here at least another couple of months. I'll have to get a job eventually. And the truth is, I really want to go back to work. I miss it."

"Yeah," I said amiably. "I don't see you as a stay-at-home kind of gal."

She smiled. Since the baby's birth, things had eased up between us. We both knew that whatever we once had was gone for good, but Alex put us back together in ways that might not have been possible otherwise.

"I might even go back to Nashville," she said. "At least I've got professional contacts back there."

"And you might find that things aren't as bad as you feared," I offered. "People have short memories. Most of them probably won't even remember that there were problems in the M.E.'s office. Something else will get their attention."

"We'll see," she said. "And I'll let you know. What about you?"

I shrugged. "As hard as it'll be to leave you two, I've got to get back to my home, my life. I've been thinking a lot lately about what's out there for me. I've been a P.I. for five years now. I've got some contacts and some experience. I could do corporate work, get into a more lucrative part of this business. You can make a lot of money if you just take the right kinds of cases."

"You can do it, Harry," she said. "I know you can."

"Besides," I added, "it's time I quit bottom feeding. No more cheating husbands and runaway teenagers."

"When will you go?" Marsha asked.

"I was thinking day after tomorrow," I said. "But I'll have to be back here for court, probably in three months or so."

"I'll miss you, Harry," she said softly. "I really will."

"You'll send me pictures?" I asked. "Make videotapes?"

She smiled. "All the time."

There was a sudden heaviness in my chest. "This is really hard," I said.

"I know."

"I hope you move back. I really would like to watch her grow up."

"If there's any way I can make it work," she said, "I will."

I reached out, took her hand in mine. "Hey, if that's the best deal I can get, I'll take it."

On my way out of town, I stopped off at Shaky Jake's to say goodbye. It was early, just before eight, but he was sitting outside in a plastic lawn chair drinking coffee and reading the newspaper as I turned the corner at the driveway.

"Hey, kid!" he called. "How ya doin'?"

"Fine, Jake," I said, taking his offered hand. "On my way out of town. Going home."

"Aw, man, I hate to hear that. Park it a sec. Want some coffee?"

I pulled up another white plastic lawn chair and sat down next to him. "No, thanks. Estella pumped me full of caffeine this morning, as well as eggs and pancakes and any damn thing else she could cram down my throa You'd think there was no food between here and the E: Coast."

Jake laughed. "Don't complain, kid. There ain't no food as good as hers between here and the East Coast."

"Look, I just came by to thank you for all your help, buddy. It's been good getting to know you. You ever get back east, you stop and see me."

"I was in Music City once, a long time ago. My boss backed a nightclub back there in, uh, what the hell you call it? Printing Alley? Print Alley? Something like that."

"Printers Alley," I said. "That's where the old clubs are."

"Yeah, and the guy was skimming the take. You know, you expect a little bit of that, but this guy was going too far. So I went and had a corrective interview with him, if you get my drift."

I smiled. "I think I got it."

"So you're driving," he said.

"Headed out right now."

"You going to see that babe you called?"

I cleared my throat. "Actually, I am going to stop off in Eureka on my way back. But just to pay a social call and say goodbye. I ain't looking to start nothing."

Shaky Jake shook his head, clucking his tongue as he did. "You know, kid, you make things too complicated. Why don't you just find a girl and have a little fun now and then?"

I shrugged. "Call it a character flaw," I said.

Jake laughed. "Hey, you wanna burn one before you go?"

"Jesus, Jake, how old are you?"

"Seventy-three," he said defensively.

"You're seventy-three years old and you smoke dope very day. Doesn't that seem a bit odd to you?"

He threw back his head and roared. "Hell, kid," he 1. "How do you think I made it to seventy-three?"

*   *   *

That night I was once again sitting over dinner with Kelly at the Jackson House in Eureka. She wore a pair of khaki pants and a white, button-down oxford-cloth shirt, her red hair cascading over her shoulders like a lion's mane. We had a drink on the veranda and talked for a while, then the hostess came and got us when our table was ready.

Kelly knew I was headed home, that I liked her a lot, but neither of us was in a position to get involved with the other.

"I'll be back through here in a couple, three months," I said. "Maybe I could stop by and see you."

"Or I could meet you in Reno," she said. "We could always grab a room at the Peppermill and I could teach you the finer points of Caribbean poker."

I grinned. "I thought you were a blackjack player."

"Well, that might take a little longer than a weekend. You could spend a lifetime learning to play blackjack."

"I'd be a willing student."

I noticed that we had two empty wineglasses on the table. I turned, looking for our waitress, and spotted Sergeant Dell Kanon of the Nevada Highway Patrol just as he stepped into the restaurant.

"Well, I'll be," I said.

"What?" Kelly asked.

"Look who just walked in."

She spotted him, smiled broadly, and waved him over. He wore a beige suit and a tan shirt with a bolo tie and a ten-gallon hat.

"Dell!" she called. "C'mon over."

I stood and we shook hands warmly. "You look like you've recovered pretty well," he said.

"I made it just fine," I said. "But, man, have I got a story for you. Join us."

"Oh, no," he said. "I don't want to interrupt your dinner. I just came in for a bite."

"C'mon," I entreated. "You don't want to eat alone. Join us."

"Really, Dell," Kelly said. "It's cool. Sit down."

He grinned, almost sheepishly, which is saying something for a guy his size. "You sure?"

I pulled up a chair. "Park it, bud," I said. "We insist."

"When'd you get in, Harry?"

"This afternoon," I said. "I'm on my way home. Thought I'd stop in and say goodbye."

"How long you going to be here?"

"I got a room at the Colonnade for tonight," I answered. "I'm leaving in the morning."

Our waitress came and I ordered a bottle of wine. The three of us wound up having a kind of celebratory dinner. We toasted my daughter and new friendships and making it through another day aboveground. The food was marvelous and the wine flowed and time went by very quickly. When the check came, I grabbed it before either of them had a chance to react and paid it gladly.

"Look, it's still early," Kelly said. "There's not a whole lot to do in this town, but why don't we go down to the E-Z Stop, shoot a little stick."

"Pool?" I said. "I haven't had a cue in my hand in years."

Kelly looked at Dell and they both smiled. "Fresh meat," Dell said.

"Straight pool," Kelly said. "Quarter a ball."

"Oh, boy," I muttered, following them out of the restaurant and into the crisp, cool Nevada night. We decided to walk down to the E-Z Stop, which took about ten minutes and was the perfect end to the meal.

We walked into the E-Z Stop to the sound of balls

thumping against rails with Hank Williams on the jukebox.

"Jack," Kelly called out to the cashier. "Got a table?"

The cashier pointed. The first of the four tables at the E-Z Stop was empty. We walked into the back room. Kelly pulled a cue stick off the rack and rolled it across the felt. Dell bent down to rack the balls. I picked out a stick and sighted down the end of it toward the other end of the room.

I stopped, lowered the cue. "Well, I'll be damned," I said.

"What?" Kelly asked.

I stared ahead toward the other end of the room. "Harry, what's wrong?" Kelly asked. She stepped over, put her hand on my forearm. "What is it?"

Dell looked up, saw the expression on my face. He crossed behind the pool table to where we stood.

"What's up, Harry?"

"Dell, you see those two down there?" I motioned subtly with my head to the last table in the room, to where two guys swilling longnecks were playing nine-ball.

"Yeah," he said.

"That's the Wolf and Greasy Blond," I said, lowering my voice. "The two guys that robbed me."

He turned, took a long look. "You're kidding."

"I don't freaking believe this," I whispered.

Kelly stared. "Are you sure?"

I looked at her and nodded. "Oh, yeah, baby. I'm sure. I never forget a face, especially not those two."

Dell cleared his throat loudly and took the pool cue out of Kelly's hand, put it back on the rack, and turned to us.

"How fortunate," he said, "that you just happen to have a Nevada state law-enforcement officer handy."

"Yeah," I said. "Lucky me."

"Kelly, go tell Jack to call the sheriff and get him over

here quick. Harry, take that pool cue and follow me. You're my backup."

I looked at Dell. "You're going to take 'em now?"

He smiled, turned slightly, and pulled his jacket back discreetly. I looked down to where a nine-millimeter sat in black leather on his hip with a pair of shiny handcuffs in the pocket next to it.

"Shall we?" he asked.

"After you," I said.

We turned and walked side by side toward the last pool table. As we approached the two, Greasy Blond looked up with a sneer on his face. Dell pulled out his badge with one hand and his pistol with the other.

"You boys want to put down the pool cues and put your hands behind your heads?"

Greasy Blond looked straight at me. I smiled at him.

His eyes got real big.

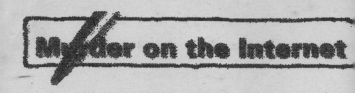